KLASIN

ON *Little*
CAT FEET

outskirts
press

Outskirts Press, Inc.
http://www.outskirtspress.com

Paperback ISBN: 978-1-9772-4661-5

PROLOGUE

The fog comes
on little cat feet.

It sits looking
over harbor and city
on silent haunches
and then moves on.

Carl Sandburg

The parking lot was nearly empty. Maggie pulled into a spot next to the sidewalk and turned around to look at the back seat. Sammy was making large loops in the air with a toy airplane; Sarah was slumped to the side of her car seat, fast asleep. Maggie felt only slightly guilty about having to wake her up.

The kids had been excited about coming to the cottage in early fall. They usually spent time with her in the summer, but had never been here this late when the sunfish had all been cleared from the beach and the colorful summer flags had all been folded and placed into storage.

She recognized the Palmers' car--they'd gotten central heat a few years back--and Doc Chard's son's jeep. He was like his father: he never worried much about the elements.

"Sarah, wake up." Maggie raised her voice a little and twisted around more to reach for Sarah's hand. "We're here."

The child's lids fluttered; she took a deep breath like a sigh, and opened her eyes with a smile. Sarah had always been easy, happy with whatever came her way. It had never ceased to amaze Maggie that her daughter Jen could have produced such an agreeable offspring.

"Shall we go to the beach before we take the bags in?"

"Yeah." Sammy dropped his plane on the car floor and began to unbuckle the straps of his car seat.

Maggie got out and opened the back door to help Sarah get out of her seat. "The water's going to be cold, now." She almost had to call this out after the kids as they abandoned their shoes and socks in a pile and ran toward the sand.

The snow fences sat haphazardly at the edge of the dune grass, utterly neglected and bereft of their purpose. She wondered why the Association put them up in the first place. It wasn't as though they kept the snow away from the front row of cottages.

The wind had already blown beach sand onto the front walk, where it would sit until late spring before someone arrived to sweep it back onto the beach. It was then that Maggie really focused on the beach. Its folds were different from the summer when human footprints crisscrossed it from all directions. This was part of the reason she loved it in fall. The wind rearranged the grains of sand like pieces of a game, building up a ridge here, creating a hollow there. She could almost picture Ben lying on his side, sleeping peacefully in the small valleys, one hand under his head, the other pushed up in the sun-warmed sand.

Maggie shook her head slightly to rid it of the memory. Where were her grandkids? She needed to get with the program. She looked up to find them tracing the waving pattern of the wet sand beside the lazy waves.

"Hey, what are you two up to?" she called.

Sarah had stopped now, as Maggie approached, bending down toward the sand. She was frowning, closing off the bridge of her nose. If Maggie had had her camera with her, this would be where she'd hold it up and shoot a wonderful natural portrait. She was tiring of all the posed portraits she'd done over the past decades, even though they had been her bread and butter. She'd always done her artful shots, though they had not made her rich. Unlike Jen, who was a genius with a camera.

"Grandma Maggie. Some don' move at all. But these two just sit and flap their wings is all."

"What, hon?" Maggie saw the answer to her question as soon as she asked it. Two colorful members of the insect world had chosen the edge of the beach to live out what was left of their lives.

"Look, Sammy," Sarah called to her brother, who was now playing a game of tag with the incoming waves. "This monarch's wing is torn. Grandma Maggie, does it hurt him? Ta have a torn wing, I mean."

"Sarah, these are viceroys, I think. Not monarchs. Viceroys have the same coloring, but they're smaller." Maggie watched as Sarah's eyes narrowed and realized she was doing the same thing she had done with her own daughters: trying to turn a time of wonder into what the educators liked to call a "teachable moment." What nonsense. They were learning all they needed to just being out on the beach.

Maggie started over. "I'm not sure, Sarah. I don't know if butterflies hurt the same way we do. But these butterflies probably won't live much longer. Their lives are not very long."

Sarah looked down at the ground, then back up at Maggie, her eyes tearing up.

"Oh, dear. Wait, Sarah. I have an idea. These viceroys are in the wind here. Why don't we take them back from the beach and put them in the clump of grass over there where they are protected from the wind."

"Yeah. Good idea." Sammy had come over and spoke for Sarah.

Maggie was afraid to pick up her butterfly at first. She had remembered being a child and chasing the white moths that fanned their wings on the clover leaves, only to fly away when she got close.

But these butterflies didn't rise from the ground at all when she cupped her hands around one. And she nearly jumped at the delicate brush of a softly unfolding wing that could no longer lift its weight from the ground. She carefully enclosed the gentle fan in both hands and plucked it from the sand. Sarah already had hers.

"Here, Grandma. Put 'em here." Sammy had run ahead to scout out the sheltered places among the grasses. Maggie set her butterfly down almost too quickly. The wings brushed her hands again, and she was sorry the wings were not strong enough to give the butterfly one last flight on the shifting air currents over the water.

Sarah was reluctant to let hers go. "Grandma, you know the ones on the beach? Are these going to die too? I mean, if we put 'em here, are they goin' ta die? Or live?" It sounded more like a pronouncement than a question, Maggie thought as she watched Sarah. How like her mother.

So Maggie answered the way she thought Jennifer would have. "Hon, I can't say, but at least we've put them in a safe place."

VI

She looked at her hands to avoid her granddaughter's sharp stare. It was there she found some slight silver-tinted dust on her hands, like when she handled shiny Christmas ornaments before returning them to their tissue-lined box after their brief stint on the family tree. It must have come from a butterfly wing. For a moment, Maggie was almost superstitious about wiping it away.

Sarah had finally surrendered her viceroy after some serious coaching from Sammy. "But we can't keep him. What does he want to be with us for, anyway? Let the both of 'em be together. Like friends."

"Yeah." Sarah spoke as she continued to bend over to watch the insects, her hands on her knees.

Maggie started to head back to the car. "Okay, time to go." They really needed to get the bags to the cottage and get settled in with a fire in the fireplace before the sun went down and they were all thoroughly chilled.

Sarah caught up with her and trotted by Maggie's side. "Grandma, can we come back tomorrow ta see if they're still here?"

Maggie was already thinking about what there was for supper. "Who? To see if who is here, Sarah?"

"You know. The vice-robs."

"The viceroys? Well, I think so, honey. They'll probably be gone though." Maggie could picture the wind scattering the moths, their paper wings skittering across the sand.

"Yeah." Sarah placed her hands together in a half clap. "They'll probably be all better 'n jus' fly away."

"Yeah." Maggie said it quietly. If you said it softly enough, it wasn't really a lie. "Let's get the cases into the cottage and get warm. I'll make us hot dogs and hot chocolate for supper. We can sit in front of the fire, and I'll tell you stories about when your mom was a little girl and we spent the summer here and she learned about photography." They'd heard these stories before, Maggie knew, but they had never tired of them.

Maggie never tired of telling them either, though it had taken her years to get to this point. It was a kind of therapy for her, she supposed, some sort of immersion or desensitization therapy where you get exposed to your phobia enough to make it familiar, to take its power away. Still, she would not be able to repeat to her grandchildren the memories that could still haunt her own dreams.

CHAPTER 1

"**M**ommy, I'm not carrying this any farther." Five-year-old Jennifer had stopped at the bottom of the steps ascending the dune and folded her arms, dropping her pink child's duffle where she stood. She spoke to the woman in front of her who was balancing a second child on one hip while clutching a bag tight against the other hip.

"Just a little more," Maggie called back, barely turning her head. Then, when Jennifer shook her head and stomped a foot, "Well, all right. Leave it for now. We'll come back for it." It was all Maggie could do to hurry up the last of the concrete steps, finally stopping at a small cottage nestled in the middle of the two rows of cottages that faced one another across a narrow walk. She dropped her own bag then deposited the child she carried in a crumpled pile of sundress at her feet, still managing to keep hold of one of the girl's small hands. She trapped the bag against one knee while using her free hand to rummage through it for a key.

Maggie managed another glance back at Jennifer, who was—by now—what her sitters would have described as "dug in." "C'mon, Jen, she called over her shoulder, sounding cross, "this is it." Then, softening slightly, in an attempt to entice the child below, "I need you to take Sam's hand."

"Well, okay." Jennifer stomped up the stairs to show her displeasure.

"No." Samantha wrested her hand from her mother's grasp and hid it behind her.

"Quiet, now. Both of you." Maggie took a deep breath and applied the key, praying she'd open it on the first try so that she could get her tired and squabbling daughters behind closed doors before they caused a stir with any of the neighbors.

The door shot open under her weight, and Maggie nearly fell forward with relief. "Well, this is it." She said this quietly, as much to herself as for her children. "Our home for the summer. See what you think. Jenny, why don't you go on up and see which room you want."

"I want a room. I want ta choose." Samantha followed her sister, hanging onto the railing and taking each step with her right foot leading, then lifting the second foot to follow.

Maggie shook her head slightly as she watched her daughters disappear. Samantha. Darling Sam. A child who often chose a corner to play by herself in a world of her own imaginings. Maggie had watched as her behaviors had regressed to those of a younger child over the last few months. On some level, she must sense that her life—as she knew it—was threatened.

"Yoo-hoo, may I come in?" Maggie jerked her head at the sound, surprised to see Janine walk in without waiting for an invitation. She had already met the Realtor, whose company handled the summer cottage rentals in Breakwater Bay. "The guard at the gate said you had just arrived, and I thought I'd better come down to make certain everything was in order." Janine was a heavyset woman with silver-blonde hair who invariably wore a long broomstick skirt. This one had Aztec-like figures embroidered around the bottom that flowed beneath a blouse of a bold color that you had to search long and hard to find in the skirt. "Is this yours?" She waved the pink duffel in her hand.

"That's mine!" Jennifer called out in alarm from the top of the stairs and began to head back down.

"Of course." Janine handed it over the stair railing and turned back to Maggie. "I also wanted to make certain everything was—oh, darn!" She looked up at the ceiling of the living room where they now stood. Maggie followed her gaze toward a light socket in the ceiling, wires protruding where a lightbulb should be. "That light still isn't fixed. I'll have to send Jason around in the morning. My son. He does a lot of work on the rentals around here. He's a regular handyman—and so much more reliable than anyone else.

"Now, what else? Oh, you poor things. You don't have to carry your bags from the parking lot. You probably didn't see, but there are these little wooden carts you can push. When you go back for the rest of your bags, be sure you get one of those. And what else? Oh, have I told you about the ants? You must keep all your food in little tins or containers of some sort once they're opened; otherwise, the ants will find it and have their feast. Believe me, the ants will find their way in faster than I can tell you."

"Thank you, Janine. We appreciate your help." Maggie was trying to think of a polite way to get rid of the woman before she was even more overwhelmed than she already felt. "You've been more than helpful. We need a little time now to get settled. I'll call you if I have any questions."

"Do you have my number?"

"I'm sure I do. We're a little grumpy right now." Maggie made a slight motion with her head toward the stairs.

Janine gave a wise nod. "Of course. I'll be back. If not tomorrow, then the next to check to make sure you've found everything you need. Oh, the washer and dryer are down-stairs—and there's a beach door off the basement too. Use that door after you've been down to the beach. That way you can keep the sand out of the house."

"Good idea." Now, Maggie leaned on the front door and held onto the knob, hoping, by the power of suggestion, to convey to Janine that she could leave. The woman took the hint.

"Just call. That's what I'm here for."

"Thanks." Maggie closed the door quickly and turned back to the girls. She lifted her bangs, then let them drop, noticing absently that she was letting them grow again, let-ting them descend low over her brow ridge so they would hood her almost too lucid gray eyes.

Samantha had stopped midway on the stairs and was staring out between two railing bars. "Is that the babysitter?"

"No, hon." Maggie felt a pang of guilt but let it pass. She had farmed out her girls more of late than she cared to ad-mit. "That's the lady who helped us find our house. Now let's see about those rooms." She followed her daughters up the stairs.

The upstairs had almost no hallway, just a landing space from which four small bedrooms radiated, one in each quadrant of the house. Three rooms had two single beds each; the fourth a standard-sized bed. She realized she'd better assign rooms if she wanted to avoid a squabble, but it was too late. Jennifer had already appropriated the room with a window that looked up the dune and was calmly un-packing clothing from her duffel into a chest of drawers, the only other piece of furniture in her room besides the beds. "Sam," Maggie turned to her younger daughter and cajoled, "this looks like the perfect room for you. See, there are zoo animals on the bedspreads."

"Yeah." Sam followed her into the room that looked down the dune, then pitched herself on a bed headfirst.

"Don't get too comfortable, now; we still need to go back and get the rest of our luggage. Why don't you two put on your shorts, so that after we get the bags, we can head down and check out the beach. Let's see, Sam. I probably have your shorts in the bag I've got here." She turned to Sam and saw Jen push her door closed. Good sign, she mused. Jen was claiming the room as her private place. "Here, Sam, here are some shorts for you. Right on top. Come on over." The child obeyed, and walked inside the circle of her mother's arms, hanging onto Maggie's forearms as she stepped into the shorts her mother held open for her: first one leg, then the other. Maggie snapped the waistband elastic over Sam's T-shirt and stood up.

She breathed in, then took stock of her own room. The wallpaper was a little rosebud design that was peeling at the seams. She could see some water marks where rain had gotten in. And the room needed a good airing. She pulled up on the two handles of the window's frame. It went up grudgingly and then had to be propped open with a short two-by-four she found on the floor under the window, apparently left there for that purpose. Maggie sighed and sank back onto the double bed, momentarily losing heart. She pictured the home she'd left behind on Chicago's west side, the white columns in front, the tall windows that let large bands of light spill halfway across the wooden floors on the first floor, the huge elm in back that guarded one entire side of the house. Part of what this summer was about would be loss, she reminded herself. She'd known that. But she could only guess at how much loss that would mean.

"Mom." Jennifer emerged from her room with matching shorts and top, her hair combed. "Can we go in the lake first? Please."

"Sure," Maggie acquiesced. "There's plenty of time to unpack later. Let's go."

"Yay!" This was cried in unison, before the two girls raced down the stairs, though the difference in their ages didn't make for much of a contest. Jenny finished by jumping the last step and pitching forward so that she had to catch herself on the floor with her hands.

"Serves you right," Sam yelled from above as she clasped the rail, descending, her right foot, again, leading down with each step.

"Okay. Enough." Maggie willed herself to breathe slowly. Her headaches often started with a sharp pain behind her right eye. That was precisely what she was experiencing at the moment. She lowered her voice, hoping to infuse a calm into the situation: "Let's go out through the basement so we get used to using the beach door."

A door in the kitchen led to a set of concrete stairs that went down to the basement. The stairs were steep with only a thin, somewhat wobbly wooden railing and ended in a small room with a concrete floor under what was the front part of the house. The only light in the room seeped through a line of dirty windows that sat at eye level with the sidewalk outside. The center of the room held a washer and dryer next to a drain in the floor. Everywhere else you looked, however, were cottage paraphernalia in varying degrees of disrepair: lawn chairs folded and unfolded, a couple of rusty bicycles on their sides, bell jars, tools, rope. Maggie stopped looking. This room was the catch-all, she decided.

The basement door opened to the side of the house, from under the front porch. It was well-placed, Maggie realized. She hadn't even noticed it when they'd arrived. "Okay," she told her daughters, "let's go. It should be straight ahead."

The girls immediately started running down the steps that Jennifer had previously complained so mightily about having to climb, but Maggie held back a moment to breathe in the air. When she stopped, she caught sight of someone behind the screened porch in the house directly across the walk from theirs. She turned her head to look, but all she saw was the hunched back of a dim female figure retreating into the house. Maggie wondered if the woman had been inspecting her new neighbors. And, if so, what she thought of them. Janine had said there were lots of kids around—that children wouldn't be a problem.

Maggie turned and hurried toward the beach. She needed to be there to make sure her girls didn't try to do any wading with their shoes on. She could see the patches of sunlight reflecting off the water even before they emerged from the rows of cottages. The lake lay just beyond a wide stretch of sandy beach. Grains and grains of soft white and brown-flecked sand..

"Oh, sparkles." Sam bent down and began sifting the sand through her fingers.

"Oh, boy." Jenny broke into a run. Sam followed. Maggie had to run to keep up. Their forward progress was hampered by backsliding in the loose sand, and the little girls gave up quickly. "Mom." Sam tugged at her arm. "Is this the ocean?"

"No, hon. Remember what I told you? It's a lake. Lake Michigan. It looks as big as the ocean because we can't see the other side, though, doesn't it?" She stopped, and they halted with her as though on cue. It was as she had remembered it. She held still a minute, drinking it all in: the gentle lap of waves on the shore, remnants of the wake of a passing motorboat, now a toy on the horizon; the abandoned sailfish lying on its side, its wet red-and-white unfurled sail sucked against the sand; a few diehard sunbathing strag-glers trying to squeeze from the sun its final celestial hour.

The last time she'd been here was the summer she was fifteen, a sophomore in high school and, at least from her point of view, too old for a vacation with her parents. It was 1960, before the height of Vietnam and the so-called Sexual Revolution, a year that her parents' generation could still claim was a time of innocence.

She and her folks had come here with some friends who made the trip every year and rented a cottage for the second half of the summer. Maggie had been the only one of the DeCour children who'd been forced to suffer this ignominy. Her two siblings had found other summer pursuits. Barbara stayed in Kankakee to work; Bryan lived with friends so he could attend a sports camp.

Maggie tried to remember where their cottage had been—something much farther down the beach, she guessed. She had dreaded a summer with her parents. She was embarrassed (though at the time she would have used the word "mortified") by her mother's strict decorum and her father's woolgathering.

That had all changed when she met some of the other teenagers from the cottages and from town who hung out at the beach every summer. And especially when she'd met Brendan. She smiled with the memory of the romance and promise that seemed to hang in the air then. His parents had owned a summer cottage at the top of one of the dunes. He was a year older than she was, knew his way around, had a car he'd bought with his earnings by working as a busboy in a nearby restau-rant. He was a regular part of the beach crowd, one of the golden boys in a set full of them. He had been only slightly taller than she was, and had the habit of standing almost too close to you when he spoke, his chin lifted a little, his chest slightly puffed up.

The summer days had had a free and easy rhythm. She'd rise late in the morning and wander down to the beach to see if there was a volleyball game or just towels of teen bodies ripening into their physical selves. Evenings were spent around bonfires on the beach or in town at a teen nightclub.

Maggie and Brendan had conducted their romance in secret. It was nearly the end of their summer stay when Maggie's mother suspected her daughter was often not where she claimed to be. At the end of the summer, Maggie and Brendan had made promises, written a couple of times, even talked on the phone. Then he'd taken up with someone else at his school. Maggie had locked herself in her room to cry. The last thing she wanted to hear were her mother's prim reassurances that this was just puppy love, that she'd soon get over it.

Looking back now, Maggie supposed part of the attraction was that Brendan had been the kind of person her mother would have disapproved of. "Disapproved of" was perhaps too strong. Her mother would have found a more insidious way of putting it, like "Well, he doesn't really distinguish himself in any way." Or, "He doesn't stand out; he isn't special." Oh, but he was special, Maggie thought, in the way that mattered most. He had liked her.

And, besides, look what happened when you ended up marrying someone with all the credentials your mother wanted, Maggie mused, not without some bitter irony.

She warned herself for perhaps the hundredth time that she wasn't here to recapture something from her youth. She wasn't here to recover a simpler time, at least not for herself. At some fundamental level, she had come here as an escape. She had come here to buy time. It would be wonderful if the girls could have a carefree summer. Heavens knows, she told herself, they were due. Especially Jen. Serious, judgmental Jen. Shades of her grandmother.

The sound of her daughters' laughter broke into Maggie's reverie. She returned her gaze to the lake, its huge expanse of water. Was this enough water to wash everything clean? To give everyone a new start? But what lay beneath that clear surface, she wondered. She sensed Jen and Sam watching her. The two had fallen silent with her own change of mood. "We're going to have a good summer," she told her daughters; yet, she knew her words were really directed at herself.

"When will Daddy come?" Jennifer addressed her with a slightly accusatory tone.

Maggie felt her jaw clench. "I don't know. We won't worry about that. We'll just enjoy things while we're here. Okay?"

"Okay." Sam clapped her hands, still looking at the lake, enchanted.

"He'd better be here by my birthday." Jennifer had gotten the bone in her jaws and wasn't relinquishing it without getting ransom of one kind or another.

Maggie looked at the child who often seemed to have some radar that was way too attuned to the misgivings of the adults around her. "Jenny, no promises. Your father has a lot going on this summer. Don't pester me with this." She tried to make her voice sound firm, final. "Let's go get the rest of the suitcases now. Then we need to get some groceries or there won't be anything for supper or for breakfast. If there's any light after supper, we'll come back down here to watch the sunset."

"Yay!" Sam jumped with glee and clapped her hands like two cymbals. Jennifer eyed her mother with suspicion, but said nothing.

⟿⟺((◉))⟺⟿

"Hallo. Hallo? Anyone home?"

Maggie's eyes shot open. Where. . .? She looked around. Her clothes were still strewn around the room. She'd been so tired, she'd dumped them where she stood before falling into bed last night. "Who is it? Just a minute," she called, grabbing a T-shirt and shorts and, pulling them on, ran a hand through her hair and her tongue over her teeth. Her bedroom was bright; it must be late.

Their visitor had let himself in through the porch and was knocking at the inside door. This familiarity must be customary for beach life, she supposed.

"Mrs. Dunbarton?" he asked when she opened the door.

"Yes."

He extended a hand and smiled wide. "I'm Jason, Janine Lurie's son. Sorry. I think I've come a little early. By the way my mother talked, it sounded like the roof would cave in if I didn't get over here."

Maggie shook his hand warily, though she wasn't sure why. She looked at him more closely. It surprised her that Janine had a son this old. And that he didn't try to be the neon sign that his mother was. The man before her had to be in his mid-thirties. He was slightly taller than average with brown hair bleached on the ends to a color beyond blond. He had the tan of someone who spent time working—or playing—outside. The tool belt around his waist accentuated a lean frame. His slightly lopsided smile made Maggie want to smile in return.

"Thanks for coming. I don't know that this is all that urgent, though. It's just some cords hanging from a light socket." She motioned at the ceiling, trying to think what it was she wanted for him to do.

He spoke before she had decided: "Say, why don't I come back later. When you've had time to be up and about. Or tomorrow. I could come back tomorrow?"

"That's fine. Whatever works for you is fine."

"Okay. But, say. I do need to give you this. My mom gave it to me. It's the name and number of a teenager who lives in one of the lakefront cottages who babysits. Annie Argersinger. I know her. She's great. And she has younger brothers. They might be someone your girls could play with." He presented her with a paper folded over a couple of times. "See you later then."

CHAPTER 2

Maggie eased herself into one of the cushioned chairs on the front porch, letting herself down with her arms. It had been a long day. But good. She was allowing herself a treat: one glass of wine. But only one, she reminded herself for perhaps the fourth time.

They'd met Annie. Actually, they'd met her younger brothers first. The boys were on their bikes and came to a screeching halt behind Jennifer as Maggie and the girls were carrying groceries from the parking lot. It was a relief to be confronted by someone, even children, after the long walk past the mostly empty white clapboard cottages where the occasional disembodied voice drifted out from a large screened-in porch.

"Hi." The taller one had spoken first. He looked a little older than Jennifer. "I'm Rodney. You new?"

Maggie could see that Jennifer was about to give him a sharp look or just a haughty turn of the head, but something stopped her. "I'm Jenny. We just moved in. Yesterday." Her tone was still full of the note of false superiority she managed so well. Where did she get it, Maggie had wondered at the time.

"I'm Stone." Not to be outdone, a smaller version of Rodney rolled his bicycle forward until it was even with that of his brother. They both needed haircuts, sported skinned knees that showed from beneath their baggy shorts, and looked full of mischief: Maggie could tell that if she'd just get past her attempts at being haughty, Jennifer might have some fun this summer despite herself.

She held out her hand, "Hi Rodney. Stone. I'm Maggie, Jennifer's mom. I'll bet Annie is your sister."

They nodded in unison.

"Well, come on over later—or we'll drop by your house this afternoon," she offered; but then Annie Argersinger herself appeared from an adjoining walk, and introductions began all over again. Annie was tall and a redhead—that explained the family's freckles. She wore shorts and a man's work shirt tied over a halter top. She'd been outgoing—had extended invitations left and right for them to come over. It had felt good, Maggie admitted to herself, somewhat reluctantly. These days, it took so little.

Rodney and Stone had carried on their own conversation with Jenny, who seemed to be warming up to them. Then Annie leaned over and grabbed Stone's handlebars. "Time to go. I told Mom I'd come find you guys and bring you home."

Rodney still straddled his bike, which seemed to be more or less a permanent part of him. "Just one more ride to the end."

"Okay. One more. But that's it." Annie's tone had a decisiveness that Maggie liked. "But not to the very end. You know where you're supposed to turn around." She turned back to face Maggie and explained, "It's Mr. Blailock. He has the last three houses on the front walk and the one at the top of the bluff. It's just better not to provoke him, that's all."

"Blailock?" Maggie had wanted to ask more, but then pandemonium had reasserted itself as the boys clattered away, standing up on their pedals to get started, their butts wagging from side to side as they rode off.

"So, do come over. My mom'd love to meet you. There aren't many summer people here yet. We're the blue house on the front walk with the big porch. Oh—and you'll know us by the noise inside," Annie called one last time as she followed her brothers on foot.

———— ((●)) ————

Getting the girls to bed that night had been the usual ordeal. Jennifer had pushed herself to the head of her bed, where she sat on her pillow and squealed that there was sand in her bed.

Sure enough, when Maggie pulled the sheet back, the bed was covered. She brushed hard to exorcize the fine grains, then calmly reasoned with her daughter, "Jenny, you probably had sand on your feet when you climbed in. It's easy to bring in. If you don't want sand in the bed, brush off your feet really well—preferably before you come into the house. Tomorrow we'll see if there's a hose outside to use to wash our feet off. That'd be even better." If *sand* were going to be the flash point, Maggie told herself, this could be a long summer.

But then, just as Maggie believed she might be able to settle down herself to relax, Sam exploded from her bed to look for Jimmie. Jimmie was a faded blue rabbit that clutched a shapeless carrot in its front feet. He shifted in and out of Sam's favor through no merit of his own. Maggie had finally found Jimmie in the toy bag still sitting, fully packed, on the floor of her room. Jimmie's beaded eyes hung dangerously from loose threads, and one seam had already pulled open.

Sam snatched him from Maggie, sticking her thumb into her mouth at the same time. "But no thumb sucking," Maggie warned. "You're going to stop, remember?"

Sam had withdrawn her thumb and leapt into bed with a giggle.

So, now, finally, Maggie could sink into one of the white wicker chairs on the front porch. She scooted another chair toward her with her toes to use as a footstool. The wine Maggie had poured for herself was a deep red leaning toward purple. It had swirled into the glass as she poured and filled it nearly to the top. Okay, only one glass, she had promised herself, but, then, make it a *real* glassful.

Maggie held up the glass to study the color. Drink slowly, she reminded herself. The trick was to make it last.

Beyond the glass, beyond the screen of the porch, her eyes caught a climbing red glow that mirrored her own gesture, lifting in a toast of its own. It took her mind a moment to resolve the red light into a coherent object. She realized she was watching the burning ember of a cigarette from within the porch across the way. It lingered, then settled back into the darkness of its owner.

Was the old woman smoking? Must be, Maggie decided. She was slightly embarrassed that her gesture had been misinterpreted as a toast, perhaps even an acknowledgment of shared vices. She drank her wine quickly and retreated back into the cottage, light-headed from the wine, a feeling she had once sought so often.

—((●))—

Sometime in the early dawn, Maggie felt herself rolled toward the edge of the bed from the weight of a child climbing in next to her. She opened her eyes and made out Samantha.

"Ghosts." Sam's whisper was exaggerated, and she grabbed her mother's forearm and tried to shake it.

"Wha—?" But then Maggie heard it too. The deep, woeful moan that crescendoed quickly, then fell away with the regularity of breathing. "Oh, hon." She pulled Sam to her and stayed on her side, breathing in a wisp of hair and the faint smell of sour milk that she so loved to smell while her girls were young. "That's a foghorn. It's a sound they make when it's foggy on the lake and hard to see, to warn the boats where the shore is so the boats don't run into it. It must mean a storm is coming in."

"Who blows the horn?"

Maggie shook her head to clear the cobwebs and smiled into the room's gray light. "It's not that kind of a horn. If it isn't raining tomorrow, we'll walk to the lighthouse so you can see it. That's where the sound comes from. It's a good sound."

"Kin I sleep here?"

Maggie's lids were heavy and she could feel herself slipping back into sleep. "Sure. For the time being."

———◦((◦))◦———

But the next morning was rainy.

Maggie had the girls seated at the kitchen table and was dishing up scrambled eggs when Jason knocked on the door. She leaned around the half wall between kitchen and living room so he could see her from the front door, and beckoned to him with the spatula in her hand, "C'mon in. We seem to have plenty of eggs here—and my girls aren't showing any particular affinity for the scrambled variety this morning."

Jason came in, lugging a stepladder. He'd slipped one arm through the rungs so one long side rested on his shoulder. Today, he'd tied a rolled bandanna around his head. Must be for effect, Maggie mused, because it wasn't really warm enough to work up much of a sweat.

"Oh, I've eaten. Thanks. I'd take coffee if you've got that."

"Sure." She disappeared back around the corner to pour a cup, calling behind her, "Black?"

"Sure. Thanks." He set the ladder down and came into the kitchen to get the cup. "Hi, girls."

Samantha burrowed her fists into her eyes and pretended to hide. But Jennifer set down her spoon and looked at him with what could only be her version of a supercilious frown.

"Thanks." Jason took the cup from Maggie. "I'll get right to work on the bulb. But I did notice a loose step on my way in. I may need to come back another time to repair that. You notice anything else?"

"No," Maggie answered him, but kept her eyes on Jennifer. She sipped her own cup of coffee. What was bugging Jen, she wondered. No matter. She knew she'd hear about it soon enough.

The phone rang, and Maggie went to answer it in the living room next to the stairs. This was the first time she'd used the phone. As she lifted the receiver, she marveled to see that the cottage phone had failed to keep up with the times. It was an ancient model with a rotary dial on the front rather than a touch tone. She shook her head in amazement. Was it supposed to contribute to the cottage décor, or was someone just cheap, she wondered.

"Hello?"

"Sister Magdalena!"

"Oh, Bryan. Hey." Maggie sank into the chair by the phone in time to see Jenny pull back from her perch at the edge of the linoleum when she heard the name Bryan. "Good to hear your voice."

Bryan cut in, a little too quickly, a little too heartily. "So, you've escaped to the seashore for the summer?"

"You think it's a bad move?"

"Hardly. Good old Sheldon had it coming." Bryan's voice took on the booming quality he used when he was trying to cajole someone.

"Well, I'm probably doing him a favor by coming here." Her voice cracked slightly as she said this, and she cleared her throat to cover up.

If Bryan noticed, he didn't give any indication. "I'm calling to see if you'd like a visitor."

"You're kidding? When could you come? That'd be great."

"Well, we should finish the job I'm on now by the end of next week, and I don't start another one for a while after that. All I have to do is pack up a few things. How about next weekend?"

"Super. We have room. You won't even have to sleep on the couch."

"That's good news." He got directions from her, then hung up the phone. Bryan had never been one for drawing out conversations.

"That was my brother," she said to Jason as she hung up, though she wasn't sure why she felt she needed to offer an explanation.

Bryan was the youngest of the three children in her family, and the darling of his sisters. That might be part of the reason they'd grown up and he hadn't, Maggie had once decided. He was still working in construction, mostly doing framing and roofing as the Dallas suburbs expanded. "I love standing on a roof and looking down," he told anyone who questioned the commitment of a college graduate who applied his cultivated intellect to shooting a nail gun. She looked guiltily at Jason, hoping he couldn't read her mind.

"Your uncle Bryan's coming to visit." Maggie returned to the kitchen to tell her daughters.

"I know." Jennifer theatrically crossed her arms and scowled some more.

"Oh, Jen, cut it out. You love Uncle Bryan. You guys always have a great time with him."

Jennifer just raised a single eyebrow at this—a facial gesture Maggie knew she herself would have had to work on for months to achieve. She laughed to try to take back control. "Finish your breakfasts. Then we'll go out and look up the Argersingers. See what's going on with Rodney and Stone. It looks like it's clearing up."

It worked. The girls raced to finish. They cleaned up and left Jason still there, at work now on the front steps.

The Argersingers' house had a huge wraparound porch, and this was where she now sat with Gertie, sipping coffee. It gave them quite a vantage point: they could see the entire front walk and the comings and goings of her girls and Gertie's boys, who appeared to be carrying wet sand up from the edge of the lake in buckets, presumably for a sand castle. Sam sat contentedly on the edge of the activity patting the sand. Maggie knew she'd be singing quietly to herself.

"Your girls are darling," Gertie commented, holding her cup of coffee close on the ridge of her ample stomach, a result of bearing children over such a long span of years, Maggie guessed. Other than the table of her stomach, Gertie was a slender woman whose face, made youthful by rosy cheeks and animated eyes, likewise made her age almost indeterminate. "My sons are always looking for someone around here to play with."

"Thanks." Maggie tried to accept the compliment without protest, but couldn't quite manage it completely. "It would be great if they'd be active enough to keep up with your two."

"Isn't that the truth." Gertie laughed. "But, you know what? Did Annie tell you she's doing a day care program for lake people this summer? It starts next week. By then, a few more families will have arrived. She keeps the kids in the morning—we even feed them lunch, if you want. I pay her to watch Rod and Stone. I love it. I can call the morning my own. But I'm around in case there's an emergency."

"How great. I have the feeling my two will be frequent attendees."

"Annie would like that. Will your husband be able to join you later in the summer? Janine said you all are from Chicago."

Maggie felt her back stiffen with the realization of the speed of the rumor mill in this small summer community. "I don't know. He's a corporate attorney, and for some reason, his caseload increases in the summer. We'll see." She looked out the screen at the far horizon, marked by an endless stretch of water. "Say, where's the lighthouse?" It was time to change the subject. "We heard the foghorn early this morning, and I promised Sam we'd go look at it."

"Oh, it's really close. The only reason you can't see it from here is that there's a dune in the way. See the end of that pier over there to the right?" Gertie pointed with her arm. "It's on the shore-end of that. It's cute. I think they even let you inside to climb the stairs on some Saturdays— when the tourism people are around."

"Maybe we'll go then," Maggie speculated. She rose to leave, but this seemed to remind Gertie of something because she stood up quickly.

"Sorry my husband Dave is not around to say hello. We own a car service place on the way into town, and he practically lives there. He's always had a thing for cars, and he's somehow found a way to make a living from it. Stop in if you ever need anything—you can't miss the 'Argersinger' sign."

"Oh, I will. I'm sure to need an oil change at some point this summer."

"Good. It may be the only way you get to meet him. You'll find him either puttering in the office or underneath the hood of a car. I tease him that he's married to those cars."

Maggie tried to smile, but the conversation had taken a turn that reminded her too much of her own situation. "Thanks again, Gertie, for your neighborliness—for everything."

"Don't think anything of it. There are a few people around here who aren't very outgoing. I try to make up for them."

<hr>

By the time they returned to their cottage, Jason had already finished. There was a new blond board in the steps that stood out from the other brown ones, and the smell of fresh sawdust was in the air. Maggie looked around, but couldn't see any shavings. She made a mental note to add "neatness" to his list of good qualities.

There was also a handwritten page attached to the screen. "I'll be back to paint the step later," it read.

The phone was ringing when they walked in, and Jennifer rushed to grab it. "Oh, Daddy," she sighed. "I've been hoping you'd call."

Oh, damn, went through Maggie's mind. She could almost hear the level voice on the other end saying, "Hello, princess," as though nothing had changed. She left the room to signal she had no interest in talking, but Jennifer ignored it.

"*Mom*my. *Mom*my. Daddy wants to talk to you."

She took a deep breath and made her way back to the living room, her top lip caught in her bottom teeth as though to say her lips were forever sealed. This was what deception—deceiving her kids about why they were here—was going to cost her. She closed her eyes as she lifted the receiver, concentrating on sounding nonchalant, remote, coolly professional. "Hello."

"Hi, Maggie? So, are you all settled in?" His voice was loud. Commanding.

Maggie held the heavy phone to her ear with her right hand, her other trapped under her right armpit. It was amazing, she thought, how exposed you could feel when the person with whom you've shared the most intimate details of your life has gone to a place where he is willing to use what he knows about you to do you harm. Her mistake had been in moving unthinkingly from intimacy to trust, she decided.

She turned her back to the room so Jen wouldn't study her every facial expression. "Yes, we're fine. Just fine." Try for professional-sounding, she told herself. And remote. And calm. And very, *very* dispassionate.

"Jen is telling me I need to visit."

Maggie tried to turn her back more. "I don't think that would be such a good idea."

"Maggie, c'mon. Ease up. Not even for her birthday? Like I told you before, you're making too big a deal out of this whole thing."

"Am I?" Too big a deal? Maggie couldn't keep the anger out of her voice. "That's for me to decide. We'll talk about it later. Bryan's coming to visit in just a couple days," she lied. "He's going to be here for a while." She knew this would cool Sheldon off.

"Oh, how nice. So, your brother can come visit, but your husband can't?"

"Yes, that's it." She wanted to add, "Yeah, but my brother didn't betray me," but Jennifer was still there, still following her side of the conversation closely, probably attaching significance to every word. She needed to end this, keep him from wearing away at her.

"Maggie, I could make this difficult for you."

Maggie could hear the edge in his voice that often masqueraded as a threat, and she felt the prickling at the base of her skull. She held the phone away from herself slightly so that her swallow was silent. She wanted to scream, "But you're the one who committed adultery!" She refrained, sensing the girls at her back.

"I could make things difficult for you, after . . . everything."

Maggie quickly glanced over her shoulder at her daughters. Jen was studying her silently. She tried to smile in their direction. *Not after I make mincemeat of you in court*, she finished the thought for him silently. "Any judge would understand what I was going through" would have been her rejoinder, but the girls would hear. She could feel the self-doubt creeping through her; she needed to end this now.

Her hesitation gave him the opening he needed. "And frankly, I'm leery of having you be the girls' only parent for an entire summer."

"Oh, come now." Maggie said this forcefully, with as much confidence as she could muster, trying to modulate the edge of sarcasm in her voice enough for him to hear but for Jen to miss. "We'll talk later. Nice of you to call. Bye, now." She replaced the phone quickly before he could begin to wheedle and threaten with all the finesse of a man who made a profession out of it.

As soon as she'd hung up, she felt sick. Surely Sheldon couldn't do what he threatened. Maggie tried not to think about it. Maybe it would go away. She shook her head in self-disgust: This was the way she had always protected herself, by removing herself, taking herself out of the loop. Go away for a summer. Sheldon might be able to intimidate her, but she was certain there was a limit to how much she was willing to compromise herself. She knew deep in her heart, she would never stand passively by if her children were threatened.

Maggie didn't know when she had become so weak, so uncertain. She could remember a time when she had been completely independent, a rebel even. Conformity and acceptance, after all, were the standards that dogged all of Winifred DeCour's children, and Maggie had lived her young adult life to defy the standards. But, apparently, now that she should be staring them down one more time, fear was her overwhelming emotion. Probably because the stakes were so high.

She now looked back on her married life as testimony to what happened when you let the circumstances of your life run roughshod over you. She had been like the belly-up, floating frog in the pot of boiling water. The frog would never have been there at all had the water not been heated slowly and imperceptibly. If the water had been boiling from the start, the frog would have never submitted to it, would have jumped out immediately. But the changes had been so gradual, had gone on so long, unnoticed . . . and were so cumulative as to worm their way through every defense.

"So, *is* he coming or not?" Jennifer stomped her foot to get her mother's attention.

"Jen." Maggie tried hard not to sound exasperated. She couldn't punish her daughter for her husband's failings, but she couldn't let Sheldon use the children as leverage against her. She tried to stroke her daughter's hair, but Jennifer pulled away.

"You want to ruin my birthday!"

"Jennifer." Maggie was getting cross now. "That isn't true, and you know it. You are not to badger me. Now, I am going upstairs to lie down because I have a headache, and you are to go to your own room and stay there until you are ready to talk nicely. And, Sam, it's time for your nap too."

Maggie hurried up the stairs. She knew if she did, Jennifer couldn't argue.

Maggie had met Sheldon shortly after her thirtieth birthday. Maybe, she speculated, that was why she had no expectations of experiencing full eardrums and stomach jitters—the ways she had always previously gauged whether she was in love. She was a young professional working for the *Sun*. She had started out as green as they came, was given a job writing obituaries—an assignment that still made her skin crawl—and had worked her way up through the usual female ranks of covering society events to the substantial position of investigative reporter. She was part of the team that uncovered the misuse of public funds by the city administration then in power. She'd met Sheldon at a party thrown by a mutual friend soon after this story broke. Somehow they'd both ended up on the patio with drinks in their hands and had struck up a conversation. He'd been impressed with her knowledge of the city's political machinery. She'd been impressed by his knowledge of the law's adaptability. They were married two years later.

So, why was it, she wondered, that she currently lacked so much confidence? Had Sheldon undermined her sense of self so completely that it had come to this? Was it her mother's everlasting curse? If she were going to do anything this summer, it would be to regain her sense of competence. It would not be an easy task for someone with her recent struggles, a husband who threatened a custody battle, and a precocious almost-six-year-old who was way too perceptive for her mother's good.

⸺⸺•((◉))•⸺⸺

They woke to rain the next morning as well. Early summer can be cool and rainy, Gertie had warned. Yeah, thought Maggie, but "cool and rainy" in this household translated into "nothing to do." She'd have to think of something to head boredom off at the pass. She could just picture the scenario that would follow if Jen figured out a way to make phone calls to her father to complain about how horrible the summer was. No, Maggie would have to keep that from happening.

She suggested to the girls that they spend the morning poking around in, and cleaning out, the storeroom. She'd seen a couple of bikes down there; maybe there was even a trike. They could see if they needed much work to get them in running order. If so, it was something Bryan could help with when he came to visit, and Jen and Sam could ride up and down the walk with Rodney and Stone. Jennifer could barely eat breakfast, she was so eager to take a look at the treasures below. She sat on the edge of her chair and launched cold cereal into her mouth.

But once they got down the stairs, it was hard to know where to begin. Things were piled up haphazardly with no attempt made to establish any reason or organization. There was a rough workbench under the long, dirty and clouded window that looked out just above ground level. The bench was full of bell jars in all sizes, clay pots in all states of disrepair, used and forgotten rags, gardening tools, empty sacks. It was hard to tell what the substance of the other piles actually consisted of, though it looked like battered beach furniture and more gardening supplies. There was no way this was going to appeal to the attention span of her girls.

"Okay." She decided to try for the camp counselor voice. "This is a pretty big mess. I have an idea. Why don't we just clean up what we need to get to the bikes in the back. We'll clear a path, get rid of the stuff no one needs. That will be enough for today."

"Yay!" Both girls had thrown themselves into it, primarily pitching things back to her, which she then had to decide what to do with. There were a couple of interesting items, including a small wooden music box, its top faded. It had art on it that looked like it could have been from her grandmother's era, all garlands of flowers framing the porcelain face of a young girl. The paint had aged and was cracked, leaving deep, dark lines across the face of the girl and across the letter "J" beneath her. Maggie lifted the lid and heard the notes of ice skating music: "Les Patineurs." The inside was a little snow globe where a small skater twirled while snowflakes fell around her.

They were practically upon the bikes when Jennifer gasped and screamed. Maggie looked up in time to see what could only be a black rat scuttle along the wall under the workbench and out a nearly invisible hole in the stone and mortar foundation.

Maggie shivered inadvertently, but tried to give the appearance of calm. Rodents were not her long suit, she had to admit. Did rats go with the territory here as well as ants? If so, where did they come from? It didn't make sense. "Oh, oh. I guess we've disturbed a visitor. All the more reason to get this cleaned up down here. Maybe that's why they call it a 'rat's nest.'" When in doubt, try humor, she reminded herself.

But Jennifer wouldn't have any of it. She stood aside while Maggie pulled the bicycles out from the pile they were buried in.

Maggie worked quickly to get a bike and a trike outside in the light. It was already clearing, just as it had yesterday. The tricycle had one very wobbly back wheel that might be too much even for Bryan. Maggie clicked her tongue when she saw it.

Sam started to reach for the bell on the handlebars and clutched her mother's wrist instead. She whimpered once, then plunged her thumb in her mouth.

Maggie looked up. Their neighbor from across the walk had come to the front of her screen door, perhaps to see what the hubbub was all about. She stood now with her face pressed almost against the screen. Even from the distance of fifteen yards, Maggie could make out the angry red strawberry mark that started from above her right eye and flowered out over one cheek, nearly engulfing half her face.

She looked away guiltily and took Sam's hand, certain the woman had seen the child's reaction. "Sam, this trike needs more work. We'll leave it in the basement and see if Uncle Bryan can fix it when he's here." She had steered Sam back toward the basement as Jen emerged, wheeling a bicycle that looked in fair shape and just about the right size. "Oh, Jen," Maggie seized on this fortune, "this may be the summer you learn to ride a two-wheeler. In the meantime, maybe we could get you some training wheels so you can still hang out with Rodney and Stone. . . ." She let her voice trail off when she realized Jen had also caught sight of the woman next door and now stood transfixed, staring at her.

Thankfully, their reprieve was already in sight, Maggie realized when she saw Jason, a can of paint in hand, climbing up the stairs from the beach. She waved at him, perhaps more enthusiastically than the situation warranted.

He looked at her quizzically, but waved back. She noticed for the first time what a gentle face he had, dark and cloudy eyes, but gentle just the same.

CHAPTER 3

With the weekend came the weekenders: families from Dearborn and Flint, fathers from Chicago and Gary. They were the interlopers, descending on the beach with their towels and umbrellas blinking unwittingly in the bright sun and rubbing suntan lotion on their white shoulders and stomachs.

A large group, probably more than one family, was moving into the corner cottage at the bottom of the hill facing the lake. There had been a steady stream of family members toting suitcases and grocery bags from the parking lot last night, organized by two overweight men in loud Hawaiian shirts who had walked back and forth on the main sidewalk, preceded by their girth. One of the men was already out this morning firing up the grill they'd positioned close to the sidewalk. Maggie nodded as she went past and wondered what in the world one grilled at this hour of the morning.

She had hoped to get out early enough to secure a spot on the beach close to the water and before the sun got too hot, but the usual things had gone wrong, and now she and the girls were having to pick their way through the sunbathing bodies decked out in sunglasses and wide-brimmed hats so they could find a place to spread out their towels. "There's a spot," Maggie blurted out, causing heads to turn. She wasn't in the best of moods, she had to admit. Pulling out her bathing suits and putting one on had been the first bitter pill she'd had to swallow in what seemed to be a steady regimen of them since arriving at Breakwater Bay.

Her present state of mind was so different from the one she remembered the last time she had been here. She felt like something that had crawled out of its hole to putter past creatures that belonged to the light, running, leaping, diaphanous creatures who were confident in their sheer young physicality, playing volleyball on the beach, running through the waves. Now she felt like a mole venturing out of its burrow and into the sun. She felt herself scuttling along and promised herself she would start walking more.

She'd lugged along a squat beach chair from the storage room and a couple of huge beach towels, which she spread out side by side. The girls had carried their shovels and pails.

No sooner had she settled into her low-slung canvas seat than Jenny jumped up and scampered over to her, circling Maggie's head with her hands like a halo. "Oh, Mommy, I want to fix your hair?"

"My hair?"

"It looks so pretty in the sun. Shiny."

Maggie laughed and patted her head along with the little hands that still rested there. "And what do you intend to do with my hair?"

"Braid it."

"Braid it? I didn't know you knew how to braid. Where did you learn that?"

"A babysitter." Jennifer had already circled behind her and was pulling on some of the long strands that often fell into Maggie's face, separating them out from the rest.

"Yeah, bade it." Sam stood up too, eager to get in on the act. But instead of joining her sister, she plopped herself in Maggie's lap.

Maggie couldn't help it. She laughed again. Whoever had said you could tell what a child's personality was from the get-go was right. Jennifer had always been royalty, in command, from the time she ordered the delivery room staff around with her cries. And then, once in a while, like today, she softened a little and showed some concern for her subjects. And Sam? Sam would have to be the quiet explorer with the outsized imagination. But it was Jen who, like her mother, had her grandmother's eyes.

Maggie often looked for something of herself in her daughters, yet so seldom found it. She supposed that was part of the reason motherhood sat on her shoulders like an uneasy mantle—that, and the fact that she hadn't had the best role model in the world. Motherhood had never been natural, never been automatic. It was hard not to filter everything through the memories of her own childhood.

"Shall I bade it?" With that, Sam pushed herself up, using Maggie's thigh for a platform.

"Ugh." Maggie gave a surprised grunt from the pain. "Okay, kids, that's enough. I'm sure I'm quite beautiful enough. Now, how about going to work on your sand castle?"

"Well, okay." Jennifer reverted to her take-charge voice. "But I don't have a rubber band for this. You must hold your head still, Mommy, or it'll unwind."

Maggie reached up and felt for Jen's handiwork. It felt a bit like knotted hair with some loose strands whorled around it. "Nice work. It feels very beautiful. Now you two go play in the sand for the time being. Okay?" Don't ask, she reminded herself. Don't give a choice when you don't want one or the other option to be chosen.

"Okay." Jen gave her mother a quick hug, then picked up the sand shovel and pail.

Maggie watched her girls for a few minutes more. Jen was already tanning bronze—like her father. She had insisted on two ponytails this morning, and her dark hair was unevenly caught in two places in the general area of the nape of her neck. Now she studied the sand serenely, as though planning her next move. Sam's vantage point was from her haunches. She squatted and went to work immediately, scooping sand furiously. Sam was so focused that it was difficult to watch her for too long without being drawn in to what she was doing. She was still full throttle in the discovery stage Maggie enjoyed so.

Maggie loved the days when her children seemed to fit into the general world order, hated it when things got cross-grained. Not that either could be predicted. Much less controlled. She opened the book she'd found on a shelf in the cottage. It had all the trappings of a beach book. There were even some grains of sand stuck between the pages. A good read was all she wanted. Was that asking too much? She didn't think so and adjusted her visor and turned the page.

She couldn't have read much more than a paragraph when a shadow fell across her page from behind. It seemed as though the world around her became quiet as well. Maggie lifted her eyes, without raising her head, to watch a woman in a two-piece bathing suit walk by as though gracing a fashion runway. Maggie was aware that several other pairs of eyes, in addition to her own, followed the woman's progress as well. Maggie tried to guess her age. She couldn't be too young; she was too stately, too self-possessed.

Once the woman got to the water's edge, she waded in a couple of steps, then turned and followed the shoreline, oblivious to the eyes tracking her. The girl—no, the woman—from Ipanema, Maggie decided. On a Michigan beach. Maggie continued to watch until the woman became a small dot at the edge of the shoreline, her footprints in the sand already erased by the constant lapping of the waves.

Maggie wondered if someone so beautiful could be a friend, then thought of Muriel. Muriel wasn't particularly beautiful. Nor did it seem to matter to her. Muriel knew how to be a friend. When Maggie had learned the full extent of Sheldon's affair, it was Muriel who had been her rock. It was Muriel who had done the ranting for her: "What a stupid, stupid man. To gamble away his relationship with a substantial woman like you!"

By late spring, Muriel had added another dimension to her rant, including the U.S. senator from Colorado who had been the Democrats' leading candidate in his bid for President and who was now contending with rumors of extramarital affairs: "Just look at the fool Gary Hart. Sheldon and Gary Hart, two powerful men who think they can get away with anything. Carrying on with floozies. Too bad all the cheating husbands of the world aren't held up to that kind of scrutiny—those standards." Maggie had just nodded in agreement, glad to let someone else share all those exhausting emotions. Yet, at the same time, feeling slightly defensive, wondering whether she ought not defend Sheldon in some way.

Before Maggie could get back to her book, she was interrupted, again, this time by a familiar voice. Apparently, an ordinary day at the beach was not in the cards.

"Hey. It *is* you. I recognized you by these two sun fairies here." Jason came around to face her. He seemed to be totally free of what her friend Muriel would call "accouterments"—no excess baggage or trimmings, no beach props. He wore no shirt, and his cutoffs were faded and worn.

Maggie couldn't help but think what a great-looking chest he had, probably the result of all the physical labor he did. She felt for the nest in her hair and tried to comb it out with her fingers while also working to hold in her stomach.

She drew a breath in that sounded like a sigh, even to her. "You're not working?"

"Nope. Even the help gets a day off around here."

Maggie thought she heard a trace of sarcasm in his voice and wondered if her question had hit a nerve.

"Time off is one of the benefits of the job." He turned to look out at the lake. "That and the water." Without waiting for an invitation, he sat down in the sand next to their beach towels, crossing his legs and resting them within the circle of his arms. "The water. Now, *that* is the main attraction." Jason didn't take his eyes off the lake as he spoke.

"So you're a fan of the water?" Maggie wanted to engage him, make amends for whatever had irritated him.

"I am. It has a life of its own." He hesitated a moment, as though deep in reverie, then slapped his calves. "But I didn't try to find you to get starry-eyed over Lake Michigan. I heard you wanted to see the lighthouse."

The image of a rumor mill churning incessantly came to Maggie. "Oh, yeah, Gertie must have mentioned it to you."

"She did." He nodded. "It's not that far. The girls might like to walk over there."

Maggie wondered why he was doing this. They had just gotten settled. . . "Jen, Sam, wanna go see the lighthouse? Sam, you know, the deep horn that sounds so mysterious?"

Sam pushed herself up from the sand, butt first, barely able to walk with the effort of carrying a full bucket of sand. "Yeah, let's see the lights out. I'll take *this*." Sam lugged her pail toward them.

"Sam, you don't want to take that." Maggie tried to dissuade her.

"Yes, I do. The sand wants to go too."

Maggie closed her eyes and took a breath.

"I'll carry this sand," Jason interceded. "This sand is so eager for a little trip."

Samantha watched her mother as she handed over her pail to Jason as if to say, "See, I was right."

The four made the trek by walking along the line of the water. The waves foamed up on shore, unpredictably, then retreated, leaving a froth at the edges. And the wet sand was darker than the rest. The girls ran ahead, daring the water to wash across their feet, then, when it did, squealing and running because the water was cold. They reminded Maggie of the killdeer bird as it ventured into the water only to screech and skitter away, making much out of very little.

She and Jason walked slowly, without speaking. Jason seemed to be watching the boats on the lake.

"Do you sail?" she asked.

"I do. Would you like to go sometime?"

"Oh, no, no, no," Maggie answered too quickly. "I wasn't trying to finagle an invitation."

"I know." He shrugged.

"A-h-h-h-h. Yuck." Jennifer had stopped in her tracks and was shaking her body in distaste.

"Wha'd you find?" Maggie called to her, coming closer.

"Uggy. Yucky." Sam had run over and was making little dancing steps on the tips of her toes.

Maggie could see it was a dead fish even before she got near, its entrails floating out from it, back and forth with each ebb and flow of the waves.

It was Jason, swinging the bucket of sand, who chided them both. "It's just a dead fish. You'll need to get used to it. You'll see plenty more before the summer's over."

Jennifer and Sam looked at him as though disappointed that he had put such an easy end to their histrionics. It was several seconds before they could bring themselves to walk on.

In addition to washed-up fish, there were heavy ropes of brown seaweed at the edge of the waves' range. These were adorned with bits of plastic trash. Maggie didn't remember seeing all sorts of refuse from her summer here when she was a teenager.

The lighthouse was visible as soon as they got around the dune Gertie had mentioned. It was a little building at the beach end of a breakwater. It was shorter and squatter than she'd expected with a fat tower on top. The building was something of a disappointment, really. An American flag and another smaller one that Maggie didn't recognize sprouted from the tower's point. The best part of the building was that it was painted red.

A concrete breakwater extended from it out into Lake Michigan. Several people strolled along the concrete structure. Most were couples, holding hands, Maggie noted.

The girls raced up the steps to the lighthouse. Jennifer pulled on the door, but it was closed and locked.

"That's a shame," said Jason. "Too early in the season, I guess. Oh well. Now that you know where it is, you can come back another time." He turned away.

Sam retreated immediately, but Jennifer had grabbed onto the door handle again and tugged at it several times before letting it go. Then she peered into a window through cupped hands. She pulled back once, then looked again. Maggie waited for Jennifer to say something. But she seemed to think better of it and let go of the handle. Or perhaps Sam's outburst took precedence over whatever Jen was going to say.

"*Ja*-son." Sam stood next to the steps, refusing to budge. "Don't forget. The *sand*."

"Of course not." Maggie was surprised at how much gentle seriousness he was able to muster. "But I'm not sure where it's supposed to go?"

"Her—" Sam started to say. Then, "No, *here*." She hollowed out a spot in the sand where she stood by, twisting her arms so they drove her feet into the sand like a corkscrew.

Jason obeyed, ceremoniously holding the bucket out from his body in the form of an offering—and then giving his blessing: "I'm sure this sand will be happy in its new home."

"Me too." Sam clapped a little as she said it.

They had almost turned to head back when Maggie stopped. It seemed so odd, really. One of the boats seemed to be heading directly into shore. "Jason, are they going to crash?"

"Wha—? Oh. The boat. It does look that way, doesn't it? But, no. There's a channel right through there that you can't really see from where we are because of the shore-line and the vegetation. It goes into a small inlet lake off the big lake. Off Lake Michigan. The marinas are all there. It's also why the lighthouse, or 'lights out,' as Sam so nicely put it, is where it is."

Another lake. Maggie was surprised she hadn't remem-bered that from her summer before. It must have been be-cause in those days her life had been all about the beach on the *big* lake. And the people on the beach.

Maggie was tired on the way back and braced her-self for complaints from the girls, who had to be tired as well. She tried to watch Jason out of the corner of her eye. Not for the first time. Who was he, really, she wondered. He seemed like such an old soul. And some-what sad—sad and tired. And why was he taking such an interest in them? Maybe he didn't have anything bet-ter to do.

⸺⸺◉⸺⸺

Maggie was grateful to have both her girls in tow as they headed for the Argersingers on Monday, more or less on time. Their tardiness had been the result of the usual early morning squabbles. She had called Jennifer twice to get dressed and come down for breakfast. The next thing she knew, Jen was standing at the top of the landing, looking down, hands on her hips, saying, "Don't call me Jennifer. My name is not Jennifer."

Maggie knew she was taking the bait, but couldn't help herself: "So, what is it, then? Your name, that is."

Jen had looked down at her mother over an upturned nose. "It's Oyster, of course."

What kind of a hell name is that, Maggie wanted to call up, but she restrained herself. "Oh. How did you *choose* that name?"

"I didn't *choose* it; it's just my name," Jennifer had explained with the bald reasoning of a five-year-old.

By now, Sam was on the landing next to Jennifer, doing a good imitation of her sister, with her hands on her hips as well. "What's a 'hoister'?" she asked. Then, "That's what I am too."

"I see." Maggie ignored Samantha and tried to sound matter-of-fact, though her patience was already wearing thin. "Isn't that a strange name for a child?"

"I'm *not* a child."

Maggie decided to steer clear of this comment. Jennifer had gone down what she called the rabbit hole of reasoning, a place where Alice-in-Wonderland logic prevailed.

"Of course you're not a child. You're Oyster. Which also means you're not interesting in watching any television." Maggie could see Jen flinch slightly at this. "Now, how about a plankton diet or will you settle for corn flakes so we can get to Annie's on time?"

"I'll settle." Jennifer was already on her way down the stairs, holding her head high as though suspended by some invisible guy wire.

———»((◉))«———

All weekend, during the days' lulls, Maggie had contemplated how she would spend this first morning without the girls. She stopped at the cottage long enough to retrieve her camera from one of the unpacked boxes in her room, slung it over her shoulder, and pocketed a couple of rolls of film she'd remembered to get at the grocery store.

Other than photos of her daughters, she hadn't been serious about photography since her working days—and, even then, though it was conceded she was a fair reporter, she knew her colleagues considered her a hack photojournalist, a dilettante.

It had been easy for her while working on a newspaper to get drawn into the darkroom. She'd had one editor lambast her for taking a photo of the mayor, telling her it was "not objective" and therefore, "not good journalism," even though he got overruled and the photo ran next to her story.

The angle from which she'd taken the photo had made it controversial. The mayor had been above her on a podium, and Maggie had crouched down some more so she could take the photo from below him, looking up. She had also held her flash attachment out from the camera, angling it up. The combination of the light illuminating his face from below and the prominent ledges of his eyebrows had given a ghoulish effect to the photo, which no doubt had delighted his detractors when it ran on the paper's front page the next day.

But today Maggie had a purely apolitical agenda. She'd decided to hike up one of the dunes to take a look at some of the cottages built above theirs. Perhaps she could find something particularly picturesque and capture Breakwater Bay's storybook quality through the tall dune grasses.

Maggie set out by heading up the stairs that went past her own cottage. She felt the weight of the camera against her hip. It felt familiar, like a part of her that was somehow restored. She tucked her palm under the lens and used her cupped fingers to cradle the camera on the climb up.

When the steps ended at the last house in their row, she struck out along what looked like the path of least resistance through the dune grass and sand. The sand's heat was fierce, and she was glad she'd worn tennis shoes instead of sandals, even though her shoes were filling with sand.

There was only a single house at the top of the dune that Maggie could see. It stood at the end of a long sidewalk, the concrete losing the battle to the encroaching sand. Tall bushes grew next to it and made it hard to see much of what was behind them. Maggie wondered if she was intruding, but couldn't imagine that. She hadn't seen any No Trespassing signs.

Once she crested the dune, she realized the sand actually fell off from the house at a sharp angle, forming a huge bowl in the sand below. A lone man, a jogger she guessed, was running away from her along what would be the bowl's lip, heading for what looked like a tire track road below.

She stood still a moment to get her bearings. She must be looking north along the Lake Michigan shore. This vantage point showed how uneven the water line actually was, jutting into the shore in some places, playing itself out in others. She could see where the channel by the lighthouse tucked into the shore. Her eyes followed what she guessed was its line of travel and—ah, yes. There it was, the inlet lake. Another container of shimmering blue, with lots of little bobbing sticks, sailboat masts rising and falling in harmony with the passing small-boat traffic. There was an open sandy area just on the other side of the channel, decorated with towels and umbrellas.

The incongruity in the entire scene, however, was what looked like a cluster of high-rise condominiums beyond the beach. The buildings' footprints were stuck in huge concrete pads that must allow for its parking lots. The structures threatened to go right to the water's edge. The contrast was startling.

Maggie smiled with the sense of discovery and crouched low in the sand, pointing her camera so the frame would show the sterile condominiums and concrete slabs offset, perhaps even eclipsed, by the delicate threads of waving reeds. And if she could just catch the sun's glint backlighting the feathery heads of the grass . . .

Deep breath in. Hold. Smooth click. She heard the shutter and pictured its sharp metal sheaves broadening to form the aperture, then closing sharply, shutting out all light. Quickly. Mechanically. Perfect. So simple. And predictable. Maggie breathed and felt herself relax; she stretched her shoulders down to lengthen her neck. Perfect.

Cartier-Bresson had been her inspiration for studies of people. Ever since she'd opened the art book of his photos her friend Muriel used to display on a coffee table, back when they were all starting out. The man was a genius, really. The way he could capture the repetition of line, even dynamics, within the frame. The human and background so closely fused. The prototype had to be the one where Faulkner stood in the foreground tensing his forearm in a slightly threatening way, his dog in the background stretching his hind legs in exact replication of the tension in his master's stance.

The wind came up suddenly. She rose, allowing a small sense of accomplishment to envelop her. It was not going to be a picture of a rustic summer cottage, certainly, but it had the potential to make a statement, nonetheless.

"Whoa—" She caught herself speaking aloud. What had started as a summer breeze became a loud eddying, a beating almost. A sand devil kicked up next to her, the grains stinging her bare legs. Sand pelted her face, causing her to shade her eyes from the grit and quickly cover her camera lens with her hand.

The steady whirring sound was loud enough to induce a visceral pumping in her chest. Maggie gave up the notion that a summer squall had come up off the lake. She looked up to see a helicopter, its spinning rotors blurred into a single dragonfly wing above its iridescent body, the sun glinting on its metal like sparks shot from flint on stone.

At first, she thought it was coming right at her, but then it hovered, suspended above the dune bowl, preparing itself to settle into the hollow. The winds from the chopper's rotors were still strong, but Maggie worked around the side of the bowl, following the path she'd seen the jogger take. Should she get out of the way, put as much distance between herself and the mechanical bird, or should she stop a minute and take a look at it through her shutter, see whether this heavy metal object against the lake presented an even greater contrast than the condos against the dunes?

The gusting from the blades made the decision for her. She hurried, shielding her eyes from the sand. She did want to see who might step out of the helicopter. Was this the travel mode of choice of one very wealthy cottage owner?

It must have been the wind and her efforts to protect her eyes that prevented Maggie from seeing the jogger until he was nearly upon her. She had no idea where he had come from, but met her several feet from the tire tracks, grabbing her arm at the elbow and jerking it up hard.

"What are you doing here? This is private property."

The noise of the rotors made it nearly impossible to understand him, but Maggie could see the grotesque face, the narrowed eyes and mouth that curled around his words. She jerked her elbow away from him and staggered back, ready to make a jabbing kick, if necessary, to defend herself.

He feinted back, then lunged for the camera. "I'll take that. No pictures."

Maggie jumped back. The noise from the copter was subsiding. It gave her the opening to launch her verbal defense. "Get your hands away from my camera. Look, I didn't know, okay? I did not take any pictures of the helicopter, for Christ's sake. I'm sorry. But you're not touching this camera. *It's private property too.*"

He twisted his head slightly in concession and held up his hands. "Okay, okay. But get out of here. Now."

"I'm going." Maggie walked away quickly, though she had no idea where she was headed. She held her camera braced against her side, and looked back a couple of times. The jogger/ bodyguard, whatever, was still there, arms across his chest, following her progress with his eyes the entire way.

She hurried down the other side of the dune. She couldn't be that far from home, but nothing looked familiar. The track road twisted around the bottom of the dune and became a one-lane asphalt road surrounded by trees. She was sure she was heading in the right direction, but wished for the world she could find a familiar landmark.

Once she was through the trees, things opened into a small clearing with two strange buildings, tightly guarded by the trees along their perimeter. Office buildings, perhaps, except that they looked more like bunkers. She kept going. There was a gate with a steel drop bar, but it seemed capable only of keeping vehicles out. She had no trouble getting around it. There were more beach houses. She shaded her eyes, then. Yes, there it was: the guard station into their community. Breakwater Bay.

She felt like making a run for it, then caught herself. How silly was that? She still had the camera on her shoulder. *Use your eyes. Look around. Visualize. It's why you came here.* She felt a small seed of determination lodge in her gut. A feeling she used to get when she was on to something in the newsroom. An overwhelming curiosity. Maggie was certain she had come close to having a glimpse of the infamous Blailock. And she intended to find out more about a man who would hire a bodyguard to keep people away from him.

CHAPTER 4

Maggie was upstairs rummaging through the shelves in one of the wood-paneled closets when she heard Bryan's fist shake the screen door a couple of times before pulling it open. "I've arrived," he called into the house as Jennifer and Sam ran to greet him.

"Uncle By!" Sam leaped into his arms, and he tossed her a little in the air, nearly missing her on the way down.

"Whoa, Sam-ski, you're getting bigger every day. You're almost too much for me to throw around."

Jen stood back a little. Maggie could see she wanted to be swung as well, but wasn't about to ask. "And, Jen. Pretty as a picture, as always."

"I made you this." Jennifer ran over to the phone stand, where she'd been keeping the sand candle they had made during the week at Annie's. The children had dug out shapes in the sand for their molds, and then Annie and Gertie had poured melted wax into them. Jennifer's was a blue star, its points small nubs clinging for dear life to a very fat center.

"Well, isn't this something? Thank you." Then Bryan turned his attention to Maggie. She could tell he was appraising her, sizing her up, calculating what the toll from the past spring had been. She tried to walk easily down the stairs, smiling, to show him she was in control. Things were just fine, thank you.

"I'm so glad you decided to pay us a visit, Bro-Bry. I suppose it doesn't hurt that your sis has a place right on Lake Michigan?"

"Not at all, not at all," he said, squeezing her at the waist and kissing her on the cheek. "So, when do I get to see this great lake?" As though he hadn't already been down to the water's edge before coming up to their cottage.

"Now, *now*." Sam was jumping up and down.

Maggie explained to Bryan over the top of Sam's head that she had had the girls doing chores this morning in preparation for his visit. But now that the biggest kid in the world had arrived, there would be no holding them back. "Your room is at the left of the stairs—the one above the living room—with folded sheets on the unmade bed, if you're really ready to head down to the beach this minute and want to put a suit on."

"A swimming suit." Bryan opened his eyes wide at Samantha and winked at Jennifer. "Nobody told me to bring a swimming suit."

"But, Uncle Bry. You have to take us in the ocean." Then Jennifer caught on to the joke. "Oh, I get it. You're kidding." She shook her head with disdain.

"Five minutes, then we're going," Maggie called to the backs of her daughters as they clambered up the stairs.

———— ❈ ————

"The cottage is nice," Bryan conceded when they were sitting on the beach watching Jen and Sam wading, stooping for shells, and bringing back everything that was larger than a half dollar. "So how are you?"

Maggie waited a minute to answer. She needed to organize her thoughts. She wanted to justify what she had done,

sound like she was on top of things here. Bryan was probably the family's emissary, sent to check on her, make sure
she hadn't gone off the deep end again.

"Things are good. Getting away was definitely what I
needed to do."

"And what's Sheldon up to?"

"You mean, besides philandering?" She looked at him
from beneath her eyebrows.

"You know what I mean."

"As of last time we talked, he thinks we're going to be
able to reconcile this. It was just a slight indiscretion—
if you listen to him." Maggie looked away because she
could feel herself tear up. It wouldn't be good to look
weak now.

It was just the image. The image of Sheldon coming out of a Chicago bistro at noon—within thirty feet
of her—the man who swore he was always too busy to
go to lunch, with his arm around the waist of Angie, the
paralegal who worked for him. Her initial reaction had
been to pull back, to avoid a public confrontation and
the embarrassment of attracting public attention. She'd
recoiled from the pair as though from a raised fist. She
must have actually taken a step backward because she
bumped into one of the café tables on the restaurant's
patio, her hand at her throat. She'd let a wave of nausea
pass, then another, before finally letting go of the table
she'd been using to steady herself. Eight years of marriage had come to this.

Maggie had driven to the bistro to meet Muriel, Rhonda,
and Joan for lunch to celebrate Joan's birthday. Now she
wondered how she could leave. She glanced around quickly
to see if she recognized anyone, if anyone else was a witness
to the shame she felt. Then she'd gone into the restaurant

straight to the ladies' room, where she splashed water on her face and studied herself in the mirror to see if her color was going to betray her: she couldn't bear it if this luncheon was the way her friends found out her husband was having an affair. Her gray eyes had looked dark, stormy almost, and hollow in their sockets. She remembered hating the sight of her own face almost as much as she hated the sight of her husband with another woman.

Bryan seemed to be watching her closely. "But, Maggie, what'll you do if you leave the guy? What happens to the girls?"

"That's what I'm here to figure out!" She sounded angrier than she'd intended. "I'm not exactly without means, you know. I had a *real* profession before getting married. And it's not as though their father is going to divorce *them*." Why was it so hard to claim your own identity when you didn't report to a workstation every morning, she wondered.

Bryan realized he'd pushed too hard. "I'm glad. So you're okay financially?"

"As if my itinerant little brother is in the position to help me out." Her anger made the comment sound mean, not the joke she was aiming for.

"Okay, okay." Bryan held up his palm in a gesture of peace. "Cut me some slack, all right? I admit, I'm not exactly in a position to raise a family. . ." Bryan's voice trailed off as he switched his focus away to some distant point.

Maggie knew Bryan well enough to know this was the end of it, the last time he'd bring the subject up officially. From here on, his impressions of her circumstances would be formed by what he saw going on.

"So, what's to do around here?" Bryan leaned back in the sand on his hands and craned his neck to look around him. "The scene looks either too young—or too old—for me."

"I thought you were here to see us." Maggie tried to look incredulous and offended at the same time.

"Oh, but I am. I am."

<hr/>

On the second day of his visit, Bryan had headed over to one of the marinas to see if there were any boats to rent. It suited Maggie fine. It meant she could take the girls to Annie's a little early in order to pump Gertie for some information about Blailock and any other local color. Maggie's reporter's nose told her she was on the scent of something, but she knew she needed to tread softly. When she'd worked at the *Sun*, she'd frequently been accused of aggressively pursuing a story when there really wasn't one to tell.

She left the girls on the front porch, where the fingerpaints and crayons were already in demand, and followed Annie's suggestion that she just head on in to the house. She found Gertie in the kitchen punching down bread dough. The smell of yeast was heavy in the air, like sweetish sour cream. As a child, she had always associated the aroma with such promise.

Gertie brightened when she walked in and gave Maggie a floury hug. Then Gertie suggested they take their coffee cups and sit on the lawn chairs on the back terrace away from the riotous noise of children playing.

Maggie breathed in the smell of her coffee and looked up the hill. They could hear the morning activities of the corner cottage. Gertie didn't have a very high opinion of the large group renting the corner house: "They come here for a couple of weeks—though it seems like a month—year after year. It's a loud, rowdy bunch that doesn't make much of an effort to get to know anyone else, especially the locals. They trash the place, then leave."

Maggie let her go on for a while, nodding and listening. It seemed as though the group was known for its love of "gear." They had been the first to bring in Jet Skis. "But those didn't last long, thank goodness," Gertie pointed out. "We got them to prohibit those things from coming too close to shore. So then they couldn't launch them from the beach. They're a danger to the swimmers."

Maggie tried not to appear too obvious as she steered the conversation to the topic she was most interested in. "Say, who is Blailock? I keep hearing his name brought up."

"Vincent Blailock?" Gertie's face hardened, and her eyes seemed to lose their focus. "In a word—he's a man with way too much money who's dead set on ruining this place." Apparently Maggie hadn't needed to employ tact in bringing up the subject. Gertie was a geyser waiting to erupt. She spent the next twenty minutes giving a diatribe on Vincent Blailock and his new vision for Breakwater Bay.

Blailock had begun his reign in western Michigan innocently enough, it seemed, training and supervising a Ponzi-style sales force that peddled small household appliances door to door. The original sales force became managers who then ran their own stable of salespeople, getting a cut of the profit everyone under them made. Blailock sat at the apex of the entire triangle and got a cut of it all. As he amassed his unlikely fortune, he was careful to cultivate an aura of largesse. He had, for example, kicked in the major gift for the city's civic center that was named after him. He'd funded children's ball fields in various parks across the city. He was the darling of the City Council and of the Chamber of Commerce. This was what made him an anathema to the citizens of Breakwater. With a few handshakes and slaps on the back, he could get a variance granted from any building code that stood in his way.

After spreading his wealth around, he had quietly, through an agent, begun to amass lakeshore property. When he'd gotten enough, he transformed this as well into tall, sterile condo buildings that housed hundreds and changed the character of the shoreline. Since he had the city in his pocket, he had no trouble getting his projects through what had previously been conservative city zoning that didn't normally allow for such high density growth or development so close to the natural beach.

But what rankled Breakwater residents most was that their precious beach and dunes were threatened. He owned two houses along the front walk and the one on the dune behind them and was slowly trying to amass every other property in the area as it changed hands. The residents had organized against him, purchasing for themselves any house that came on the market and then re-selling it to like-minded buyers themselves or holding it as a rental; but Blailock had fistfuls of money to throw at every property. The temptation to sell out was too great for some.

When Gertie finished with the story, she took the end of her apron and wiped it across her forehead as though the air around her had suddenly become too close. "Oh, we know we can't keep things from changing some. We know that. It's just that we have a piece of heaven here. We're not trying to hitch the shoreline to a towrope to pull it straight. We're not trying to flatten these sand hills, or spray the reed grass out of existence. We don't want our lives to alter the balance. It just seems so worth keeping the way it is." Gertie fell silent, and smiled absently at Maggie.

Maggie felt compelled to speak. "It is a beautiful spot. One well worth protecting."

"And it's so hard when you're up against the big money of the world. But you know what is so odd about all of this?" Gertie was still speaking to some imaginary spot beyond Maggie's head. "People say he grew up around here. How can that be? How can someone who grew up with the lake on one side and the dunes on the other ever want to destroy it the way he is? It's beyond me," Gertie sighed, then seemed to return to the present. "So, have you set eyes on him yet?"

Maggie considered telling about the helicopter incident, but thought better of it. "No."

"And you probably won't, either. He's a real mystery man." Then Gertie seemed to become conscious that she had delivered a railing monologue. "Oh, but if it's history that you want, don't talk to me. Talk to Vernon Chard—or 'Doc Chard' as he's known around here. In the yellow cottage on the front walkway down at the other end. He'll talk your ear off—on a good day. And a lot of it is from personal memory. He has been around here longer than anyone." Gertie grew silent as her thoughts seemed to trail off, and Maggie guessed she'd stayed long enough.

Maggie waved to her girls when she left the Argersingers. Jen barely looked up from the table where she was gluing dried kidney beans in a circle on some poster board. A slight boy, fully a head shorter, stood beside her, intent on his own work of art, warily licking the sunflower seeds before dropping them into a pool of glue. He reminded Maggie of Kent Rhoades, a boy in her own third grade class and the first male to declare his love for her on notes he hid in her coat pocket in the school coatroom. Those were the days of innocent young love, Maggie thought. Right now, that seemed so long ago. She wondered if she'd ever be brave enough to let go of her daughters so they could grow up.

⸺⸺◦((◍))◦⸺⸺

Once outside, Maggie walked partway down the beach and stared at the expanse of water in front of her. What was the lake's attraction, she wondered. Was it something primordial, a life force? Was it that water created such an obvious point of transition, from solid earth to fluid liquid, the two so startlingly different? Was it because water was the medium of baptism, the means by which we could all wash ourselves clean? Or, more likely, reflections were the initial attraction, images of ourselves served up to us. But that was only on the surface. That was so you'd get sucked in. Once you'd immersed your toes, it only took a little effort to wade out a little farther . . . and then a little farther than that . . . until you were something that could let go of its earthly existence, weightless, yet heavy; you became something else entirely.

Maggie wondered whether she might be able to capture water in all its guises in photos. With photos it was all about light, and certainly water served up light in spectacular ways. But water was also dark and brooding, and that might be a more difficult mood to catch. Maggie looked up to see where the sun was.

Gray and blue clouds drifted overhead, creating a dappled effect on the water. More movement. This superficial impermanence made Maggie remember again her own confrontation with Sheldon after she found out about his relationship with Angie. She'd waited several days after seeing them together. By then, she had gone through his jacket pockets; looked back over credit card statements; done everything she could think of to unearth additional incriminating evidence.

When she thought about this now, she wondered whether her actions stemmed from a fundamental disbelief in Sheldon's infidelity or because she needed to create the airtight case: If she was going to confront him, she needed to out-lawyer the lawyer. But her obsession with the discovery somehow altered its nature. The more time that passed, the less determined she had become and the more culpable she herself felt. By the time she had actually confronted him, the wind had gone out of her sails. Maggie found she had not been able to summon enough indignation and outrage when she confronted him because, by then, what she had felt had been simple resignation.

Their own courtship had lasted nearly two years. At first, it had been casual, two professionals who didn't have time for messy commitments. They would go out to dinner, sometimes sitting shoulder to shoulder at a sushi bar, occasionally taking in the theater, often using the other as a partner at a professional social function. Their mutual friends had urged them both on, she remembered. She'd been flattered. And slightly embarrassed. Why did everyone else have such a keen interest in her romantic fate? It was as though the unattached person were an affront, incomplete, something that needed to be fixed. It must have worked, because she herself had felt a measure of relief at the conformity of what had been her married life.

Initially, her relationship with Sheldon had been one of peeling back layers, the excitement of getting to know another person intimately. One came to see life filtered through the eyes of the beloved. But, then, once the layers were gone, what was there? Had it all been too meager? Perhaps it had just gotten too familiar.

When Maggie and Sheldon reached that stage of final intimacy, the task became something else entirely. What followed was a reversal of the process: taking up the discarded layers and, with concentrated and exquisite care, trying to pull them back over the flimsy core, removing to arm's length what had once been so accessible, taking pains to hide from yourself the knowledge that the core had been so unsubstantial, had hardly been worth the effort. Oh, and the children had aided and abetted. By demanding attention, they had been the distraction that allowed the steady re-accumulation of layers to continue, to become complete until you felt as if you really didn't know the person you were living with.

Occasionally, Maggie would watch Sheldon as he leaned close to the bureau mirror to get his full Windsor just right. She would wonder who he really was and where his thoughts took him. And whether she was ever in them.

If marriage could be graphed scientifically, like the rise and fall of the Roman Empire, then Maggie believed theirs would had to have been in that final stage of decay where all was strictly sumptuous display for the benefit of an admiring public, all show without any substance. The rotten smell came from within, and no one was aware of the creeping stench because it had been around for so long that everyone was used to it by now.

After going from promises to make another's happiness one's lifework, they had gotten to that next to the last stage where substantive communication was mostly secondhand. It was either what Maggie termed the Morning Meeting in the Mirrors, the conversation over teeth brushing and shaving when their eyes met in the looking glass. Or it was at the perennial cocktail parties, where Maggie learned what Sheldon thought of her from the barbed stories he told to casual acquaintances about her latest debacle, things like forgetting Sam at day care, or about her publicly shared current fault, wastefulness.

We settle for so little, she thought, after expecting so much. Although the world had been party to their coming together, she wasn't ready yet to have the rest of the world bear witness to their falling apart. Self-righteous indignation was the face she wore for the rest of the world. But what she really felt was much more difficult to acknowledge, much harder for her to deal with: her own responsibility, her own part in this. It would have been so much easier to make Sheldon the sole transgressor.

But she suspected the reality was far more complicated than that. Still, moral indignation would have to serve until she could work through this in her own mind. Before Sheldon moved away from her, he'd kicked a leg out from under the stool she was on, and now she was teetering precariously. Maggie had seen herself as part of a couple for so long, she had no idea who she was without it. This is what she had given herself a summer to learn. She wondered if these few months would be enough. What she hadn't counted on was Sheldon's lack of remorse over his infidelity. She supposed this went along with his insistence that his affair was just a fling. This, and the vindictiveness he'd shown when she tried to claim some part of her life as her own.

The sky's trick of falling off into the water at the horizon seemed too vast somehow, too overwhelming, and she thought of her parents' marriage compared with her own. She hadn't actually told her mother yet that her summer plans were more a separation from Sheldon than a lakeside vacation with the girls. She winced inwardly at the possibility that Bryan had already taken the explanation upon himself.

Her parents still operated in the generation where foibles and faults were met with weighty forbearance and martyrdom for which payment was extracted later in unrelated and irrelevant ways. If her father had shown too great an interest in another woman, small things would go to ruin around him: The dinner would be overcooked; socks would go missing; his wife would be preoccupied whenever he spoke to her.

"They are so secure in their pathologies" would be Maggie's assessment of their parents' generation's passive-aggressive score settling. But who really knew whether this lack of acknowledgment was better. Perhaps bringing the truth out into the open and exposing the raw flesh was worse. Because once the wound was in full view, it required radical treatment, massive surgery. Whereas her parents' generation seemed to believe the application of a simple Band-Aid could hide a great deal of fault.

You're not really the best judge of this, she chided herself. She hadn't exactly succeeded where others had failed.

The clouds were still casting their jigsaw reflections on the water when Maggie turned away and headed back for the cottage. The interlocking cloud shapes passed over one another as though searching for the perfect match. The images were strong and conjured up in her half-formed beings condemned to the task of trying to join themselves together in order to become whole, which made her wonder if marriage itself was the problem, a gigantic excuse for never coming to terms with yourself.

Maggie brought an end to her reverie with a thought that had haunted her ever since she had first uncovered

Sheldon's affair. What she hated most, she supposed, was that she had wanted to be the first to tell him—tell Sheldon—even before she had seen him with Angie, before any of this had happened. She had wanted to be the first to tell Sheldon just how unhappy *she'd* become as his wife.

———◦((◦))◦———

Maggie started when she opened the door and found the television downstairs left on. Then she heard the cottage floorboards squeaking overhead. She took a quick breath in, then realized it had to be Bryan. He must have beat her back. She felt relief. "Bry?" she called up.

"Sis." He appeared at the top of the stairs without a shirt, then ducked back inside his room, sending "You'll never guess" her way. When he reemerged, he had on work clothes, cut-offs, and a ripped T-shirt spotted with paint. "Guess who I ran into? Guess who has a boat?"

"Someone I know. And I don't know too many people around here. Yet."

"Yeah. Jason. I ran into him on the dock. He seemed to know who I was even before I said anything. I'm going to trade some elbow grease helping him varnish the deck for some sailing on the big lake."

"Oh." Maggie felt like making a snide remark but checked herself. What was the matter? Bryan had made plans that didn't include her. "What kind of boat is it?"

"It's a sloop. You know, with two sails and one mast. She's got a beautiful mahogany interior. What a pain to maintain. But Jason swears by her. Want to come? I'm sure he could find a job for you."

"Naw." She glanced at her watch. "I need to get the girls before long." But that was only partly true. She knew the real reason for her refusal was that she didn't feel like sharing Jason with someone else, including her brother.

Bryan hurried downstairs, but stopped momentarily in front of the television. "Have you been following the Gary Hart story? He's the senator from Colorado who was making a run for the Democratic candidate for President."

"We barely turn the television on."

"I'm sure you know the press caught him with a woman in his apartment. They practically cornered him. Can you believe it? Now it's looking like his bad judgment will ruin his chances at the presidential nomination."

"You're calling it simply 'bad judgment'? How about betrayal?"

"Okay. You're right. Sorry." Bryan walked over to the television set and turned it off. "I was being too easy on him. But he is certainly going to pay for it, one way or the other. I guess if you're in politics, the public gets to know if you're having an affair."

"Hopefully, this was not how his wife found out." Maggie tried to make her voice sound grim, but it seemed to be lost on Bryan, who was already out the door.

The sense of abandonment after Bryan so calmly announced the Hart story, without staying to see if the story had disturbed her, made Maggie throw herself into her plan. She headed for the storeroom. She stood at the foot of the stairs and looked across the room. It seemed like there was junk everywhere, but she knew she could bring order out of the chaos. Some lined, heavy black fabric to cover the window—that's all she'd really need to purchase. Well, that and the equipment. The shelf just below the windows would be her workspace. The huge utility sink on one side wall would be perfect for washing her prints. She could smell the developer now, feel the slippery solution or the sting of the stop bath on her fingers when she pushed a print fully into the chemicals. She let herself think about what kind of lens she could use to create a photograph where the waves would look sharp, the water dark and angry at the injustices heaped upon its shores.

Maggie had been hatching a plot in her mind. What if she could use photography to capture the spirit of this beach community on film, make a visual statement that argued for its worth. Maybe she could get her photos published, the locals would be grateful, and then . . . well, who knew where it might lead.

She had just begun to clear miscellaneous cottage clutter from underneath the windows and stow it under the steps when a pair of legs crossed her line of sight out the window. They seemed to have come from the house across the way. Maggie ducked to see if she could catch sight of the rest of the person, but the window was too narrow and there was too much clutter to see any higher than his thick waist. She guessed the person was squat from the length of his legs, which were short and massive inside a pair of black sweatpants.

The legs hesitated for a moment before her, as though the person were looking back to where he had just been. Then they turned back toward the beach and quickly withdrew from her view. Maggie wondered briefly who it might have been. Probably a friend who had been visiting the old woman.

———((•))———

"Mommy, I can't sleep," Jen whined. Her very tone grated on Maggie's ears—and on her nerves.

Maggie was sitting alone on the front porch with her back to her daughter. Bryan had gone into town to see what there was to do on a weekday night in the summer, most likely to drink beer. She downed the rest of her wine quickly and turned around.

Jen stood on the upstairs landing, bent over at the waist with her hands on the railings.

Her hair was matted on top like she had been sleeping on it.

Maggie patted the seat next to her. "Come on down, and we'll talk." Jen came, but walked slowly as though she would bolt at any moment. Maggie held out her arms. "What's up?"

"It's too hot."

Maggie hesitated, taking the measure of the temperature. She wanted to point out that oysters liked the heat, but resisted. "Is your window open as far as it can go?"

"Yes." The whine again.

Maggie looked at her watch. It was just eleven. "Well, then, we'll just have to get Sam up and go take a midnight swim."

Jen gave her mother an incredulous look and cheered. "Yay! I'm getting Sam."

Maggie couldn't decide if this was good mothering or something that would put her on social services' blacklist, but she didn't care. The girls had their suits on and were ready before she'd rinsed out her glass and stashed it in the back of the cupboard.

"Sam. I think you've got your suit on inside out—well, no matter. It will do for the time being. Let's go."

Sam had started to tug a strap over her shoulder, then—noting her mother's change of heart—pulled it back up.

The moon was a luminescent sliver hanging from the faintest suggestion of a circle. It cast a thin, wavering band of light across the water. In contrast, the water that lay outside the uncertain moonlight was a deep brackish green that faded away into a dark gloom. Maggie put her fingers to her lips. "We have to be really quiet. We don't want anyone to know we're going swimming." Sam began to walk tiptoe across the sand, and Maggie laughed.

The beach was strangely quiet, in retreat, as though it had been caught in the nude. The daytime smell of fish had left with the sun. And it was cooler by the water than Maggie had anticipated. Maggie looked around, expecting to see other walkers, even lovers under blankets. But there was no one. "Don't go too far out, now. I want to be able to see you." She sat down and buried her feet in the sand in search of a warm spot. The girls were content to wade to their knees and splash each other.

"Bet I can make you yell," Jennifer threatened.

"Bet not" was Sam's reply.

At first the splashing was fast and furious, but the two tired of it as soon as they were both drenched. Then there was some conspiratorial giggling. "Hey, what's going on?" Maggie asked in a stage whisper. She suspected a plot against herself, but her daughters headed away from her toward deeper waters.

Maggie stood up. "Hey, Jennifer. Samantha. Don't go too far," she called to them.

But Jen just splashed forward a few more steps and then lunged.

"Got it," she called out. She sounded elated.

"What is it?" Sam had stopped. She would soon be out of her depth, and she knew it.

"Lookie here." Jennifer returned to shore slowly, dragging a short wood plank draped in seaweed. "I think there's been a shipwreck," she told her mother when she got close enough. "It's a piece of a boat."

"It certainly looks like something from a boat," Maggie allowed. "But I doubt there's been a shipwreck."

Sam stopped and stamped hard. "You don't know. You don't know that." She sounded stern, even angry.

"Yeah," Jennifer confirmed, and as she spoke, Maggie could sense she was forming a plan to tease her younger sibling. "It's probably a plank. From a wrecked pirate ship."

"Jennifer." Maggie wanted to nip this in the bud before Sam became too frightened. "There are no pirate ships around here."

"Yeah, Jennifer," Sam scolded. "And, anyway, it is named a plankton."

"Well, a plank is different, Sam. Never mind. It can't be a plank. If it's part of a ship, it's from a regular boat. We'll keep our eyes open the next few days. See if anything else washes up." Maggie pulled open the large beach towels as she said this and wrapped both girls up. They sat down on either side of her. Sam quickly lay down with her head in her mother's lap. Jennifer stared at the water.

Jennifer and Maggie heard the sound at the same time, the quiet lapping of the water against something almost directly out from them. Instinctively, they both grew quiet and listened. As if on cue, Maggie felt the breeze coming from the cool lake water blow across her face, chilling her. She looked at her feet and could almost see the fog deepening before her eyes. The small tongues grew out of the water, spreading over the sand like an eerie stage effect preceding a sinister scene. Mother and daughters stood up as they became surrounded, the tongues collecting around their ankles, entrapping them where they stood.

"We need to go," Maggie told them.

Maggie looked across the lake and thought she could make out the shape of a boat about sixty yards from the shoreline. No sounds were coming from it; there just seemed to be a shape in front of them much darker than the general gloom. The shape was that of a sailboat with its sails lowered, bobbing quietly on the water's surface. Maggie imagined it carried a pair of lovers who had escaped the shore to wrap themselves in each other's arms. Even still, she could feel her skin crawl.

"Mom?" Jennifer broke the silence first, but it was a whisper.

"H-m-m-m?"

"Are you going to die? Are you and Dad going to die?"

Maggie pulled back and tried to see Jen's face. But it was too dark to read much of anything, and the fog was slowly climbing up their legs. "What made you think of that?" she asked.

Jennifer shrugged. "Nothing. Well, this dream I had. You were in the bed and Daddy came in and found you, and you were dead."

Maggie felt the small snake of dread circling in her stomach and became conscious of her own breathing. "We're not going to die, Jennifer." She tried to say it with conviction. "When we get old—very, very old—maybe. When you are way grown up. Then we will think about dying. But not before then."

"Okay." Jennifer sounded relieved. "That's what I thought."

But Sam had been following their conversation and wasn't satisfied. "What about people with face sores?"

"Face sores?" Where'd this come from, Maggie wondered.

"Big face sores." Sam made a circular gesture with her hand that took in the entire right side of her face.

"Oh, yes." Maggie knew Sam was thinking of their neighbor. "Hon, the lady who lives across from us has what you call a birthmark. It doesn't hurt her. She was born with it. That's why it's called a birthmark."

"Oh." Sam fell silent, her mouth still pursed.

"What does it mean?" This from Jennifer.

"Nothing. Nothing at all. Some people are born with those marks—and sometimes the marks are on their faces."

"Why doesn't she erase it off?"

"I don't know. Maybe because it's so close to her eye. Maybe it'd be dangerous to try to get it off." Yet in her own mind, Maggie was conjuring her neighbor up as a victim of a self-prescribed penance worthy of Nathaniel Hawthorne.

Maggie reached over and stroked Sam's head. It felt so small, as though you could almost palm it like a basketball. The dimensions of the questions had exhausted her. "But now it's time to go home to bed. Safe in bed," she added for good measure.

Just then they heard a moan from the direction of the lighthouse. Even without a choreographer, the three turned in unison to face in the direction of the sound, listening. Sam placed her hands over her ears. Maggie could have sworn the intervals between the burdened sounds were shorter than usual. Without a word, they all began walking back across the beach.

Maggie noticed as they walked away from the water that the edge of Sam's towel was dragging behind her. She started to tell Sam to pick it up, but then asked herself why. What did it really matter, anyway?

When they were almost to the front walk, Maggie looked up the hill and noticed a single light on in the house at the top of the dune. She watched as it flickered on and off. It must be some branches blowing across a lighted window, she guessed. And yet, there seemed to be coherence to the flickering, like that of a meaningful pattern. *You're tired*, she told herself. *Stop imagining things.*

CHAPTER 5

I t was Saturday. Maggie woke earlier than she'd wanted. It must have been because of the sound of the foghorn. The foghorn? She started up. It couldn't be raining. Not today. She lifted herself high enough to see out a window. It wasn't. So, why the foghorn? Maybe they were just testing it. It was Saturday, after all. Tour day. They were going to make an adventure out of it. Pack a picnic lunch and walk over, see the lighthouse, then meet Jason at his boat for a sail.

The boat had been launched into the water late yesterday afternoon. She'd been there for it: the ropes attached to its sides, the dock hands, a couple on either side, to help steer it down the ramp and into the water.

Jason's boat was far from the largest in the marina. Actually, it was on the smaller side; yet it had been magnificent when the boat's keel had touched the water and slowly become submerged, stopping with a slight splash and a moment of gentle bobbing. It was the motion of a living thing settling into its nest, Maggie thought. Jason had grabbed a wire (a "stay" Bryan told her) on the side of the boat to balance himself as he leaped onto the deck, where he lowered the motor and prepared to steer the boat under motor power into its slip at the Yacht Club dock.

Bryan and Maggie had walked along the dock, watching the boat's forward progress. They reached the slip at nearly the same time the boat did. Maggie stood on the dock and shielded her eyes with her arm, thrilling at the sensation of the slight bobbing of the boat in time with the sun's shimmering on the water.

Thinking about the boat ride to come, Maggie headed absentmindedly into the kitchen to start the coffee, tiptoeing to keep from waking the girls. It was nice to have some of the early morning to herself. She took her cup of coffee and headed for the front porch, thinking how good it would feel to sit in the square of sun that usually bathed one of the stuffed wicker chairs at this time of day. She stopped short just as she reached the porch, nearly spilling her coffee. The woman from across the way was standing on her top step with her back toward Maggie. She had a long duffel bag that she slowly dragged with her as she backed down the steps, feeling her way with one foot. The bag made a muffled thud each time it fell to a lower step.

Maggie leaned backward to stay within the shadows of the house, hoping not to be seen. She needn't have bothered. The woman didn't look around her when she reached the bottom step. Instead, she continued to walk backward, lugging the sack around the cottage to the trash area, bent over from the weight of her load.

When the woman's figure disappeared behind the partition that jutted out from the house, Maggie looked up and saw another person whom she hadn't seen initially because he had been sequestered by the porch screen. The man seemed to be short—and round—and when she glanced his way, he coughed erratically into the top of his fist. It was difficult to distinguish any of his features, even his age, but he seemed to be watching her. She wondered how long he had been there. Maggie took another step back into her house, both hands around the coffee cup to keep them warm. She wouldn't sit on the porch after all, she decided, looking around the living room for another quiet spot.

But then the morning's silence was broken anyway. Sam came down the steps, dragging Jimmie behind her, one thumb stroking her upper lip, getting dangerously close to fitting itself into her mouth.

"Sam, come here," Maggie whispered. She pulled the child into her lap. "We're going to visit the 'lights-out' again today, see if we can get inside this time."

"Yay." Sam leaned against her momentarily, then pulled away. "I want breakfast."

"Okay. But let's be quiet. We'll let Uncle Bry and Jen sleep some more—for the time being."

"Yeah. Just us. For breakfast."

Maggie sat Sam on the counter next to the mixing bowl and let her pour in the Bisquick by herself.

<hr>

The trip to the lighthouse seemed much shorter this time, probably because they had an idea where they were going. It was open for business. A small sign hung from a chain at the top of the stairs that said "Open for Tours 10:00 a.m.–2:00 p.m." The girls paraded up the stairs and pushed open the door. As she approached the stairs, Maggie noticed windows about knee high off the ground that were like small portholes in a ship. *How quaint*, she thought as she entered the structure. A slight man, with thinning gray hair that had been meticulously combed and glasses as thick as his hair was thin, was leaning on the display counter reading a magazine opened in front of him.

The building's interior was an unfinished wooden floor and contained almost no furniture. Besides the counter, there was a rocking chair and a display case that housed what looked like old navigating instruments. The man must have decided to finish reading the paragraph he was on, because it took him a moment to glance up. "Here for the tour?"

"Yeah, sure." It was Bryan who answered. "Is it a self-guided tour, or are you the guide?"

"A little of both." The man laughed. "I tell you some history, and you get to look around.

"Let me start." He stepped away from the counter and went into autopilot. "You know this lighthouse was built in 1901. Originally, it was a completely wooden structure with a gas lantern that was lifted into the top tower by a set of pulleys. It had to be rebuilt in the early 1930s after it burned down. How it burned down is something of a mystery. Perhaps you remember what that era was like: it was Al Capone, shoot-'em-up gangsters, Prohibition." The guide looked closely at Jennifer when he made this pronouncement and pretended to twirl two six shooters at his hips. "We know all about the rum-running that took place in the Caribbean, but we had our own small version of that here. The early residents suspected the lighthouse was used as a transfer point: a shipment of hard liquor from Canada would be dropped off to be picked up under cover of darkness by private ships headed for the Chicago speakeasies."

Maggie noticed both Jenny and Sam perk up at the word speakeasy. She wondered where she might encounter such a graphic word next. Perhaps Jen's next pseudonym? Bryan backed away from them and looked out a window. Probably bored or just eager to get to Jason's boat, Maggie thought.

"The story goes that there was a terrible storm on the night of one transfer. The ship was loaded with booze and hit terrible waves in the middle of the lake. It sank. Though a couple of bodies and pieces of the ship washed ashore, all of the liquor sank straight for Davy Jones' locker."

Sam was pumping Maggie's hand now. Maggie looked down and knew that eventually she'd surely be called upon to explain what Davy Jones' locker was.

"The lighthouse caught fire shortly after that. Some people think someone set it deliberately. That they were trying to cover something up. Others said it was just that gas lantern and all that wood. At any rate, the structure was rebuilt later, out of ship metal, primarily. And, of course, the gas lantern was replaced by electricity. About thirty-five years ago, the authorities decided to tear the place down, but the locals wouldn't let 'em. Got together and made the case for its historical value. So, we've preserved the light-house to this day. The light still comes on; it's set by an as-tronomical clock and goes on and off automatically. And the foghorn comes on for testing and in the fog—that's partially a romantic touch, I guess."

Sam, who had long since lost interest in the thread of the story, took a step toward the counter. "Were there ghosts, then? From the pirate ships?"

"Ghosts? From the *pirate* ships?" The man laughed without smiling. "Well . . . perhaps. Not all the bodies were found after the wreck, you see. You will want to climb the stairs to the little walkway at the top. That's where people could watch for troubled ships. Or see the weather on the lake."

"What a funny story." Maggie shook her head as she took Sam's hand. "Let's take a look at this tower. See what we can see."

"Yeah, see what we can see," Jennifer mimicked as Sam and Maggie headed for the stairs. "See if there's ghosts."

"There won't be ghosts. Ghosts are just make-believe, remember?" Maggie assured Sam while trying to keep an eye on Jen, who had wandered over to a door opposite the desk and seemed to be playing with the door handle. Maggie could tell Jen's curiosity was irritating the attendant, because he came around the counter seemingly ready to say something. At that moment, the door opened in Jen's hand. By then, the attendant was there pushing the door back closed. He turned to Jen as though to scold her, but Maggie beat him to it. "Jen, the stairs are over here. C'mon." Best to get her away from there—and him—she thought.

The stairs were narrow and spiraled upward where they opened onto a small room surrounded by the lighthouse's uppermost windows. The girls held onto the window ledges and pointed to a couple of boats on the lake. "There's the ghost ship now," Jennifer informed Sam.

Maggie shook her head at her older daughter. "C'mon, Jen, don't start that. Sam doesn't need to hear that."

Jen made a sour face at her mother and tossed her head, angry from the reprimand. Maggie took a deep breath. She knew she had her work cut out for her now: She wondered how long it would take her to bring Jen back from the ranks of the uncommunicative.

⟸•《◐》•⟹

They followed a path that paralleled the channel connecting the two lakes to reach the marina. At the midway point the girls declared they were already tired of walking.

Bryan had tried carrying Sam on his shoulders, but the height had frightened her, and she'd pleaded to be put down.

By the time they reached the boat, Maggie was as out of sorts as her daughters. She couldn't stop herself from scolding Jen, dredging up what was already old news for a soon-to-be six-year-old. "Jen, you should not have gone snooping in the lighthouse, looking in places without permission. That door was closed for a reason."

Jen glared at her. "I didn't open it."

"What do you mean you didn't open it? I saw it open."

"Yeah. But I didn't open it. Someone on the other side pushed it open." And with what she must have intended to be a dramatic delivery, Jen wheeled around, turning her back on her mother, and hurried after Bryan.

Maggie followed, uncertain how to handle this piece of news. Among her other transgressions, was Jennifer now also guilty of lying?

Jason was busy at the boat when they reached the marina. He stood up from what he was doing and came to the side to help them board. He stood with one foot on the deck of the boat and one foot on the dock and extended an arm to Jennifer. "Here, Jen, give me your hand." Jennifer seemed proud to be chosen first. "Now take a big step onto the boat. That's right. I've got you."

When they were all on, Jason gave the girls a short tour. There were steps to the small cabin below that consisted of a couple of benches with cushions on either side. There were small windows above them that were only slightly above water level. A storage bin in the center of the little cabin had a broad lid which also served as a table. The toilet was sequestered in something the size of a stingy broom closet. At the very back, behind the stairs, was another wider bench with a thick cushion on it. Maggie supposed it would be possible to lie down on it—if you kept your knees up around your chin. What Maggie liked best was precisely what Bryan had liked as well: the mahogany interior. The wood was a dark reddish brown and polished to a high shine.

Jason opened the lid of the storage box, pulled out life jackets, and helped everyone into one, including himself. Maggie tried to signal her gratitude to him, but he was too intent on the work at hand to notice.

They positioned themselves in the boat's cockpit to get started, except for Bryan, who moved around at Jason's command, loosening ropes and stowing things under the deck. "Okay," Jason ordered, "I'm about to raise—pull up—the main sail, this big sail here. When I do, it will start to luff—shake—a little, even swing back and forth. You need to watch out and not get hit by the boom—this board on the bottom of it." Bryan tapped the board to show what he meant.

"Boom. That's a weird name." Jennifer had her hands on her hips as she said this, almost as though to reinsert herself into the situation, Maggie thought. "Is that 'cause it can hit you?"

"Naw," Jason laughed, "though it should be. That's a good thought. Here, Jen, I'm going to let you hold this rope. It's the jib sheet. The jib is the little sail in front. Just hold it loose in your hands," he cautioned as he saw her clamp her fingers down on it. "You want it to be able to slip through your fingers—but not get away from you."

"Sheet?" Jennifer said this with incredulity. "How'd it get that name?"

"Oh, Jennifer, you're going to test me with your questions," Jason called to her as he swung himself around a small wire attached from the top of the main mast to the deck of the boat in order to untangle some "sheets" on the bow of the boat.

The preparations to set sail seemed beyond comprehension to Maggie, but at last Bryan walked along the deck to guide the boat out of its slip; then he climbed aboard, and they were off. Jason held the main sail close to the center of the boat with his left hand, cranking it around a short wooden pedestal to take up the slack, while he steadied the boat's tiller in his right.

The sound of the bow breaking through the water, the sharp feel of the wind against her face bringing tears to her eyes, the spray that occasionally found its way across the deck all worked their magic on her. Maggie laughed and succumbed to the oldest sailing cliche: this was the feel of freedom.

Jason let them all take a turn at holding the tiller while he sat next to them to grab it if the going got rough. He held Sam in his lap with his large hand over hers as she pretended to steer, but with Jennifer, he let go. Maggie could see by the tilt of Jen's chin how proud she was of this feat.

When it was Maggie's turn, Jason gave some instruction: "Don't just let yourself meander; steer for a specific spot on the shore or the horizon and hold to it."

"Why?" Maggie couldn't imagine why it made a difference.

"Well, a day like today, maybe it doesn't matter as much, but often a fog will come in while we're out, and it really is the only way you have of figuring out how to get back."

"Okay." Maggie tried to sound convinced as she concentrated on steering toward a house on shore with a bright blue roof.

<hr />

They'd dated nearly eighteen months before Sheldon had invited her to meet his parents. He had rarely mentioned them—and then usually in relation to their age.

He'd been a twilight child, Maggie gathered. A surprise to a couple who had assumed they would never have children. Sheldon would make a joke of it if pressed, that his first bib had been a crocheted doily, his first baseball bat the straight end of a cane. Maggie would wonder sometimes at this humor. She would try to draw him out when they lingered over their last glass of wine in a restaurant, asking what it felt like to be an only child. He'd usually shrug and say something noncommittal like, "It felt like it feels for any kid." She couldn't decide if this was due to a lack of self-reflection or a fear of self-disclosure. At the time, she hadn't thought much about it, since she had yet to meet a man who could or would speak with much self-insight.

So, Maggie didn't know what to expect the weekend Sheldon had driven them to Detroit. He gave her the now-familiar snort when he saw how much she'd packed. "We're only going to be there for two days," he reminded her as he heaved her suitcase into the trunk with more force than was necessary.

It was late fall, and Maggie spent most of the four-hour drive looking at the leafless trees that lined the interstate, watching hapless raindrops get splayed open as they hit her window.

For his part, Sheldon didn't acknowledge, or perhaps didn't realize, he'd made her angry. He was silent as well for most of the trip, answering her rare questions with one or two words, adjusting and readjusting the windshield wiper speed the entire trip.

It was a relief when they finally arrived at a house on Detroit's north side. The house was brick with a large, ill-fitting porch. He took his hands from the wheel, slapped both thighs, and turned to look at her for the first time in at least two hours. Raising his eyebrows in what she by now knew to be his deepest announcer voice, "Okay, folks, it's *show* time."

Betty Dunbarton wasn't old in the way Maggie had expected. Her skirts weren't long and plaid and pleated. Her hair wasn't curled just around the nape of her neck and her ears. She was old in the way she'd frequently take both sides of her sweater and pull them across her chest in what often seemed a nervous gesture. She was old in the way that she lived in a resigned sort of way, afraid, or at least not willing, to take any chances.

Betty opened the door wide to let them in, but then caught Sheldon at the elbows before he could get past her and rose slightly on her toes to kiss him on the cheek.

"Hello, dear. And you're Maggie." Betty had taken Maggie's right hand in hers. Rather than shake it, she'd pulled it slightly toward her and patted it with her other hand. The gesture had surprised Maggie enough so that her quick withdrawal had been more of a reflex than a calculated move.

Sheldon walked directly to his old bedroom. Maggie found herself maneuvered toward the den, where she would sleep. Betty again held the door open for her. Maggie entered and realized she was surprising Reggie Dunbarton awake from an afternoon snooze. Sheldon's father had a football game on television—the University of Michigan, Sheldon later informed her—and had nodded off in the confines of his easy chair. Maggie strode over to shake his hand. She stood there with her hand out while he stiffly pushed himself out of his chair. "Hello, Maggie. Looks like I'd better get out of your room."

"Oh, dear, no. I'm displacing you." Maggie couldn't believe she'd only been in the house five minutes and already felt like a burden. "Stay where you are. I just need a place to put my suitcase for now."

So she had talked a few more minutes with Reggie. He'd asked her questions about work, her own family, often looking past her to the Wolverines on the screen while she answered him.

The weekend hadn't been a complete disaster, though there were moments when Sheldon seemed determined to make it that way. It was almost as though he wanted to sabotage any relationship she might develop with his parents, or maybe he wanted to make certain Maggie saw his parents as he saw them.

On Sunday, the sun came out and Betty took Maggie's arm and led her around the yard, pointing out the flowerbeds that seemed to be one of her main preoccupations. "It's too bad you're here now and can't see what all this looks like in the spring." She had sighed and nodded in silent recognition. "I do cosmos here—and delphinium over there. I call them my heirlooms. They're descendants of my mother's flowers. I gather the seeds every fall, just like she did."

Maggie was impressed and told her so.

"Are you a gardener?"

Maggie had to tell her no, but added she'd love to get into it when she had a house with a yard.

Maggie had sat at the kitchen table with Betty in the afternoon while Reggie and Sheldon camped out in the den. This time it was in front of the Lions' game. Betty had waved her hand in the direction of the television when she heard that this was how the men were to spend their afternoon, and took Maggie with her to the kitchen, where they sat and drank tea. Maggie had repeated some stories about herself and listened to some about Sheldon's boyhood. His mother was clearly proud of him, and also somewhat mystified about where he had taken his life. "His father was a salesman," she'd said more than once. "For Nabisco. He worked for them all his life and then retired."

They'd headed for home as soon as the Lions lost. The ride back was nearly as silent as the ride going had been. Maggie remembered what someone had told her once: you can tell what kind of a husband a man will be by looking at how he treats his mother. Remembering how invisible Betty Dunbarton had become, Maggie believed there might be some truth in that. It was too bad she hadn't paid more attention at the time to his apparent disregard for his mother.

Betty had given Maggie flower seeds from her garden after Maggie and Sheldon were married, snapdragons and cosmos, descendants from her mother's garden, she said. The seeds produced flowers that had faithfully reseeded every year since. Maggie imagined this would be the summer they'd finally die out, with no one to look after them. No one to water them.

———⋯((•))⋯———

Maggie had her feet up on her favorite stool—one of the wicker chairs. It felt great to be so tired. Bryan was sacked out on the glider, a partly read newspaper draped over his chest like a thin blanket. She had gone straight to the refrigerator after the girls were in bed and grabbed a beer. She could feel Bryan start to say something, think better of it, then walk over to take out a second one for himself.

"I think it was the combination of the wind and sun that did me in." She aimed this at her brother under his newspaper tent.

"H-m-m?" He shook his head as though to clear it. "Oh, yeah. That and all the exercise. So, now what do you think of sailing?"

"No wonder you love it."

"Then the bug has bitten you too?"

"Maybe so." Maggie ran her tongue around the rim of the bottle, looking for the taste without actually taking a sip.

It had been a wonderful day in every way. They'd sailed around the little lake. Jason advised it was better to stay where there was a little more protection on their maiden voyage. That, and the weather forecast was for choppy waters on Lake Michigan. He wasn't sure how well the girls could handle that.

They'd dropped anchor in a small cove about twenty yards from shore. Jason and Bryan slid off the boat into the water, then had Jen and Sam jump into their waiting arms. Maggie slid herself off the boat on the shore side, hidden from view, in case her entry into the water was clumsy. She was suddenly conscious of how awkward she felt.

The water near the shore was warm. Bryan and Jason took charge of the girls, launching them from their arms into the water, then waiting while Sam and Jen paddled back for more.

While the others played, Maggie allowed herself to lie on her back in the water: it lapped gently around her, supporting her weight. She marveled again at the attraction of water. Today it would have to be because it was comforting, like amniotic fluid, supporting her, lulling her back to the safety of the womb. She imagined the lake as one gigantic cradle, gently rocking its occupants until their cares slid off and floated away.

The sail back to the marina was more of a chore. By now, the lake was full of sailboats, even some motorboats with skiers, and Jason had to concentrate to maintain some distance from them all. He did what he referred to as "tacking" or crossing through the eye of the wind, while his passengers did what they could to avoid the sweep of the boom. As they had neared the dock area, a huge boat, which Maggie would have described as a yacht, motored slowly by. Maggie could see three women in two-piece suits already settled into lounge chairs in the area at the stern of the ship. Maggie imagined that a boat this size could only belong to Blailock, and she tried hard to look inside the cabin to see if she could get a glimpse of her notorious neighbor. But it was impossible to see anything through the small windows.

It had been the kind of day that made people return to the same spot year after year to try to reenact what they had loved about the last time they were there. She wondered if Jason had been as conscious of her as she had been of him, sitting at the stern of the boat surveying the waters ahead, his back almost too straight, his body now taut, now relaxed as the wind emptied itself into the sails, at one with his boat. She tried to picture Sheldon there, but the thought was almost ludicrous. He would have needed to be the master. She conjured up how he would have to stand on the bow, balancing himself by holding onto the mast, trying to bend both the waves and the wind to his will.

"Maggie?" Bryan interrupted her reverie. She started, and nearly spilled her beer. Bryan was eyeing her as though trying to read her thoughts.

"You want to meet that guy? Blailock?"

"Sure." Maggie settled back down and cradled her beer against her waist. "You know I do."

"Talk to Jason. He has an invitation to the guy's Fourth of July bash. Maybe you could talk him into taking you."

"H-m-m-m. . ." Maggie tried to sound noncommittal, but privately wondered if she'd get up the nerve to ask.

"I hope you're not up to one of your harebrained schemes. I haven't heard good things about the guy."

"Yeah. Me neither." Maggie let it drop. It wouldn't do to let on to Bryan what she was thinking.

———((◊))———

Maggie was proud of herself. This was the third morning in a row she had managed to get up early enough to take a walk along the beach. Bryan's presence had given her the luxury of being able to steal out of the cottage in predawn light. She pulled on a sweatshirt and tied a scarf around her head against the wind that often seemed to come up at night and create new patterns in the sand.

The cottages were silent at this time of day, their screen doors still; the voices within silent. Once, Maggie had followed a trail that left the dunes and had taken her deeper into the woods. She'd stepped over a fallen log across the trail and stopped to pull cobwebs from her face. She sensed someone watching her, and wondered for a terrifying moment if she was being followed. But when she looked up, she spotted a deer peering out from a stand of bushes, its gaze directly on her. It was motionless except for the twitching of a single ear. Maggie tried not to make any sudden moves so she could savor the sight as long as possible.

She'd gone along the trail a little farther, then, afraid of getting lost, turned around, and returned the way she had come. On the way home she'd taken a shortcut across what was probably private property and headed down a dune. Occasionally, she'd turn back around to look up the hill behind her, realizing how visible she was to someone at the top of the dune.

Today she just followed the beach and tried to pick up her pace. The killdeer were out in force, screeching and running away in mock fear whenever she approached within fifty feet of them. There were several gulls out as well, wheeling and diving toward the water when they detected something floating on its surface.

Maggie headed inland on her way home, following a narrow paved road that again climbed up, winding its way through several cottages that were some distance from the beach before ending near the entrance to Breakwater Bay. The path got steep and even narrower on the way down, and the trees had become dense enough to make it seem dark as well. Maggie walked quickly, watching her footing to keep from sliding on the sand that had accumulated on top of the pavement.

Just as she was emerging from the trees, she caught sight of a strange pair ahead of her. She recognized the woman walking in front as the one who lived across the walk from her. The person following her struggled to keep up. *I should really introduce myself*, Maggie told herself, feeling embarrassed that it had taken her this long to do so. She hurried to catch up to the trailing figure, calling "Hello," as she went.

The unknown man turned first at the sound of her voice. The flat face and open mouth, the small round eyes. Maggie stopped short. It was a young man with Down syndrome, she realized, but not before the older woman had turned to face her, her lips held tightly together in a small, thin line, her eyes hidden beneath her straw hat. Was this the figure who kept himself deep within the shadows of the porch? It dawned on her why the woman was so private: she was ashamed of her son. She was trying to keep him out of sight.

Maggie couldn't be an accomplice to this game of pretend, even if she'd wanted to. It was too late. The woman had seen her and surely knew who she was. "Hello," Maggie ended up saying. What followed sounded lame, she knew. "I just wanted to say hello. I'm—we're—your neighbors."

The woman nodded, then turned her back and called to Maggie over her shoulder, "I'm Helen." And kept walking without checking to make sure her son was still behind her. She knew he would be.

Maggie stood several moments more to watch them disappear behind the guardhouse into Breakwater Bay. Then she chose her own, longer route home, realizing she may have discovered the real reason her neighbor was so reclusive.

CHAPTER 6

J ennifer held the phone tight against her ear, opening her eyes wide or nodding occasionally as though the person at the other end of the line could see her. Maggie pretended to be busy in the kitchen, occasionally glancing over at Jen, listening closely to hear her side of the conversation.

"No." Jennifer's "o" hung in the air longer than was necessary. "Okay. Yes. Okay." Then, "Mommy, it's Grandma."

Maggie had known she was due for this sooner or later and steeled herself as she walked to the phone. "Hi, Mom."

Winifred DeCour was a proud woman who'd aspired to a social standing that was, as the wife of a high school coach and English teacher, always out of her reach. Perhaps it was because of her mother's social aspirations, but for as long as Maggie could remember, her mother's life was one in which social conventions and matters of moral significance frequently became blurred. So, of course, when it came to her children, any act that deviated too greatly from the current social norm received the full brunt of her self-righteous censure.

As they got older, Maggie and Bryan often referred to their circumscribed upbringing as though it were someone's typing style. They called it the "hunt and peck" method. They went through their childhood with one eye on their mother's face. A grim upper lip, teeth compressed tightly, eyes narrowed meant they'd gone too far, stepped over some invisible boundary. And it was time to stop. To retreat. To try something else. A passive, disinterested face meant they could continue.

Is this okay? How about this? They read the answers by watching their mother. Maggie wondered which expression her mother was wearing now as she held the phone to her ear.

Maggie knew only too well how much of her own life was a response to this upbringing and that it had endowed her with some character deficits she hated. Her personal rebellion against control had made her an aggressive investigative reporter, true, but it certainly had not prepared her for motherhood.

"Hi, hon. Jennifer and I have been having quite the chat. She sounds good."

Maggie pictured her mother standing in the laundry room, the phone trapped between her ear and shoulder while she folded clothes. Score one for me, Maggie thought, as she answered, "Oh, we're having a great time here. It's all working out. Of course you know Bryan arrived a few days ago." Of course her mother would know. Bryan was probably the one who had instigated this call. He would have delivered his report by now. Maggie wondered how she had fared. "And he's discovered sailboats."

"So it seems." Three words, but still Maggie could hear the censure they carried, probably because, for her Calvinistic mother, sailing would be seen as a solely recreational pursuit, one without any redeeming economic or social value. Her mother had become quiet at the other end of the line. Maggie knew her mother wanted to give a larger voice to her disapproval, but couldn't decide how to go about it. Having no desire to make it easier on her, Maggie kept silent as well.

Winifred would have shifted her phone to the other ear by now in order to initiate a new tack. "So, how's it going, hon? What do you hear from Sheldon?"

Maggie didn't rush in. *Try for a place between concern and nonchalance,* she told herself. "He seems fine. Is busy—at work. We talked with him the other day. H—" She started to say that he might make it to Jen's birthday, but why throw her mother this bone when Maggie intended to do whatever she could to prevent a visit.

"And the girls?"

"The girls are great, Mom. They've made some friends here. There's a college-age girl who does a morning day care program at her house just down the way from us. Jen and Sam have a great time there. Do lots of stuff."

"Do you leave them over there a lot?" Maggie could hear the rise in her mother's voice. She had probably stopped folding laundry at this point, and taken hold of the phone in earnest, with both hands.

Maggie allowed her fingers to go to her face, where they flitted above her right ear. She could feel a piercing, like the opening of a small hole in her temple. She tried to ignore it.

It was too complicated really. This thing with her mother. She knew her mother was expecting her to be experiencing some guilt, paying some sort of penance. But she refused to provide anyone, including her mother, with this satisfaction by showing it.

Maggie's mother wore her motherhood like a suit of armor. She saw herself as the epitome of the self-denying wife and mother, a perception that had become, for her, an identity badge and a yardstick. She had the proof of her own goodness—all those years of self-denial. No one else could really compare. No one else could measure up to the sacrifices she had made for her children. Not even her own daughter.

"They're at Annie's most mornings, Mother—while I work. It's great for them to be with other kids. And they love it." Maggie cleared her throat slightly to indicate she was changing the subject. "And how's Dad?"

Winifred didn't answer right away, and Maggie imagined her surveying her surroundings to fix on something solid before answering. "Oh, about the same, I guess. I was just there yesterday."

About the same. "About the same" was as good as the news got, Maggie knew. And as much as anyone could hope for, though who knew if her mother was making things sound better than they really were.

Randall DeCour resided in the dementia wing of a nursing home, and had for almost two years now. His symptoms had begun over six years ago, shortly after his retirement from the Kankakee school system where he had taught high school English and American history his entire life. His children had mistaken his lapses as attempts to absent himself from his wife's stifling control.

Winifred had continued her vigilance even after his mind had deteriorated enough to require nursing care, by visiting her husband nearly every day, though he no longer gave any sign that he knew who it was sitting before him.

The last time Maggie had seen him had been early spring. He'd been nearly catatonic, his hooded gaze deeply internal, his face completely slack. Occasionally he would rock to his own internal rhythm, and even more occasionally he spoke as though emerging from some great depth, the words rescued only with great effort, one by one, from the lair where they lay trapped. His sentences would be non sequiturs, yet containing just enough meaning to seduce others into hanging onto some false hope that he knew what he was saying.

When Maggie and her siblings had encouraged their mother to visit less often—it just didn't seem to matter to Randall that she spent long afternoons there—Winifred became indignant at the suggestion. "Oh, I do it for the staff," she defended herself. "To keep their spirits up. They need someone around they can talk with," though Maggie suspected the visits were really for appearances' sake.

While Winifred's children had learned the techniques for controlling others' lives at their mother's knee, they had long since given up trying to tell her how to run her own life. Eventually, they'd dropped even the incidental protests.

Maggie hung up the phone feeling dissatisfied and lonely as she always did after speaking with her mother. She massaged her temples and went into the bathroom, closing the door behind her. She repeated something she had often done as a teenager, looking at her face in the mirror and searching for the features she got from her mother, eagerly lighting on those that had no resemblance. Maggie had intense gray eyes. Her mother's. A slightly long nose. No one's. Thin lips. Her mother's. Unless she smiled. Her chin was strong. Maybe that was her father's. Her dark hair, rather than making her look severe, made her seem mysterious, her friends used to tell her. In the days of her adolescence, when she tried to distance herself from her mother, she'd worn bangs. She supposed it was to help cover up any resemblance. Those days were long gone. Now, she just worked to resist that trait of looking at the world so critically. Maggie took a deep breath. *How could a phone call from her mother reduce her to feeling like a child*, she wondered.

———⟫(((•)))⟪———

The shoreline meandered aimlessly, and Maggie tried following the wave line exactly, where the water had just pulled back from the sand and the sand was packed and firm under her feet. Gulls circled, their stubby bodies tubular projectiles with wings. Nothing romantic or pictur-esque about those, she decided, not even tempted to lift her camera to her eye.

She wasn't sure what she had gotten herself into. She'd called Noreen a couple of days ago—out of the blue—told her she was in the area for the summer, would love to stop by for a visit.

Noreen had been a sorority sister in college, in the class ahead. President of the sorority, in fact. One of those bright women in college and, though she'd had her hands in nearly every campus activity, she was pinned by her junior year, engaged her senior year, and set on a track for marriage and mothering. Oh, she might teach while her husband went to graduate school, but when he was done, she'd quit to raise her children. Maggie wondered whether Noreen's life had unfolded according to plan. She occasionally read the alum-nae section in the sorority newsletter, enough to know that Jerry, Noreen's husband, was in the biology department at the University of Michigan. She'd also learned that Noreen moved to western Michigan at the beginning of each sum-mer, and Jerry joined them as his teaching schedule and re-search allowed.

It was partly Jerry who Maggie wanted to see. If she remembered correctly, much of his work was in the area of environmental biology. But she was also curious about Noreen. Maggie wondered how changed Noreen would be. Would there be a kindred spirit there?

She had decided to walk to Noreen's. It was a bit of a drive by car, heading out the long road leading from Breakwater Bay, then on to the grid of county roads which didn't follow the lake's shoreline. But by walking along the beach, it would only be a couple of miles. People walked it all the time, according to Noreen. There was some private beach, but the public was allowed to walk across, if you stayed close to the shore.

Maggie had slung her camera bag over her shoulder, something she was getting adept at remembering. She had some notion about capturing the lake in a composition that was consumed by water with only the barest hint of horizon at the very top of the frame. She wanted the water dark and brooding and boiling over, though the chances of getting something like that today were slim, since the day was bright and sunny. There would be no darkened sky to give the lake a greenish, fiendish cast.

Maggie carried her shoes and went barefoot. Strands of seaweed occasionally caught between her toes, and she stopped frequently to see whether the bits and pieces of shell that washed up carried something living. None did. She photographed a clam-like shell that lay open and empty, its iridescent interior glistening form its recent submersion in water. There were a couple of smooth stones close by, and Maggie used the backwash line of shell bits to create a linear backdrop behind the large shell, to give the impression that it was bound to its setting, both visually and historically, not an isolated phenomenon, but part of something larger, part of a pattern.

Point, frame, sustain the breath, push. Click. Capture the creation. Simple. Perfect. Maggie marveled at the satisfaction her photography was giving her. What was it? she wondered. Control over at least one small corner of her life? Or did she also love the sense of creation it gave her? This was a world of things she designed. No one, not even Sheldon— not even her mother—could come in to make corrections, to tell her how it *should* be done.

Maggie kept her eyes on the dunes as she walked,

wondering if she could pick out the one that she and Brendan had escaped to that summer long ago. They all looked the same now. Then, there had been a couple without any houses. By hiking up the dunes and walking straight back, you found yourself all alone in the woods. Brendan would put a blanket over his shoulder and they'd hike up the hot sand to lie on the blanket, their bodies eager, stretched out against each other. It had seemed so simple then. Life was about their relationship. That was the central thing. The first kiss had been quick and awkward, but had led to longer, slower ones. His hands had started by stroking her back and then had found their way under her bathing suit top. She supposed their summer explorations would have gone a lot further if their summer visit hadn't ended.

She stopped. There was a sharp glint between the trees at the top of the dune. Most likely off of someone's window. The woods above were probably filled with houses by now.

Something cold between her toes returned Maggie to the present. The thin trickle of water that flowed beneath her feet. It looked dark with pools of a greasy film swirling on top.

Maggie looked toward the beach. A tiny rivulet snaked its way back from the water's edge, quickly disappearing into the dune grass and then into the undergrowth beyond this. What was its source? Was it just a private cottage flushing effluvium from some household project, or was there something else going on?

She aimed her camera at the oily pools as they formed, swirled, re-formed. What would she call this, she wondered when she realized the shot wasn't going to produce the ominous impact she wanted. The floating shapes were much too light-hearted, and the sun caused sparkles to dance and bounce off the water.

———◦«(◉)»◦———

The sun was nearly overhead by the time Maggie saw the sign for Sunnyside and the interminable set of wooden steps that led from the beach up the dune. She glanced at her watch. It'd taken her longer than she'd thought, but no matter. Noreen knew she was walking and wasn't expecting her at any particular time.

Maggie was winded by the time she reached the top step, and she held onto the railing to catch her breath. Noreen lived in a community of summer cottages that opened onto a common grassy area. A couple of children rode bicycles along a path between the cottages, their calls to each other strangely out of place in what was otherwise the scene of a lazy summer day.

Noreen had described a large white house with green trim that sat at the top of a hill. There was no mistaking it. The entire hill had a groundcover of ivy. It was a shiny green and gave the impression of still being damp from the morning's dew.

Noreen must have been watching for her, because she stood in the doorway with the door held wide open as Maggie approached.

"I was hoping you'd get here in time for lunch." Noreen balanced the door with one hand and hugged her with the other. "Maggie DeCour—or Dunbarton, now, I guess. Right? I couldn't believe you just called right out of the blue. We have some catching up to do."

Maggie remembered now what a knack Noreen had had in college for taking charge, setting the social tone in any situation. Apparently, she hadn't lost the knack.

Noreen stood back and surveyed her. "Yes, I think I

would have recognized you in a crowd. You haven't changed all that much."

"You either, Noreen." Maggie smiled as broadly as she could to cover the lie. In college, Noreen had had the sculpted look of someone who could wield an eyebrow pencil as though her life depended upon it. What Maggie saw now was the untied version of this: baggy sweats, hair clipped hurriedly on the back of her head, no sign of an artificially arched eyebrow here. She had moved a long way from the button-down collars of those sorority years. Noreen's only nod to having put some preparation into her appearance was a gold sailboat charm that hung from a red cord around her neck. "So, you're a regular summer resident here?"

"Oh, I may be more than that if Jerry has any say in the matter. We're thinking about winterizing this place and re-tiring here. Or, at least Jerry is. I'm not sure if I could stand winters here. Too cold—and too quiet." Noreen laughed at herself. "But what about you? Are you just here for a sum-mer at the beach?"

Maggie hesitated. She could tell Noreen the truth: I caught my husband with another woman, and now I'm running away from him for a while to decide what to do. She was sure Noreen had a whole network of college friends she kept in touch with. "Actually, we are here on vacation—yes. But also to work on a project. I'm working on a photo essay."

A slight frown registered itself on Noreen's forehead. "Oh, a working girl. And how's it going? Tell me more."

"Well, I'm trying to capture some of the natural beauty of the area—highlight it. Things seem to be getting devel-oped around here so fast. Actually, I thought Jerry might be able to help me. Fill me in on some of the environmental background I need for the piece."

"Oh, will he ever." Noreen folded her arms in front of her. "That man lives his work. He'll talk you blue about his work. If you walk into Jerry's office, be sure you have an exit strategy."

They shared a laugh that Maggie supposed was directed at male foibles, though she couldn't be sure. The differences between Jerry and Noreen were evident the minute you stepped into the cottage. It was a tug of war between what Noreen probably wanted to be an attempt at early American and what Jerry's habits had turned into the absentminded professor's weekend retreat. In the dining room where they now sat was a hutch whose shelves contained a cup and saucer collection, but whose top was strewn with papers and folders. Next to that was a stack of newspapers a foot high. The two styles must have achieved some kind of detente by now, Maggie supposed, since Noreen seemed so at ease in her summer home.

"Let's eat first," Noreen suggested. "Then I'll turn him loose on you. Otherwise, we won't get a chance at all to talk."

Noreen had prepared a chicken salad, and the two women sat on her porch, their forks clicking while Noreen explained how she spent her summers. It seemed to be by committing nearly equal parts to beach life and community activities. Apparently, Sunnyside had a guild that devoted its energy to the local arts community. The guild held a fundraiser every year, a bazaar in the nearby town's armory that drew visitors from as far away as Lansing. Noreen was proud of it. She was vice chair this year and was immersed in generating the publicity for the event. "You might want to put your photography to use by taking some pictures of artists working, Maggie."

"It's not really what I had in mind," Maggie wanted to

say, but let it drop. Who knew? Maybe there was an opportunity there.

———————— ((•)) ————————

Jerry crossed his hands behind the back of his head and leaned precariously back in his chair. He took a deep breath and whistled it out, sending a few stray hairs on his forehead into the air.

Maggie imagined this might be the preparatory posturing before a lecture—a studied act which focused attention on him. "A quick answer to your question." He leaned forward, with the speed of a pounce, as though propelled there by the back of his chair, catching her off guard. "That's a tall order. But I can try." He took another deep breath, started to say something, changed his mind, and started again.

"I'm sympathetic to what you're saying, Maggie, I really am. Though some of what I'm going to say will sound as though I'm not. Sounds like you've fallen under the spell of Lake Michigan—nothing wrong with that. You've probably noticed what's been going on along the lakeshore, and you see it as a microcosm of something lots larger. What you're saying—I think—is that to some of us it seems so clear. What we are doing to this earth—at least what Western civilization is doing—seems to be instigating changes that are messing things up? Right?"

She nodded.

"We seem to have this view that the earth is at our disposal—our playground, our warehouse for resources, or whatever—there for our use, for our purposes. We take the tops off mountains and strew the waste down our valleys. We pump our refuse into our air and our water. We look at the environment as something to make a quick buck off of."

"Exactly." Maggie felt something like relief to hear someone else put it into words. It was reaffirming. She knew he wasn't through, though, and waited.

"People in my field who find fault with this human activity think the problem is our attitude. It's our attitude that produces our hegemony—this huge sense of entitlement—over the environment." He pursed his lips again, as though to think.

"That—and because we can." Maggie spoke up. She had intended to lighten the mood a little, but Jerry didn't seem to notice.

"We behave as though there's some hierarchy here, and we're at the top. We are at the apex, so we get to dominate. We can only see our world through our own self-centered—our own human-centered—point of view, as something just for us to use—however we see fit." Jerry had turned his back on her now and began to pace. Maggie almost felt like he was not really speaking to her as much as arguing with some alter ego.

Jerry went on. "Yet this attitude—or so the argument goes—is bankrupt. Look what has come of it. *We're* creating an atmosphere that is no longer healthy or hospitable for *us*. What we need is a new respect for the other members of this environmental community of ours. We are just regular members of this biological community with no more significance than anything else. We need to curb our activities: if we're going to mess around with this community of ours, it had darn well better be for some reason other than the inconsequential one of feeding our own greed!"

"Exactly." She smiled at him. She knew she sounded too enthusiastic, but couldn't help it. His words had felt so empowering.

Jerry hesitated when he saw her smile, then turned to

look at some faraway spot out his window; his shoulders sagged almost imperceptibly. When he turned, his voice had changed: "But, Magdalene, don't you see the lack of logic in this?"

The alter ego had won the day, Maggie realized. This wasn't what she wanted to hear. By way of a retort, she wanted to point out logic's limits, but she didn't. She waited for him to go on.

"We're humans. We are creatures of this world. If we say we must prohibit ourselves from engaging in human activities, it's *then* that we're treating ourselves differently, it's *then* that we're setting ourselves apart from our world. It's our *nature* to apply our 'know-how' to the world and modify it to suit ourselves. All living things affect their environment in some way or other: we just do it more—or more visibly, anyway."

"Yes . . . but." Maggie didn't know how she was going to respond to this, but she knew she couldn't let it go by unchallenged. Jerry picked up the thread where he had left off, so, once again, she didn't get to explore her own misgivings.

"Humans are creatures that are able to transform their environment. This is what we *do*; this is who we *are*. We just can't seem to get around that fact. And, if we're contributing to the destruction of the biosphere, the biotic community, that itself may be just the natural progression: the universe itself is heading toward entropy, after all."

"That can't be all there is, Jerry. That feels all wrong." Maggie was out of her depth and she knew it. But she couldn't help launching some kind of protest.

"Oh, yes, well . . ." Jerry sat himself back down in his chair and leaned forward. "Perhaps what you want here, what you're searching for, is some way to find value in nature in and of itself, independent of what any human thinks of it. Something intrinsic. Value apart from how *we* humans value it."

"That's it." Maggie sighed this more than said it. The world didn't rotate on a human axis; the sun didn't set by a human timepiece. Who and what did we think we were? Yet, once again, she knew she'd spoken too soon.

Jerry sighed also. And though Maggie knew full well the sun was still high in the sky, it felt like a long evening shadow was finding its way into the study they shared.

Jerry smiled almost ruefully at her through vacant eyes. "Maggie, showing that the world has some kind of intrinsic value is not as easy as it sounds. You can't just wave your arms and say the earth is valuable for its own sake. What's the basis of this? The basis that we keep coming back to is that people think it has value. That's our best hope. People will see our own well-being is tied up with that of our surroundings and will stop some of our foolishness."

Jerry must have decided he'd gone on too long, Maggie decided, because he went silent and placed his palms together, then rested his index fingers against his lips as though to silence them. Or perhaps he was offering this gesture by way of making peace.

Another day, Maggie might have let the whole subject drop, might have given a self-deprecating smile and deployed her "exit strategy." Not today. She wasn't ready to give her plan up so easily. And she was seething. This helped her find some courage. "But, Jerry, why worry about the intellectual tripe," she challenged him. "That's fine for you academics. But that isn't what moves the earth." She was daring him, she knew. "Why can't we just rely on how we feel to tell us when we're right?"

He'd nodded knowingly to show this had also occurred to him. "So, whoever feels the strongest about what they want is the one who's right?" It was a rhetorical question because he didn't wait for the answer. "But do you really believe that the developers and oil tycoons aren't as impassioned as you are?"

It was Maggie who now took a huge breath and then blew it out. He was right. His point was devastating, she knew. She suspected what she had just witnessed was the winding down of some long-running battle he'd waged with himself and which had finally snuffed out any idealism he'd once had.

Maggie didn't have an answer. Not yet. What Jerry had done for her, she realized, was to understand what she had to go up against. She knew there was no way her gut could be that wrong. She just had to work at it. "Thanks, Jerry. You've been a great help. You don't know."

"Sorry not to make things easier for you."

Maggie sighed as she thought about the many ways in which life was not easy for her. "No, it's good for me." She said this with more conviction than she felt. She rose to go.

"And, so, have you met Blailock? Your cottage is close to his." He said this quietly, as an afterthought.

"No," she admitted.

"When you do, you'll see. That's what you're up against."

Maggie said goodbye to Noreen, then headed back along the beach. If she was going to find the answers, she might as well start now.

————)«(»(————

Maggie felt some relief to be free of Noreen and Jerry's cottage as she left the way she came, down the steep wooden steps to the beach. She watched her feet while she descended the stairs, searching there for an answer that seemed to elude her mind. She could see the weakness in answering every issue by claiming it felt right. But damnit! This one did.

When she reached the sand, she looked up in surprise at how far across the sky the sun had traveled. The shadows from the beach umbrellas had wheeled around the sand, and now sat on the other side of their handles. It was later than she thought. A gull squawked repeatedly in mid-flight as though another bird had stolen its catch right out of its mouth.

The reason to protect the beach, Maggie told herself, was that its beauty made your heart leap up. But this sounded flimsy even to her. Try saying that, and you'd be laughed out of both Sheldon's and Blailock's courts of law.

⸻ ⧉ ⸻

Maggie wondered if her meeting with Jerry had so soured her that everything just seemed to go wrong or if it were really as bad as it seemed.

Her daughters were the last to leave Annie's, and Maggie could tell that they had overstayed their school time. Annie clearly had someplace else she wanted to be.

When they got home, Maggie walked into the kitchen and stopped short when the black streak extending across the linoleum floor began to weave from side to side. "Ants." She tried to say it loud enough to get the attention of the rest of the household. The outbound lane led unerringly into a slit between the molding and the floor. The inbound lane led directly to a now-congealed red puddle by the refrigerator.

"Samantha, Jenny, come here," she called without turning her head. She wanted them to see the mess for themselves. Hearing the tone of her voice, the two approached hesitantly, standing close to one another, side by side.

"Look at this, will you? Someone spilled juice here, and now we have this battery of ants."

"Battery?" Jenny said it softly, inquisitively.

The ploy made Maggie lose her temper: "This mess of ants in the kitchen! Look at it." Maggie put her hands on her hips to emphasize her sense of indignity, though she knew the theatrics were clearly stupid and ineffective. She knew it had been Sam, could almost picture the child pulling the heavy plastic bottle from the refrigerator shelf and aiming it toward an uncooperative cup, making a mess of the attempt.

"Who do you think did this?" Maggie looked directly at Sam.

"Bevin." Sam said this blandly and without guile.

"*Bevin*. Who's that?"

"The one who did it." Again Sam answered lightly, no hesitation.

The battle that followed was not the one Maggie had been prepared to wage. Rather than dealing with a child's remorse, Maggie had exhausted her anger trying to get Sam to give up her fictional character and admit her own culpability, had tried to get her to understand actions and consequences. When Sam finally understood that Bevin had been stripped from her, she burst into tears and ran to her mother, burying her face against Maggie's legs and sobbing, "Don't look so *ugly*, Mommy."

Maggie bit her tongue and stroked Sam's head, sick with herself.

⸺◈⸺

The memory of Sam's tears made Maggie try to take extra care tucking the girls in bed that night. When she went to kiss Jen, her toe kicked an object under the bed. "What's this?" She'd bent down to look. It was the music box they'd unearthed in the storeroom. "Jen, did you bring this up?"

Jennifer didn't quite meet her mother's gaze. "Um-hum . . ."

Go easy, Maggie cautioned herself. "Well, that's okay. But let's not keep it under the bed. How about putting it on your dresser?" Maggie assumed Jennifer's silence was acquiescence, and placed the box there. The box had gotten cleaned, somehow, Maggie realized. Jennifer must have done it herself. If Jennifer was taking that great an interest in an object, Maggie knew she'd better delineate the territory from the start. "Remember, hon. This doesn't belong to us. You can enjoy it this summer, but when we leave, you need to leave it here. Okay?" Silence. "Okay, Jennifer?"

"Lady Bug."

"What?"

"Lady Bug. My *name* is Lady Bug." She pronounced it almost haughtily, with the emphasis on "lady," turned over, and pulled the covers up over her head.

CHAPTER 7

Maggie pulled the heavy curtains across the storeroom windows and studied the effect. There were no slits of light that she could see. She'd taken down the tattered fabric that had served as curtains and traded them out for a heavy black material she'd found on the sale counter at a craft store in town. She'd also found a used safe light in the photography store. It swung from the light socket overhead, producing a nearly surreal bloodred cast on everything within its sphere; the effect was one of embers asking to be fanned.

She couldn't believe how perfectly the storage area worked as a darkroom. She'd pulled up an old potting table, the enlarger on a card table next to it. The long, narrow wooden table under the windows would serve as her developing area, the "wet" side of her new lab. The utility sink in the basement, a cast-iron tub on legs, was actually on the far wall, but at least there was a water source nearby so she didn't have to go up and down the stairs every time she needed water.

The chemicals had been tricky to come by. Phil, the owner of the photo store, explained there was so little interest in developing one's own photos these days that he had stopped carrying darkroom supplies years before. But he warmed to Maggie's plight and readily ordered a small supply of what she needed. Maggie suspected he had not made much of a profit off of her but was pleased to have a customer who took her craft so seriously. He had even given her the name of another customer who had an old enlarger he wanted to sell. She'd called and gone to his house to look it over. The man was elderly and limped noticeably as he took Maggie into a back room to look at what he had. The enlarger was a relatively new Leitz. Maggie reminded herself she could always replace the lens if it didn't live up to expectations, and she paid the price he had asked for.

As Maggie poured the developer and stop bath and fixer into their trays, she breathed in to let the familiar smells penetrate her nostrils. The stop bath prickled, and she had to pinch her nose to keep from sneezing. Where had she read that smells brought on our strongest memory associations? Her mind returned to her early days on the paper, her short initial forays into the darkroom there. A couple of the regular photojournalists had taken her under their wing. She wasn't certain she was really ready to fly alone, but how else would she know if she didn't try.

She knew local newspapers were often folksy places. Maybe she should try there first to run a photo essay on the shore area. What if she were even able to get a photo of the phantom Blailock, the culprit who threatened to disrupt life as usual? It could make the whole thing very powerful. A plot was beginning to hatch in Maggie's mind. If she could convince Jason to go to the Fourth of July party with her, she would smuggle her camera in, somehow. She'd try for something like the Cartier-Bresson effect, capture a moment that revealed the soul. Or, perhaps in Blailock's case, she would reveal the lack of one.

A photo could carry the day—maybe even better than watching heavy machinery bulldoze under lakeside cottages. Single moments rarely registered on the psyche; our eyes didn't normally focus on the single frames but on the continuity of the series, the overall effect. To be able to pick out and hang onto the frame that captured the soul of a person or of an event—that was genius, Maggie knew.

She was itching to try a couple of prints . . . nothing monumental . . . to get the feel. She placed a negative in the carrier, then fitted it into a slot in the enlarger and flipped on the instrument's light switch. The image virtually vaulted out on the easel below. Wildly wonderful was the way she always saw it. The photo spread beyond the easel, onto her makeshift countertop, ignoring all boundaries. She cranked the lens down enough to shrink the image so that it fit on the easel below, bringing it into focus.

<hr/>

The negative she started with had nothing to do with the Blailock project. It was a portrait of her daughters on the beach, kneeling beside a sand castle. Jennifer was primly shaping a single turret on the castle, while Sam was sitting back on her heels with her hands buried in the sand behind her to admire their handiwork. It had been late in the afternoon, and the shafts of light breaking through the clouds over the lake made the lighting uneven. Maggie adjusted the level of the lens and the focus once more. Then she flipped off the switch.

She reached under the table to the shelf where she kept the photographic paper in a light-safe pouch, carefully lifted out a piece of paper, and lined it up on the easel. Then she set the timer and turned the enlarger light on. Even though it was on only a matter of seconds, it always seemed like an eternity. Would it turn off when it was supposed to? Or go on too long and ruin things? Maggie was a terrible judge of the length of the time—her own innate distrust of all things mechanical was strong, and she consciously had to keep her hand from reaching up and manually shutting off the light. When she was certain she could stand it no longer, the light turned off automatically. Grateful, she lifted the easel frame and took her print out with her left hand, then transferred it to her right, careful to keep her left hand dry as her right hand slid the print into the developer.

She used two fingers to rub just slightly over the area where Sam's face was beginning to take shape, as though looming up from the depths of Lake Michigan itself. Maggie hoped to speed up the development of that spot in order to get a little more detail out of her daughter's delight. Maggie couldn't help but be proud of the look of pure contentment that was so clearly registered on her Sam's innocent face.

Maggie repeated the process with a few other prints, taking them through their chemical baths and then leaving them in a pan in the sink with water gently flowing over to rinse them off.

She was about to whip the curtain back open, when a sharp scraping sound caught her attention. It seemed to come from the corner of the basement. Her throat contracted. The rat, she thought. It was back. She stamped her foot and shouted, "Get out." She heard some shuffling above her, but when she heard the scraping sound again, she realized that sound was coming from outside.

Maggie quickly lifted the curtain to look. She found her eyes at the level of the cuffs of someone dressed in navy suit pants. He was stopped on the steps in front of the house of the woman who lived on the other side of the walk. The screen door was open, and he seemed to be talking with someone inside. Maggie bent down until her head was nearly level with the gardening table to try to see who would wear suit pants to a lake cottage on a summer's day, but it was no use. The window was too narrow, and the table kept her from getting any closer to it. All she learned was that he was also wearing a suit coat in June. At the beach. A mystery visitor.

While Maggie watched, the screen door was closed, and the cuffs climbed down the stairs. She shook her head at herself. *What's wrong with you*, she thought. *Spying. I'm letting the investigative reporter in me develop the backstory and gain too strong a foothold on my imagination. As usual, I'm seeing intrigue at every turn.* Maybe she was letting this business of exposing Blailock take on a life of its own. She chastised herself. Some objectivity was necessary, after all.

Next, she'd be talking about the guy in a navy suit carrying a violin case and wearing spats, unloading booze in the lighthouse. She laughed at herself and was about to let the curtain drop back down when the suit coat turned abruptly and just as quickly mounted the steps to her cottage. This action was so swift, Maggie was startled by the knock, loud and insistent.

Who in the world *was* this, she wondered. Just some random sales person? She supposed she should answer the door, then get rid of him as quickly as possible.

She glanced around to make sure she was not leaving any unexposed paper in the open before climbing the stairs. Maggie barely had her foot on the first step when she heard her front screen pulled open and footsteps on the porch.

At a later time she would question why she had continued up the stairs to confront a stranger who had essentially entered her home uninvited. It had never even occurred to her it could be someone dangerous and she should get away from him, leave by the basement door to get help.

She hurried up the stairs. By the time she reached the living room, she found the man with his hand on the banister looking for all the world as though he were going to head upstairs. Maggie wondered whether a face could match this particular suit, but his did. It was long and, aside from dark, piercing eyes, expressionless.

"Who are you and what do you want?" Maggie knew she sounded like a dime store novel, but these were the first words that came out. She couldn't be sure whether the stranger was actually going to climb the stairs, but it seemed as though his weight shifted back when he gave her a careful smile.

"Oh, I'm sorry. I got confused about where I was. I'm looking for my brother's place. He's in a rental around here. I must have the wrong house. Forgive me. I had no idea." He seemed to bow a little with the apology, backing toward the door. "I thought he said he lived in a cottage up this walk . . . but it must be the next one over."

"What's his name? Perhaps I know him." The man's apparent discomfort made Maggie sympathetic.

"Oh, I'm sure you don't. He just got here."

"But I know some of the rentals."

"Oh, that's all right." His hand was already reaching for the screen as he said this, pushing it open. "Sorry to disturb you."

Maggie stood on her porch watching him until he disappeared down the walk. She was relieved enough to see him go that she didn't question his story until later. Much later.

━━━━◦《◉》◦━━━━

"You sure you can't stay a little longer? Help me with Jen's birthday?" Maggie knew wheedling never worked with Bryan, but she could tell already how much she'd miss him once he left.

"Sorry. This has been great. But time to return to the real world, sis."

"I know." Maggie realized Bryan had already stayed longer than he'd intended. But the timing was especially bad. It was so close to Jenny's birthday, and she needed to make it clear to Sheldon that he was not to come. That would be so much easier if Bryan was still around.

"Get Annie to help you do a party with the kids—or get Jason to help you out. He seems good with kids." Bryan tossed off the suggestions as he pulled himself around the banister and up the first step. "I heard from Dante. They need roofers on a new subdivision, and if I can get hired, I'll have work for the rest of the summer. Can't miss out on this."

"I know." Maggie watched him for a moment, then turned away. She hated goodbyes, hated the sadness produced by a lingering sense of loss, the sense that there was something missing. Now, she had two favors to ask of Jason. She wondered if it would seem too forward. And she didn't really care if it did.

Jennifer, Rodney, Stone, and Daphne, a girl close in age to Jennifer from Annie's day care, walked ahead with Jason through the gaping clown's mouth that was the entrance into the Silver Sands Park entrance. Sam hung back, clinging to Maggie's hand. She stepped through the opening quickly, trying not to glance up at the clown's white teeth hanging overhead. Once they were inside, they could hear the carousel's music blaring over the speakers, and the older girls immediately headed toward the painted horses as though drawn by some magic spell.

"Looks like we're going to start at the merry-go-round," Jason noted. Maggie smiled at him. It hadn't been hard at all to convince him he'd like to spend an afternoon at an amusement park with a bunch of six-year-olds. Maggie had started to explain that Sheldon hadn't been able to make it here for Jen's birthday and she didn't feel that one adult was enough to ride herd on five children, but Jason didn't need any convincing.

"That's my old stomping ground," he'd told her. "We used to spend every other Saturday night there in the summer when I was twelve, thirteen. It was where we went to meet girls," he'd unabashedly admitted. "You know this is the last summer for the place. It's slated for the wrecking ball. Too old now. It loses money. This can be my farewell trip."

The carousel was slowing down, the ride over. The children broke into a run, and Maggie hurried to catch up, pulling out her billfold as she went. There were only about ten children in all, waiting for their turn, so Jennifer got the all-white horse with blue studded reins and saddle she had her heart set on. The ride operator climbed onto the ride's platform to help lift Sam into her horse's saddle. Sam leaned forward and wrapped both arms around the pole; then the music began again and Maggie watched as her daughters circled before her eyes, waving as they came around.

"Thanks again," Maggie told Jason.

"Don't mention it." He turned to look at her. "Your husband wasn't ever planning to come, was he?"

Maggie knew she was coloring. "That's not quite what's going on." She felt cornered. Had Jason suspected something all along? Maybe Bryan had said something. She felt strangely vulnerable. "It's not really something I want to talk about, but I'm here for the summer to get away from him. He wasn't invited to the party at all—at least not by me."

"Oh, I see." Jason said this slowly and returned his gaze to the merry-go-round, as though considering the possibilities this confession conveyed.

Hoping it would bring an end to further questions, Maggie directed her attention to the rising and falling horses as well, the breathing of the machine, the waving children, the colors swirling before her. She could feel Jason looking at her again, sense his desire to speak. But he said nothing.

Rodney and Stone were off their horses almost before the music stopped. "That wasn't fast enough," Rodney complained when the group had reassembled. Jennifer concurred. Maggie glanced over at Jason for help.

"Then what we need is Ghost Mansion," Jason said. "Follow me."

Sam tugged at Maggie. "You said there weren't ghosts."

"Sam, it's pretend. But you don't have to go on this one. You and I will just sit this one out—okay? Now, no thumb sucking."

Maggie took Sam to the concession stand with a cotton candy machine while Jason and the others headed for the ride. The group was seated in one of the ornate Victorian motif cars moving down the ride's track and into a darkened building by the time Maggie and Sam walked back. Sam held Maggie's hand tightly as they waited at the ride's end, watching the cars make their last turn out of the dark exit and into the light, slowing abruptly, the safety bars clicking open as the riders emerged. Maggie and Sam scanned the faces when the cars came into view. Some riders had their heads thrown back. One little girl had her hands over her eyes.

Then the car that held Jason with Daphne and Jen on either side of him emerged. Jen had her eyes shut tight. Rodney and Stone were next. The boys had clearly enjoyed it. "Whew." Rodney was first to speak. "Did you see the lady in the black dress at the end? She had cobwebs all over her." He imitated whatever it was by holding his arms over his head, and leaning toward Jennifer as though to envelop her.

Jen let out a small scream and pushed him away. "She was yucky. I think I felt her hair on me. It was terrible." The boys laughed with glee. Maggie smiled despite herself.

Jason came over and rested one arm on Maggie's shoulder. He spoke softly so only she could hear him. "Why don't I take these four over to the bumper cars. You and Sam can head for what's called the Kiddie Area, where the rides are for younger children."

Maggie was so conscious of him, could almost feel his arm hairs on the back of her neck, that she wasn't sure whether she'd answered. But she must have because the four older children headed off with Jason.

"Sam, come with me for the time being. I think I see a little airplane ride you're going to like."

Sam was watching her sister go with doubt in her eyes, but she allowed herself to be herded toward a small, enclosed area with a few downsized rides. There were only about five children in the whole enclosure, but all seemed bent on taking the airplane ride with stubby, primary-colored planes attached to steel arms that radiated out from a center pole. Sam clambered into a blue plane, grabbing the steering wheel and turning it when the ride started up.

Each plane was outfitted with a silver laser gun that swiveled on its base. The children twisted these at each other as the planes lifted from the ground. Maggie could hear the "pow" sound from the guns each time someone depressed a trigger. Sam seemed to be taking aim at a little boy directly across from her who was returning fire. Sam squealed with delight each time her gun went off. So much for nonviolent girls, Maggie thought.

When it was over, Sam insisted on a second plane ride. From there, it was on to the boats floating in a large tank of water. The guns in this were actually squirt guns with a limited range. The trajectory of water indicated the direction in which the gun was aimed, but there were no direct hits. This one delighted Sam as well. Maggie loved it. She loved seeing her daughter's confidence grow. Hopefully, the older children wouldn't brag too much about their own rides.

It was about half an hour later when the group gathered in front of the games of chance. Rodney and Stone were betting Jason that he couldn't hit the assembly line of dented, flat metal ducks that moved in formation continuously across the back of the booth. Maggie could see that Jason was tempted. He looked at the boys and winked.

"Okay. Here goes." Jason placed some money on the table and looked over the rifles lying on the counter. The booth operator leaned forward quickly and swiped the money into his hand before Jason could change his mind. He wore a wrinkled white T-shirt and jeans, and the sign of a stubble was beginning to show on his face below bleary eyes. Maggie suspected his evenings off were most likely spent at local bars.

Jason chose the longest rifle, though they were all extremely short, and held it to his shoulder so he could look through the sights. As Maggie watched him take aim, she could have sworn that the ducks speeded up.

Jason must have shared her perception because he lowered the rifle from his shoulder for a moment and watched the birds skirt across his field of vision. Maggie wondered if he'd say something. Instead Jason turned to face the operator for a moment, as though taking his measure, the hint of a smile playing at the corners of his mouth. Then the rifle went up to his shoulder again.

Jason fired the five rounds without wavering. Maggie supposed it was an amazing display; she knew so little about shooting a gun that she couldn't say. But they heard the rapid "ping, ping, ping" five times in short succession as all five blanks found their mark. Then Jason lowered the rifle and turned toward the operator. "Well?" he asked. "Does that win a prize?"

"Where'd you learn to shoot like that?" the man asked as he turned and took down a gaudy fuchsia monkey from the ranks of monkeys hanging from a pegboard. "You been in the service or something?"

Jason didn't answer. He shrugged and turned, awarding the stuffed animal to Jen and winking at her. "For the birthday girl." Jen grabbed the pink animal eagerly and hugged it close to her. Then, laughing, Jason turned to Rodney and Stone to let them grab his arm to feel his biceps. Maggie hung back as the group headed for their final stop at the roller coaster. It would not do to fall for this guy, she told herself. It wouldn't do at all.

———— ◦《◉》◦ ————

The children were still bragging about their grand finale on the Silver Sands roller coaster when Maggie pulled her van into the Breakwater Bay parking lot. "That first hill," Rodney reminisced, "creeping up, up, and then over the top and bam! My stomach was up to here." He held a hand under his chin.

"Mine was up to here." Daphne held her hand over her head. They all laughed again.

"You can just let me off here," Jason said when he saw Maggie would be hunting for a parking space. "I have a job I need to get to. It was fun. Thanks all," he called back, swinging out of the car.

"Bye, Jason, bye," they called. "Bye, Muscle Man," Stone added for good measure.

More laughter from the back seat.

Maggie shifted uncomfortably in her seat, though she didn't know why. She eventually found a parking space close to the south end of the lot. The children emptied the van quickly, and she had to talk fast to make sure they got everything they'd brought out of the car. Rodney and Stone started to run ahead; the older girls quickly followed. Maggie was glad that Jennifer was out of earshot and couldn't hear what happened next.

"Yoo-hoo!" Janine materialized from between two cottages, waggling her arm in the air as she walked. "Yoo-hoo. Maggie. There was a man here—your husband, I assume—asking directions to your cottage. I gave them to him. Saw him head that way."

Maggie stopped short, forcing herself to smile. She could feel the knot already forming in her stomach, feel her shoulders ascend toward her ears. "Thanks. We'll see if he's there now."

But when she and Sam had nearly reached the cottage, they were greeted by Jennifer, who had changed her shoes and was heading out. "We're riding bikes. Rodney and me. Okay?"

"Are you sure that isn't too much? Maybe Rodney and Stone would rather be by themselves for a while."

"They asked. 'Sides, it's my birthday."

"That's true. It's your birthday. Go ahead." The thought of turning around for more exhausted Maggie. "Don't go too far. Be sure Gertie knows where Rodney is." She felt like saying, "Keep your eye open for your father," but maybe Janine had been wrong. Still, who could it have been?

—————))(())((—————

Sheldon had chosen the wicker chair to sit in, reclining against the back and stretching his long legs out as far as they would go into the porch. *Of course he'd choose that one*, Maggie thought. *My favorite. Contaminate it, will you?*

Now he stretched his arms up in the air and, crossing them, rested them on top of his head. It was a gesture that was accompanied by self-satisfaction, Maggie knew. She had never had to ask him if he'd won a case. All she'd needed to do was watch for that characteristic gesture accompanied by a short exhalation of air from his nose. Like a snort, was how she described it to herself. She'd come to hate the sound.

How was it that she had let him in the door, she'd wondered. She'd heard the girls' excited calls to her from the walk and had hurried out. Sheldon was coming up the walk with Sam riding on his shoulders, timid Sam—who had once begged Bryan to put her down—now holding onto large fistfuls of her father's thick dark hair for safety. He carried his daughter as he might wear a crown, the triumphant conqueror. The hero coming back from doing battle. And Jen was the admiring entourage crowding around his feet.

He must have just walked in, Maggie thought. She must have just stepped back from the door, and he must have just walked right through. The girls had run around, showing him every inch of the cottage, showing him their summer projects, before they'd all settled on the porch. Maggie had felt violated. How dare he so casually invade her privacy this way. She was thinking of her unmade bed and the two changes of clothes strewn around the room.

"So." Sheldon brought his arms down and leaned forward with an air of what? Authority? Superiority? "How about some wine, Maggie? I would almost bet you have some around."

"Sure." She got up, eager to get away from him for a minute. She escaped into the kitchen and took down a glass, then glanced around before taking out the bottle hidden behind some things on the top shelf of the cupboard. It wouldn't do to have him stay. How would she manage to get rid of him? Maggie felt her strength seeping out of her. She'd have to think of something, some way . . .

She could hear them on the porch. Hear the girls talking about their day at the amusement park, going through the "pows" and the screams all over again. "And then Jason shot the gun and hit the duck," Jen told him. "He won me a monkey. I'll show you." She came into the living room to get her monkey, nearly bumping into her mother carrying the glasses of wine.

"And who's Jason?" Sheldon asked with raised eyebrows.

Maggie had started to speak, not certain what was coming out of her mouth, but Sam interrupted her: "Oh, he patches things?"

"Patches things?" Sheldon directed this straight at Maggie.

"He's the fix-it man around here—for Breakwater Bay. He does the small repairs on the cottages." Maggie handed him his wine.

He took it without comment, nodding smugly and settling himself comfortably back into the wicker chair. Maggie wanted to smile. How like him, she thought. Easily dismissing the manual laborer. He wouldn't see any need to worry about a handyman. No competition there, he'd think. How wrong he might be, she decided, wondering silently if this was a promise or a threat.

"Ha! That's great." Sheldon took the stuffed monkey from Jennifer and held it, sitting it on his lap. The monkey was a foreign protrusion against his khaki pants. "Now, why don't you and Sam go outside and play," he told Jen. "Your mother and I have to talk. Then we'll walk to the car to get Jen's present from me after we're done."

Jen looked at him suspiciously, but the weight of the bribe was not lost on her, and she did as she was told. "C'mon, Sam. Let's go look for the boys."

"If you don't find them, come right back." Maggie followed them to the steps. "Don't go that far." She was feeling vulnerable, for some reason. She had a sense of foreboding, of doom almost. She knew it had to do with Sheldon. His sheer physical presence had taken some of the glow away from the summer.

Maggie hung onto the screen door to make sure the girls headed toward Gertie's.

"Oh, you don't have to worry, Maggie," Sheldon said lightly, mockingly, she thought. "I'm not going to stay. I have too much to do to hang around here." He tipped his head back as though to dismiss all of Breakwater Bay. "Actually, I have a client here. A big one." He hesitated to let this sink in before going on. "And I thought I'd kill two birds with one stone. I was just up the walk to see him. Perhaps you've heard of him. His name is Blailock. Vincent Blailock." Sheldon leaned forward as he said this, balancing his arms on his knees, as though confiding in her.

Maggie hadn't ridden the roller coaster that afternoon, but she suspected she knew what it had felt like. She waited a moment before allowing herself to speak. Aim for nonchalance, she told himself. "Sure I've heard of him. Everyone has. He's a big name around here, but he's not popular. People around here don't like him much at all." Maggie was proud that she'd managed this slight. It wouldn't be lost on Sheldon. "So, what'd he hire a corporate lawyer for?" She tried to make it sound as though she couldn't care less.

"Ha." The snort again. Sheldon scrunched up his face in disdain. "I can't tell you that. Attorney/client privilege. Just that it will be interesting. Very interesting." He looked at her directly, too directly, she decided, then drained his wine.

Maggie wondered why this felt like a threat. She was still vulnerable; she knew this.

"So, you'll be seeing me again, most likely. When I come here to meet with Vince."

Maggie steeled herself, took a breath. Was he really on a nickname basis with the guy? Maggie knew she needed to try to set some boundaries. "Well, if you intend to stop by here, then you need to let me know in advance. Call ahead to say you're coming." It wasn't much of a show of courage, she knew, but it was something.

"Yeah, yeah." Sheldon's tone of voice was almost taunting, but then he seemed to shift gears. "Maggie, be reasonable. I know this has been hard on you. I know you think you're doing the right thing by coming here—for the entire summer. But I have every right to see my daughters. I probably have more rights than that. But I'm not pressing for those. At least not for *now*." His tone had become more insistent.

Maggie let her lids drop momentarily. Her resolve seemed to be nothing more than beach foam, small bubbles the wind easily blew away. This was always the way it was. Sheldon allowed himself to be more human, and she allowed herself to weaken. His affair had been justification for getting away from him. But it wasn't the only reason. Maggie knew she needed to continue to project outrage at his betrayal if she was going to be able to stay away from him.

Sheldon must have read her silence as a refusal to acquiesce, because he stood up, hitching up his slacks around his waist as he did so. He was still trim. Not beefy like many of his middle-aged partners. He had been on the second string basketball team in high school. It was probably his athletic poise that made him so formidable in the courtroom, Maggie supposed. He would gracefully move in front of the jury box as he made an argument, like a jouncing boxer waiting to land the perfect punch.

Maggie had almost wished that he had gone puffy, had lost the physical prowess that now made him so formidable. He seemed to take up too much room in the small porch, and she was relieved when he stepped out of it and back into the living room to gather his jacket.

"I'll say goodbye to the girls, give Jen her gift."

"I'll go with you."

"Don't trust me?" Sheldon made the motion of lowering his head to look at her. "Ha."

CHAPTER 8

Years later, when Maggie looked back at her summer on the lake, she equated July Fourth and the coming of the alewives as the line that separated the good part of the summer from the bad. She wondered whether the arrival of the small, bristly fish had cast a pall over everything or simply brought out the worst in people.

Of course, if she had given it more thought, she would have remembered that the tiny, bloated bodies floating on the lake's surface hadn't technically arrived until later, and she might also have remembered that events prior to the Fourth were the precursors for most of what followed. And if the alewives hadn't arrived, she might not have shuttered herself in her darkroom to work on the Blailock photo.

She had indeed finagled an invitation from Jason to attend the Fourth of July party at Blailock's home, mostly by just expressing a genuine curiosity. Typically, when she asked him, Jason had shrugged at the entrepreneur's ability to remain so elusive. It was the power of money, he said, the ability to move in different circles from the rest of us.

But Maggie was exultant. She'd finally get to see and size up the man who people described as a threat to his community—and worse, from Maggie's own point of view—the man who gave Sheldon a reason for appearing at Breakwater Bay unannounced. What was he like, she wondered.

She really wasn't using Jason, she told herself; she really was looking forward to spending some time with him. He had been the one to suggest that they take his boat out afterward to watch the fireworks from Lake Michigan.

The girls were at Gertie's and would be for as long as needed. Jason dropped by the cottage to pick her up. Maggie liked it that he had dressed casually for the party, short-sleeved shirt and khakis. Maggie supposed it was possible that he didn't even own a sports coat. They headed down the front walk side by side.

"I usually don't go to this thing," Jason confided. "Not my idea of entertainment." He glanced over at her with a look that seemed to imply he was doing it for her.

"I owe you one, then." Maggie smiled back.

Even though they arrived fairly early, it was clear that for some of the guests, the party had already been going on for some time. The redheaded bodyguard who had accosted her at the helicopter landing took their invitation and entered their names into a log book. Maggie wondered if they were being vetted against some master enemy list. She looked past him, hoping he wouldn't recognize her.

Blailock's home was sumptuous, and, whether intended or not, it made a travesty of the beach house look—gone were the wooden siding and dormer windows. This home featured arched doorways and marble floors, more fitting for something in Beverly Hills. "You wonder how a guy can become this wealthy from small appliances." Jason sounded almost envious, Maggie realized.

A strange, life-sized sculpture of Poseidon astride two lurching stallions occupied the center of a huge entryway. Poseidon held a long trident in an arm that was drawn back behind his head, taking aim at a serpent entwined in the stallions' legs curling upward so that its head was above god and horses. Water jetted out of the serpent's mouth engulfing a horse head. Maggie gave the sculpture a wide berth as she walked into the living area.

They'd only been there a few minutes before Maggie made the assessment that by far the majority of guests were women of a certain age—and look. Jason spoke to her over the crowd noise, saying he'd go get their drinks. What was she drinking?

With Jason gone, Maggie directed her attention to the room she was in, working her way round to a collection of photographs on top of a baby grand that sat in one corner of the room. A short, stocky man who Maggie assumed was Blailock dominated nearly every picture, posing either with celebrities, politicians, or alongside large fish hanging from hooks in exotic seashore settings. If the photos could be believed, Vince Blailock was clearly a man whose fortune had helped him buy his way into power.

One photo in particular caught Maggie's eye. The man she supposed was Blailock loomed large in this one as well. He was receiving a medal of some sort from a dignitary who looked, what? French, maybe. But in the background was a woman who looked vaguely familiar until Maggie realized it was the woman she'd seen on the beach early in the summer, the Girl from Ipanema, who had quieted the other sunbathers as she passed by. Was this Blailock's wife?

Maggie looked up, then, thinking this would be a question she needed to ask Jason. She was in time to catch sight of him in the dining room, drinks in hand, making his way back to her. He was still at some distance when a tall woman in a red sundress, whose dark hair was pulled back from her face, grabbed his arm, causing him to hold the glasses of wine he carried away from himself to prevent them from spilling. The two exchanged a quick—and familiar—kiss. She said something, then bowed her head to hear Jason's response. They seemed to hold each other's eyes in a promissory gaze for several seconds before Jason turned away.

Maggie sighed and shrugged. Gads, if that was her competition for Jason's affection, she was doomed. Here, all along, she had supposed he had shown some special interest in her. How could she have been so naïve, she wondered, turning her head toward a window. If Jason happened to look this way, she could pretend she hadn't seen the exchange.

"Thanks," Maggie said, regaining her composure as Jason reached her and handed over a glass. "Say, tell me something. Is Vincent Blailock married?"

"He was." Jason took a sip from his own glass, watching her over its rim with some curiosity as he did so. "Do you mean you haven't heard the story yet?"

She shook her head.

"Well, the accepted version is she was killed in some kind of boating accident a few years ago." Jason gave her a half smile. "You sure you want to hear this? It's the usual stuff people love to tell about Blailock."

Maggie nodded while sipping her drink.

"Course, Blailock's detractors believe he was somehow responsible for her death. But that hasn't been proved. The boat capsized in bad weather. According to Blailock, he tried to save her and wasn't able to. Her body washed up on shore days later. A young couple came across it. It was so bloated, according to the press, the couple could barely stand to look at it—a detail the paper should have left out."

Maggie was surprised at how angry Jason sounded. "How awful. So who's the woman in the photo over here?"

Maggie took Jason by the arm to lead him over. If some woman in a red dress could take him by the arm, so could she. Maggie pointed to the photo that had caught her attention.

Jason barely glanced at the photo. "Yeah, that's Julia."

Maggie looked at Jason hard. "That can't be. I think I saw her. It was that day you walked to the lighthouse with us."

Jason laughed. "No, you're not seeing ghosts. But you did make a rare sighting. You're not the first one to be fooled. That was Jersey, Julia's twin. She doesn't come around here much anymore. They were quite a pair, I guess. Julia and Jersey, I mean. Grew up near here. They were great water skiers. Used to perform in tandem for the guests of a huge hotel that was once here—right where we're standing, actually. It burned down years ago and was never rebuilt. I've always thought there must be some connection between Julia's association with the hotel and Blailock's interest in this property. Course there's no love lost between Jersey and Blailock. I'm sure Julia's twin blames him in some way—every way—for Julia's death."

Maggie could feel her reporter's instincts clicking in; could feel herself itch to talk with the sources for what had to be a good story: "I should talk with Jersey, then."

"Oh, don't count on that," Jason warned her. "She's as elusive as Blailock. Comes 'round here, but no one knows when she'll drop in. And she doesn't take up with any of the locals."

Maggie felt herself hesitate with disappointment, but her interest had been piqued. "Well, did they have any children?"

"Blailock and Julia? Yeah, there was supposedly a son. He's grown, I think—I don't know what became of him. He's not in his father's business—as far as I know."

"And this heavyset man in all the photos is Blailock?" Maggie pointed at the nearest photo.

"No." Jason laughed. "Weird, isn't it, that the world's biggest egomaniac doesn't have every wall decorated with his own mug shot. That's his business partner—or was his business partner. The two parted ways not long after Julia's death. People blame it on Blailock, that he was impossible to work with after Julia's death."

"That *is* odd," Maggie agreed.

Maggie turned from the wall and saw the red-haired guard in the hall watching them. Perhaps they were showing too much of an interest in the photos. "Don't look now but our red-haired friend who checked IDs when we came in is keeping an eye on us."

Jason smiled. "Yeah. Blailock hires him to be the heavy."

"I know." Maggie thought again about how aggressive he had been with her.

They had stayed at the party another hour, long enough for Maggie to wander through the open rooms, but Vincent Blailock never made an appearance. Jason confirmed he sometimes didn't hang out at his own parties; they were for show, a way he rewarded business associates—and to give the impression that he had a stable of attractive young women.

Jason introduced her to a few people he knew, all Blailock employees, or former employees. Maggie didn't get to meet the woman in the red dress, however.

Just as they were heading toward the front door, Maggie's head jerked up to the stairs leading to a second balcony at the sound of a familiar voice. She was all but certain that the voice coming from the dark recesses of the upper level was that of Sheldon. Typically, he was speaking a little bit too loudly, and she caught the word "regrettable," then, "can't be helped." Without completing the actual thought, she knew Blailock must be there as well. This could be her only chance to get a photo of him.

While Jason walked on ahead, she wheeled around so that her back was to the balcony. She lifted her camera over her shoulder, held it at what she hoped was the right angle, and, bracing her hand on her cheek in case the aperture lingered open in the dim light, managed to push down the right button on top.

Without looking up, she pivoted back around, walked quickly to rejoin Jason, and, taking his arm a little too forcefully, moved them toward the door. She silently hoped this whole maneuver had not been too obvious, but at this point she didn't care. Just so she could escape with whatever she'd caught on film.

But their exit got waylaid. The woman in red had positioned herself by the front door as though she had just cast a net and was waiting to see what swam by. She reeled Jason in when they drew near. And though Maggie and Jason were clearly leaving together: "Don't make yourself so scarce," she told him, once again resting a hand on his sleeve.

"Stephanie." Jason allowed her hand on his arm to stop him. He turned to Maggie then back to the woman in red. "This is Maggie. She and her daughters are at Breakwater for the summer."

"Hello." Stephanie looked at Maggie briefly, as though appraising her and dismissing her at the same time. She turned back to Jason. "See you soon." She said it as though confirming a prior arrangement.

"Yeah. We'll see you." He moved his hand in a truncated wave.

They'd only walked a few yards down the front walk when Jason stopped, turned her to face him, and leaned over for a slow, soft kiss before walking on.

It took Maggie a moment to get her bearings, catch up. She didn't know what to say, and Jason was silent on the walk back, giving Maggie time to consider that Sheldon might put in an appearance at their house that night but also to picture Jason in some ongoing relationship with the woman named Stephanie. What had the kiss meant? Was she being used as some kind of ploy to make Stephanie jealous?

The two thoughts combined to convince her to ask Jason if she could bring the girls along to watch the fireworks that night. This would preclude any chance of a romantic evening, she knew, but at this point, given her own confusion and what she had just seen, that probably wasn't going to happen anyway.

Maggie knew in her heart that this spontaneous decision had not earned her the moral high ground, should not be cause for self-pride. It wasn't as though she had consciously made the decision to keep her relationship with Jason a friendship. It would be a pretension to think she was somehow morally superior to Sheldon by not actively pursuing an affair of her own. She admitted that there had been a time when she hoped her relationship with Jason would amount to something more. And, if she was being truly honest with herself, maybe she still did.

⸺⸺«◉»⸺⸺

The fireworks were memorable in retrospect: it would be the last time in weeks when anyone could go out on a boat when the waters appeared clear, not littered with bobbing silver fish bellies wherever you looked.

She and the girls had met Jason at the slip behind the Yacht Club. Jason was talking with a man in the slip next to his who was also readying his boat for a sail, pulling the sail cover off the main sheet and boom.

"Where's the Ought Club?" Sam had asked Jason. "Mom said we were going there."

Jason had clearly been delighted with Sam's version. "Sam, you sure called that one. Personally, I try to stay *away* from the *Ought* Club as much as possible."

"Sam," Maggie interjected, if only to set the record straight. "It's 'Yacht Club.' A yacht's a boat."

"Are we going on Jason's yacht like last time?"

"You sure are." Jason had lifted the girls onto the boat, then helped Maggie in, giving her a wink.

The man with a boat in the slip next to theirs helped push them back, but Maggie was proud that she was able to do most everything else with careful instructions from Jason.

They sailed through the small lake, but then dropped sail at the mouth of the channel and motored between the concrete siding and onto the big lake.

Hundreds of boats were already there. These had settled on the waters offshore and dropped anchor to wait for the show.

The crowd had not been disappointed. The bursts of color and noise had lasted nearly half an hour. There were red, green, and blue explosions, silver ones that rang out like bullets, and swooshing ones that rained sparkling comets and curlicues. Sam clapped gleefully with nearly every blast; then, worn out from the excitement, she fell asleep on the ride home. Jen, Maggie knew, was enchanted, but wasn't going to show it. Jason helped carry Sam back to the cottage and up the stairs to her room.

He'd given Maggie another quick kiss before he left and before she could protest—or respond in kind. "See you around." It had almost sounded final, Maggie later thought to herself. As though he knew something she didn't. She watched Jason as he walked away and thought how dark the night felt, such a short time after the fireworks had lit up the entire sky.

———◦((◦))◦———

That night a deep fog rolled across the eastern shore of the lake. It provided cover for the aquatic intruders to steal in. While Breakwater Bay slept, the alewives filtered into the Great Lakes. Sometime earlier, the first of the migrating ocean fish must have become disoriented and turned in to the mouth of the freshwater St. Lawrence Seaway. The ancient vetebrae made their way upstream along the several channels that formed the Seaway from the Atlantic Ocean to Lake Ontario.

Had the rest of the schools all blindly followed a few confused leaders? Or just been attracted to the opening in the shoreline? No matter. The result was the same. The fresh water claimed the lives of hundreds of thousands of the small, silver-scaled fish when they followed this deadly route, choosing a path that ultimately led to their own death.

Within days, the bodies of alewives began to wash up on shore, first just at the edge of the water line where it touched the sand and drew back. Before long, the bodies began to pile up, sometimes several inches deep across the entirety of what had been beautiful sandy beaches. When the breeze blew onshore, the stench was unbearable.

The coming of the alewives was a catastrophe for tourism along Lake Michigan. Nature had found a way to ruin the beach for humans to a far greater extent than Blailock's wealth and influence ever could have.

Eventually, bulldozers would come in and turn the sand over and push what was left of the alewives, the bristly curved spines, to the perimeter of the beaches where they dried and bleached and cracked in the sun. People would stumble back onto the beach, blinking at surprise in the sun, lugging their lawn chairs and sun umbrellas back to the water's edge. But that effort was still weeks away when Maggie and the girls woke up that first morning to low-lying fog and thousands of unwanted visitors littering the shores. They had to adjust their lives to a long, hot July without the respite of the beach and Lake Michigan.

Rebuffed from the beach, Maggie poured herself into her photography with a real sense of purpose. Noreen had let her know that she was welcome to be part of the arts and crafts show—this would be the first time they would have a photographer as part of the show, but why not. Annie's day care program now included trips into town to the park or to tourist concession stands at the mall not far from the State Park on the other side of the channel. And, of course, there were still the art projects that Gertie helped Annie dream up.

————))((((————

Maggie's legs ached. She'd been on them too long, she guessed, catching the photos as they fell from the drum of the dryer. It was an old dryer, not very satisfactory. She still ended up placing the prints between the pages of a heavy book she'd found in the cottage, to make sure the prints were flat.

She surveyed her prints critically, appraising their visual impact. Not bad, she thought. But did they create the effect she wanted? Who knew.

In the end, she'd relied on something of a metaphor. She'd placed some children—her own girls and others from day care—in the photos. The children were beautiful, simple, unaffected. There was no clutter behind them, only open waters and endless sky.

The next series of photos she'd used a double exposure, exposing the photographic paper to two negatives, one at a time. She'd had to line up the negatives in advance to make certain the composition was perfect. In the second series, superimposed behind those same small children were Blailock's high-rises, like so many menacing multi-eyed monsters, their windows reflective lenses that hid what was behind them, their mass threatening to engulf whatever lay before them. The children, clearly, were the innocents who would be no match. They, too, would be wiped away.

But of all the photos, the real treasure, Maggie believed, was the photo she had gotten of her neighbor's son, the young man with Down syndrome. She'd come across him lying in the swale of a small sand hill. He'd fallen asleep in the tall grasses and so was nearly invisible until you were almost on top of him. He lay on his side, his mouth slightly open. He had snuggled into the sand, and one hand cradled his head. The other hand, rather than clutching a security blanket, had buried itself in the sand. It was clear that this was the world he was a part of, a world that didn't include pity or disdain. The photo's focus was as crystal clear as the Michigan sky.

Maggie held the photo at arm's length. This was the one she was most proud of. Until a spot on the print's background caught her eye.

Crap! Had there been some dust on the negative? Was the negative defective? That would be terrible.

Maggie set the print down and pulled the negative from its sleeve. She couldn't see anything on it. It looked fine.

If it wasn't the negative, what could it be? It was almost as if a small point of light had found its way into her darkroom. But how could that be? None of the other prints were marred. And she always checked all of the curtains before starting. She refused to display a photo with even a small defect.

Maggie looked around the room, half expecting to uncover some new secret it held. Now she'd have to re-do her best photo. The thought exhausted her and made her put off working on the photo she'd taken at Blailock's party until she had more energy.

⟫•⟪

Maggie had just pulled her darkroom curtain open when a pair of legs clad in red stretch Capri pants under a shortened broomstick skirt crossed her view, followed by a strong knock on the screen door. That's got to be Janine, she thought. She wiped off her hands once more and went upstairs. What in the world could she want?

Janine had actually knocked, Maggie realized, as she rounded the corner into the living room. Maggie was feeling generous with her time because she wasn't planning to work anymore today, and it was so much easier to be welcoming when someone didn't take it for granted you would be. Maggie opened the screen door wide. "Hi Janine. Come on in. What's going on?"

"Oh, hi." Janine said it as though she were surprised to find herself at the Dunbarton cottage. "Just checking up to make sure things are okay. I haven't paid a visit in so long . . . really. Forgetful of me . . . really."

"We're doing fine, thanks. I mean, the cottage is fine." Then Maggie surprised herself. "Do you want to sit down?" *But draw the line somewhere*, Maggie told herself and stopped short of offering something to drink.

As though reading her mind, Janine continued on, "Oh, thanks. I won't be but just a minute." Then, belying her own words, Janine crossed her Capri-clad legs after settling into a comfortable chair. She absently looked around the room. "Things are okay?"

"Sure. Yes. We did have an ant episode, but I think I've taken care of that."

Maggie bit her lip. Don't get the ball rolling, for heaven's sakes. But Janine still didn't rush into the opening Maggie had unwittingly offered. What was going on, Maggie wondered. Had she undergone some sort of radical personality therapy?

A few seconds passed before the Realtor spoke. "Well, good then." Janine took hold of the chair's arms as though preparing to push herself up, then relaxed her grip. "Oh, well, I meant to say." Then, slightly louder: "I meant to say, Jason, my stepson, is taken by your girls. He's always had a soft spot for kids."

"Yes," Maggie agreed. "He's been good to them. And helpful to me."

Janine did not acknowledge Maggie's words. She appeared not to have heard them. She looked up at the new fixture in the ceiling, then out the window. "He, uh, he sometimes seems like a kid himself. He was a good kid, really. But, uh. Things in his life were not that good to him. Or rather for him."

"H-m-m." Maggie wondered what Janine was talking about, but tried not to appear overly interested.

"He spent a fair amount of time in Vietnam."

"I didn't realize he was in the service. He never talks about it."

"Oh, yes. He came back changed. You know. World-weary. Unable to focus for long, unable to commit . . . to anything. That limited his options. I mean, commit not just to anything . . . but also to anyone." Janine shook her head slightly. Then finally looked at Maggie. "I met your husband. Did I tell you?"

"Yes, you did tell me."

"He, uh, he was walking along the front walk looking for the cottage. I hope it was all right. I showed him the house."

Maggie wanted to give up the pretense. Tell Janine she'd made a mistake. But Maggie knew that was not why Janine was sitting here, in her living room.

"Jason. Jason gets taken with summer people. He likes them, you know. Sometimes I think it's because he knows they will leave . . . eventually. So, there's no need for real commitment on his part. I guess he saw too much. In the war, I mean. Nothing holds his attention for too long. Or his affection either."

It finally dawned on Maggie what Janine's real purpose was in coming here. "Yes, I imagine that could make commitment difficult for Jason, Janine. I see what you mean."

"Right. I'm glad you see that. I like people who come here to have a good summer." Janine finally pushed herself up. "But Jason does care for children. Is good with children. So, let me know if you need anything."

Maggie walked out with Janine and down the stairs to the walk, wondering if Janine would reveal anything else.

"I'm glad you're doing so well. When did you say your husband would be back?"

"I'm not sure, really." Maggie decided to be halfway honest. "He has a client in the area, so he sometimes surprises us."

"Oh? Well, yes, I suppose. Bye now." Janine kept walking, picking up her pace slightly, seemingly absorbed in her own thoughts.

Maggie turned back to the cottage and let out a sigh. Had she just been warned off of Jason—by his stepmother? Or been given some sort of moral rebuff? What a busybody that woman was. As though Maggie had even heard from Jason since the fireworks on the Fourth. All had been terribly quiet on the romantic front, as far as that went.

Maggie shook her head as she walked back into the house. She spotted Jennifer standing at the top of the stairs. "Jen. I didn't know you were here. When did you come home? Why did you come home?" She couldn't believe her daughter had managed to get in the house without her hearing. Had she been trying to sneak in on purpose.?

"Just to get somethin.' Annie said it was okay. Who was here?"

"Janine, Jason's mom." Maggie could see Jen held something under the sweatshirt she was wearing. "What did you come to get, sweetheart?"

" Just this." Jennifer pulled the music box out.

"Jen, are you sure? Remember, that does not belong to us. If you take it to Annie's, you must be careful with it. Okay?"

"Aren't gifts mine? Like the toy monkey Jason gave me?"

"Of course. But this is something we found here."

"Um-hum." Jennifer gave one of her worldly smiles as she came down the stairs and out the door, letting it slam behind her.

Raising the girls alone might just prove too difficult was the thought that crossed Maggie's mind. Maybe she was not cut out for it. Maybe she'd head back downstairs and work some more. She needed a focus to keep her mind from her own neurotic worries.

Maggie returned to her darkroom, trying to decide whether to work on the shot from Blailock's party. See if she'd caught anything or anyone worth catching. She could see from the negative that the foremost figure was indeed Sheldon. But it was impossible to discern anyone else in this small—and backward—format.

She was still trying to decide what to do when another female figure walked by her darkroom window, stopped briefly, then mounted the stairs to Helen's porch and walked in. The gait had looked familiar. Maggie told herself, then realized, it reminded her of Jersey, Julia's twin. Maggie leaned on her table with the feeling of vertigo that came over her. Something was going on that was surely more than coincidence. All the comings and goings at Helen's was like watching some kind of circus car stuffed with way more clowns than it could hold.

Okay. Maybe it was time to put the photography on hold and return to her investigative intuitions. She could just hear Sheldon telling her she always made too big a deal of things, saw meanings where there weren't any. No matter. She looked at her watch. There wasn't enough time to pay a visit today, but it was time to go see Doc Chard, the historian who lived at the end of the walk whom Gertie had mentioned. Maybe he could set her straight. Besides, she needed to find some better company after having her wrist slapped by a busybody Realtor.

CHAPTER 9

M aggie still had over an hour before the girls returned from Annie's. Now would be as good a
time as any to see if she could catch Doc Chard,
the local historian. She got her notepad and pen and
headed down the front walk past the entrance to the
very end. Gertie had told her that the house was yellow
and off the main walk, but still had an unobstructed view
of the lake.

Maggie knew the house the minute she saw it. Unlike its
counterparts that were painted white or gray or a workman-
like brown, this one looked like it had recently been painted
a sunny yellow with white window frames. But more interesting than the color of the paint was the structure of the
roof. Although it was two stories, the second story was tent-
like, creating a shape with a very sharp peak.

There was a railing all around the second story, a line of
bright flags flying from the top of the peak down to what,
for all the world, looked like a huge wooden steering wheel
with handholds at each spoke, something from shipping's
past. It took her a minute to pick out the pole sitting at the
roof's peak with its footholds, to realize she was looking at
what was designed to be a crow's nest. She was still smiling
when she knocked on the screen door.

Doc Chard himself answered, responding to her introduction with "I have been expecting you. Gertie told me you might stop by. It's been awhile since I've been able to show anyone my photo collection. Come on in." Doc held the door open for Maggie. He was short—Maggie towered over him, and she looked down on a head of white hair disheveled enough to suggest its owner had recently been napping.

Maggie and her host spent the next half hour slowly making their way along a hallway where Doc displayed a series of old photographs from the early 1940s and 1950s, when Breakwater Bay had sported a large wooden frame hotel and before private summer cottages had been built. The tourists in those days had come from the same upper Midwest cities as the tourists of today, only they traveled by train, then by trolley along an interurban which dropped them off within blocks of the old hotel.

Photos showed these tourists lounging on the large porch that ran the length of the Haskell Hotel, seated in Adirondack rockers, hands folded on their laps or clutching a book, one hand with a finger in the book to mark their place while they smiled at the camera.

The best photos, however, were those of the water ski shows. There were a couple of skiers taking a ski jump, but the majority were of multiple skiers holding onto multiple tow ropes behind a single boat. The skiers were either side by side or in pyramid formations.

"Were these local kids?" Maggie asked him.

"Well, some were. Lots also came from St. Joe's or Muskegon. They got up here in early summer to practice their shows. They also doubled as waiters and maids in the hotel. It was probably a pretty glamorous summer for a teenager."

"I imagine." Maggie thought of her own summer spent in the company of kids hanging out at the beach. "I heard that Blailock's wife, Julia, and her twin, Jersey, were part of these performances for some of the summers."

"It's true. They were from Grand Haven and worked at the hotel for a couple of summers, though I've heard their family actually had a cottage around here. Look, here they are." Doc pointed a finger at one grainy photo that showed two teenage girls who looked to be around the age of seventeen standing on the shoulders of three boys about the same age. The girls were standing side by side, each one straddling between the shoulders of two boys, gripping her twin's arm and holding the outside arm in a high wave.

"That looks dangerous," Maggie commented. "How in the world were they able to get into that formation in the first place?"

"Good question. Beats me. Crowd pleasers, though."

"And the hotel burned down?"

"To the ground. Might have been faulty wiring. Maybe arson. Nothing was proved. In those days, the fire trucks were a long way aways, and the place was pretty much a total loss by the time they got there. All that water sitting right there in the Big Lake, and no way to get it up to the hotel other than a bucket brigade—which they tried, of course. Not that it mattered much. Structures in those days were pretty much wood, just waiting to go up in flames. Luckily, it was slow enough starting that no one was hurt."

"So, they never rebuilt?"

"No, the owners decided subdividing and selling off the land was more profitable, and they were probably right." Doc smiled then, opening his arms in a gesture that seemed to take in his surroundings. "Made me happy. But, say. Why don't we go out on the porch where we can talk, if you'd like. I'll see if June will bring us some lemonade and join us."

With that, Doc called toward the back of the house, and then led Maggie out to the side of the house that faced the lake. They eased down into white plastic deck chairs. Maggie stood to shake hands with June when she appeared. The woman looked a lot like her husband: plump with a head of very white hair that she had twisted into a loose bun in back. They talked for a few minutes about summer and the alewives before Doc turned back to speak directly to Maggie.

"Gertie tells me you're curious about Blailock."

"I guess I am pretty transparent," Maggie admitted.

"I try to keep my ear to the ground as well. The rumor is that he's got some big new project, the subdivision of that open area right before the Breakwater Bay entrance. The problem is he wants to build houses on smaller lots than's allowed. This time around he may just have a tougher time of it."

"But I heard that Town Hall likes him and tries to give him what he wants."

"Oh, this may be different," Doc explained, "because it would be a zoning change that could open the township up to even more requests for change. It will involve a couple public hearings. People could come and say some pretty negative things about his doings, open him up to real criticism. The word is he's hired some high-powered attorneys to work on this."

Maggie put down her lemonade glass a little too quickly on the plastic end table. She massaged the back of her neck. If the locals learned Sheldon was representing Vince Blailock, what would that do to her friendships? She turned to look directly at Doc. "Do you think he has a chance?"

"Oh, sure, Blailock always has a chance. But a lot of us are preparing to speak at the public hearings."

"Doc, as you were talking about the old hotel, I kept wondering: why do people object to Blailock's tall apartment buildings when there had already been a pretty large structure around here."

"Good question. I think it is because he builds huge structures without regard for his surroundings--he has sacrificed a lot of beach grass in his day. And because these buildings just devour resources. And, then, usually, the people who move into them just want something fancy and impressive. They don't have any regard for what was displaced. The old hotel. . . Well, people stayed there because they *loved* the setting."

Maggie nodded as he spoke. "Do you think he had anything to do with his wife's death?"

Doc leaned back in his chair and looked up at the sky. Maggie followed his eyes and saw small wisps of clouds overhead, but the sky to the west was darkening. An airplane flew overhead, too high for its sound to reach them. "I like to think of myself as an historian, Maggie. I try to deal in facts, not rumors. But about the time of the boat accident, there was a rumor going around—and I am probably one of the few who remember this since I've lived in these parts so long—that there was some question about Blailock's son's paternity." Doc raised his eyebrows as he said this.

"What?" Maggie was incredulous. "Who was the other possible father supposed to be?"

"His partner, Phillip Tobias."

"Whew!" Maggie tried to let this sink in. "But I've seen photos of the guy—Phil—he didn't really impress me as that attractive, as a ladies' man."

"No, I think that was right. But I ask you, if you don't like your husband, and you want to hurt or infuriate him, who would you choose to have an affair with?" With this, Doc scooted his chair around to face the lake, and pulled himself up to a telescope mounted on the porch railing, its long lens lined up with a boat some distance off shore. "Scuse me. I just have to check this out." He fiddled with the lens' focus for a few seconds and then turned back, smiling. "Sorry. I always like to know who is out on the lake."

"Wouldn't you think Julia'd be too smart to do that?"

"Maybe. But let me tell you another Blailock story that is very instructive. This incident took place a good twenty years ago, in Vince's younger days. We used to have sailing races on Lake Haskell, you know, friendly Sunday afternoon kind of races. Frequently, there wasn't even enough wind, and all the boats would sit dead in the water. But one race in particular stands out because it was the perfect sailing day, both sun and wind. Blailock was sailing in the Class JY race, doing pretty well, when he tried to get too much speed out of his boat, pulling in the sail and sailing too high upwind. He just tempted fate a little too much: The boat went over. But this wasn't an easy over that could be righted; his boat turtled with its mast pointed straight down, probably stuck in the sand at the lake's bottom."

Maggie could imagine, without being told, how the proud Blailock would despise the ignominy of not just defeat, but also the shame of making so elemental a sailing error.

"That old boat with its centerboard sticking straight up in the air could have been a shark. Vince pulled himself up on the keel of the boat and yelled to his handyman on shore to bring him an ax. No one knew exactly what he was up to. We suspected he was going to try to chop the mast off so he could right the boat. But we were wrong. He took that ax and hacked at the bottom of the boat for all he was worth, ripping up the wooden keel—for no other reason than the boat had made a fool of him. Those of us on shore watching couldn't believe what we were seeing. He just wrecked a perfectly good boat because it didn't do what he wanted. People re-told that story for years after, but always with a little discomfort, glad they never worked for the man. If he would do that to a boat that thwarted him, what might he do to a person who made him look like a fool."

"That story does show a temper. But maybe he's mellowed some since then."

Doc just shrugged at this. "I wouldn't know. Truth is, he didn't spend a whole lot of time around here, didn't build that behemoth house, didn't have notions of building skyscrapers next to the beach, until after Julia's death. Maybe there's some vindictive streak in him. Maybe this is some kind of jealous payback to destroy a spot she loved."

Maggie shook her head to buy time, but couldn't come up with a way to segue into her next question, so she just asked it outright: "What reason does Jersey have to spend time around here in the summer?"

"So, you've spotted her?" Doc nodded a few times, rocking with the effort. "I'm not sure. She's a bit of an apparition. Here—then gone again. I think this is a spot she likes, too, and is familiar with. Maybe. Maybe she returns to get under Blailock's skin. Hard to say, really. Say, aren't you staying in one of the cottages on Blue Sky Lane?"

"Yes, we are."

"I think that was where Julia and Jersey's family stayed when they were here in the summer. Wouldn't that be a coincidence?"

Maggie laughed. She imagined the historian loved to see coincidences everywhere. It made for such a good story, one where everything fit into place.

Maggie only stayed a few more minutes, talking about the alewives and the people at Breakwater Bay that summer. She left as soon as it seemed polite.

She needed time to think. She thanked the Chards, then hurried up the walk toward Gertie's. The ax story paired with the possibility that Blailock's son was not his seemed a disturbing juxtaposition. Still, the idea that Blailock's son had a different father seemed preposterous somehow. What would a wealthy person do with that kind of information? Wouldn't you just consider divorce? Except that you would not want to chance losing the son. Or would you?

Maggie had difficulty thinking through this possible wrinkle. The idea that a spouse might make an affair choice based upon doing the most collateral damage left her puzzled. She thought about her own situation. She was sure this was not behind Sheldon's choice; he wasn't actively trying to hurt her, was he? It wasn't as though she was some kind of threat to him. He had always considered himself superior to her. He had just found someone he was more attracted to. Hadn't he?

⸺◍⸺

Maggie got to Annie's a little early; Annie was still reading a picture book to the children. Maggie gave a little wave to Jen, who sat cross-legged on the floor facing the door. Jen looked up momentarily and waved back.

She found Gertie in the den sitting in an easy chair with her own book in her lap. "Hi. Mind if I join you."

"Not at all. Sit down." Gertie put her book aside. "Can I get you something?"

"No, thanks. I just wanted to talk for a few minutes. I've been needing to tell you something for a while."

"Sure. What is it?"

Maggie decided if she spoke quickly, she could get it out without shame or embarrassment. "I didn't say anything before, but I'm here because my husband and I have separated. Well, not legally, but in practice. He had an affair—or is maybe still having an affair, and I came here for the summer to try to make some decisions for myself." Maggie stopped and took a breath.

"Hm-m-m." Gertie nodded. "I wondered. It seemed like you had something on your mind."

"Right. I didn't want to say anything because I don't want people second-guessing me. But I learned something from Doc Chard today that makes me think I need to tell you. I think my husband, Sheldon, is representing Blailock in Blailock's latest development scheme, and I want you to know I am not part of this at all. My husband doesn't care who or what side he represents: Business is business."

Gertie was still nodding. "Are you able to influence your husband—Sheldon—at all?"

Maggie looked sharply at Gertie. This seemed like an odd question. "Well, no, he doesn't consult with me—not about business matters, anyway. And certainly not at this point in time. I just want people around here who are my friends to know that I am not part of this. I don't agree with what he's doing. In fact, I think representing someone of Blailock's stature around here gives him a chance to gloat—and also unnerve me because it means he is entitled to come around here, even if I don't want him to."

"Your description of him doesn't make him sound very attractive." Gertie smiled a little, and Maggie realized she must have sounded as angry as she felt. "But then, you might want to be someone who speaks against Blailock at the hearing."

Maggie hesitated. She couldn't imagine facing off against her husband in a public hearing. "I'm hoping the photo essay I'm doing for a crafts show in town will make that case."

"Don't worry." Gertie wiped her hands on her legs out of habit before standing up. "Those of us who know you won't let your husband's actions reflect on you. You have always seemed to me like someone with a great deal of integrity."

"Thank you, Gertie. It felt like Sheldon was going to be able to get back at me by isolating me from people I like."

Gertie nodded in understanding, though Maggie couldn't imagine a scenario where the placid Dave would ever venture too far from his cars or his family. So how could Gertie really understand?

———— ((●)) ————

Maggie and the girls had been seated next to the window at the Lakeside Restaurant. The little café was misnamed, really, because it was actually separated from Lake Haskell by the true beachfront properties and a road, and their window looked out on the restaurant's parking lot.

Jennifer was doing her best to read the menu. Finally, she opened it toward Maggie. "Mom, do they have pizza?"

"Yes, they have all kinds of pizza. What do you want?"

"Cheese."

"Yeah, cheese," Sam agreed.

"Are you sure you don't want to add something to that? Like sausage? Or pepperoni?"

"Okay. All right." Jennifer sighed and let her menu tip over toward the table. Then she took her spoon and began to fish around in her water glass for a large piece of ice.

Maggie willed herself not to harp on Jennifer for as long as possible. There was nothing wrong with eating ice, after all. Her eyes drifted around the room at the other diners. This was clearly a sunset crowd. Hers was one of only three tables where there were children. A door opened in a partition wall opposite them. Must be a space for private parties, Maggie supposed, as she watched Jason step into the room, turning his back on them to close the door behind him. She continued to watch as he stopped by the checkout register to speak with the woman behind the counter briefly, then exited the restaurant without looking back.

Maggie didn't have time to wonder what the explanation for his departure was because a waitress was there to take an order. "Lemonades all around and a medium cheese pizza with sausage and pepperoni. You can pick off the sausage, if you don't like it," she reminded Jen when she saw that Jen was about to protest.

"Yeah, you can pick at it," Sam echoed her mother as soon as the waitress left their table.

"Don't tell me what to do." Jen turned to Sam with folded arms. Maggie could see Jen was spoiling for a fight and knew she needed to nip this in the bud.

"Sam, why don't you come over here and sit by me?"

"Okay." Sam scooted to the edge of the booth seat and slid off.

"Fraid-y cat. Fraid-y cat," Jennifer hummed under her breath. "Mommy's little *ba*-by." Jen kicked the booth bench with her heels in time to the chant.

"Enough, now!" Maggie hissed. "If this is how you two are going to behave when we go out to eat, then I guess it means no more dinners out."

"No!" Sam protested.

"All right then. Let's play a game. I saved a menu. Let's see who can find the letter 'B' on the front cover."

But before there was an answer, Jennifer said, "There's Jason!" She had spotted Jason heading back into the building, and jumped up to intercept him.

Maggie tried to call, "Wait," without yelling across the room, but it was too late. She sat and watched as Jennifer caught up with Jason, then watched the exchange between them from across the room.

Jason had a set of long, rolled-up papers in one hand, which he switched to the other as soon as he saw Jennifer descending on him. Maggie realized she was looking at someone she thought she knew, in a totally different context. She would never have guessed that the Breakwater Bay handyman owned a sports jacket.

Jason patted Jen on the head, then looked across the tables until he spotted Maggie. He waved at her with the long scroll of paper, then bent down to say a few words to Jen before re-entering the door behind him.

Jen skipped back to their table, delivering the message from Jason even before she had reached them. "Jason said if we're still here when he gets out of his meeting, he'll come over and say hi."

Maggie had tried to drag out the meal, but when there was no sign of Jason after nearly half an hour, and the girls were again bored enough to get on each other's nerves, she knew it was time to go.

⸺⸺⸺◦((◦))◦⸺⸺⸺

Maggie leaned on the kitchen counter for leverage so she could reach her stash of wine on the top shelf of the dish cabinet. She pulled one bottle of red down, then a second, thinking surely that would be enough to make her feel better.

Her conversation with Doc Chard had inspired her finally to go back underground to the darkroom to see how much resolution she could get out of the impromptu photo she had managed to shoot at the Fourth of July party.

Now she had to get back down to business. Not that this would be an award-winning photo—she'd be lucky to have anything. She just wanted to satisfy her curiosity about Vincent Blailock.

It was a difficult negative to coax into a print, really underexposed. She had tried to rescue the detail from total darkness by waving her hand across the area where faces should be to uncover any detail that was there. There was some detail, but it was far from great. All she wanted was to be able to recognize who was who.

After working to get as much detail as she could without obliterating other objects, she had placed the sheet in the stop bath and then in the sink, where water flowed over her feeble attempts. Only then did she turn on the light.

One look at the photo told Maggie way more than she had ever wanted to know.

Maggie pulled down a drinking glass—forget the shallow bowl of a silly wineglass. Might as well go whole hog with this, she decided. She cut the foil on both bottles, crushed them into unrecognizable balls, and pitched them in the trash.

Well, if her other benders had been a result of being disturbed, even destroyed, by what was going on around her, then what she had witnessed in this photo could certainly justify *whatever* she did.

Maggie wasn't proud of her past. She'd be the first to admit that she had drunk herself numb on numerous occasions. All those nights when Sheldon "worked late," even after Maggie had found out about his affair with Angie, she'd often waited for that numb feeling when finally the most difficult task before her was just to make it down the hall and into the bedroom. She had fallen into bed, some-times so drunk she was unable to pull the covers up over her. Then, waking in the night, still not sober, holding onto things to find her way to the bathroom.

It hadn't taken Sheldon long to realize she was abusing alcohol. One night when he came across several empty bot-tles, he read her the riot act. Told her if she expected to be a mother to his children, this had better not continue.

And, then, he had done the unthinkable. He had called Winifred. Under the guise of seeking information about whether there was alcoholism in Maggie's family back-ground, Sheldon had given her mother one more reason to be disdainful and superior toward her daughter.

Maggie couldn't stand it. She had decided right then and there that she needed to find another place to direct her restless anger. She was still looking for that answer when they'd come to the lake. Photography had almost worked— but now photography had betrayed her. It had told her way more than she could bear to know. The negative had been damning in more ways than she had anticipated.

But damning to whom, Maggie wanted to know. In any case, the proof was there—in black and white.

Maggie knew it was possible to use trick development techniques to insert an entire person into a photo. But she was the photographer here, and she had been the one in control of the negative from start to finish. The negative did not lie.

Sheldon had been there. Even a poor image of him was recognizable to Maggie. There had also been two men coming up behind him, and also darker because the light there was poorer. The one farthest away wore glasses, because they had caught a glint of light. His shape was oddly familiar, but Maggie was unable to place him. It was the other man, slightly ahead of the pair of glasses, who Maggie clearly recognized. He was the intruder she had found in her home—uninvited—that day she was working in the darkroom, the one she had caught going up the stairs. And if this man *were* actually Blailock, as she suspected, then he clearly knew his way around. He was not someone who could have been mistaken about where he was the day she had surprised him on the stairway after he had just let himself into the house.

If this weren't disconcerting enough, there was something even more incriminating as far as Maggie was concerned. The worst part was the woman on the landing who seemed to be waiting for Sheldon to walk to her. Even though her face was mostly in profile, Maggie recognized Angie. And even though—or perhaps because of—the loose shift she wore, Maggie could tell the younger woman was pregnant. Very pregnant. And Maggie did not have to think too long and hard to know who the father was. There was no question of paternity in this case!

What kind of man did this? What kind of father did this? Maggie swallowed hard to keep her gorge down. He had children. Why in the world was the person she had called her husband be starting another family—while they were still technically married? Couldn't he have waited? What was he thinking? What a dupe she was, Maggie chided herself. It meant Sheldon wasn't just divorcing *her*—he was also divorcing his children.

Still, Maggie thought. *Still*. What upset her most was that, once again, she was not able to make one of the central decisions in her own life. She knew that now there was only one outcome possible from this new twist. She had left Chicago to go somewhere where *she* could sort things out. Decide what was best for *her*. And, now, once more, Sheldon's actions had made a choice, one that meant she didn't have a choice of her own.

This latest transgression made Maggie realize that here, all along, she'd been fooling herself. She'd told herself she'd come here to make a decision about her marriage. But that wasn't really true. She'd known all along the reality was that her marriage had been crumbling for a long time. She had really come to Lake Michigan to see if she was actually able to raise her daughters by herself.

Maggie already had the corkscrew in the cork, had already made one twist, when she stopped. There was one more thing in the photo that had caught her attention, but which just now she realized was also significant. The photo was no masterpiece. Obviously. But it, like others before it, had a streak in approximately the same place it had appeared in her other photos. Maggie realized this was too great a coincidence.

She stood on her toes and pushed the wine back into place. She needed to be sober to head back downstairs and figure out once and for all what was causing this dark slash on so much of her work.

CHAPTER 10

The shadow from the house up the hill was long and gave Maggie shade as she rested on the third step of their stairs and stretched her legs out to the walk. The hydrangea on both sides of her were now in full bloom, their heavy blue and white heads, comprised of tens of tiny flowers, bowed on their spindly stems. What a strange flower, she thought. Such an ostentatious blossom, yet one with no scent. As though it needed to make up for the lack in one area with an overabundance in the other.

Maggie heard a buzz next to her ear and swatted at it. Her hand came up empty. There must be an onshore breeze that was sending the mosquitos inland.

How was she ever going to do this, she wondered. Make Jen understand that a six-year-old sneaking in and out of the house was not safe.

Maggie had been outraged when she'd finally enlarged the Blailock photo. How could Sheldon wheedle *her*, threaten *her* about wanting the girls while carelessly propagating somewhere else? Propagate. The word fit—it sounded unseemly, another "gate" of one sort or another, something very close to "profligate," the crossing of yet one more forbidden threshold.

She'd gone back downstairs to the darkroom to solve the mystery of the streaked photos, after coaxing every detail she could out of the black and white photo. A really good picture would have contained all the shades of gray in between stark white and a deep, opaque black to bring out every detail. How appropriate that this poor quality photo, like the truth, was just a single tone, a single measly shade of gray: sad, predictable gray. Nothing at either end of the scale and precious little in between. How fitting that her discovery had come from a negative. Very negative.

She didn't even need a magnifying glass to tell that Angie was pregnant. Speak of an olive on a toothpick.

How could they? How could *he*? Threaten to take the girls away, for god's sake. What a fake. Just thinking about it made her want to upend the darkroom. Take the goddamn developing table by its fat legs and dump the lot. Let the developer slam into the stop bath. Stop bath? Someone should empty *them* into a stop bath. Down the drain. Swirling down the convenient drain in the middle of a cement floor. Exposure. . . overexposure. No fucking lie. What was it all for?

Maggie could hear her father tell her to take a deep breath. Not get too carried away. She could obsess on old hypocrite Sheldon later. That was not why she had come down here.

She wheeled around, her eyes searching the dark corners of the room. Settle down. Settle scores with the bastard later.

She grabbed two of the nearest botched prints and held them up together. The overexposed streak was in almost the exact same spot on both. She placed one print on the enlarger's easel on her table and tried to judge the wall behind her. If it had been a slit of light, where had it come from?

Her negatives had all been clean. She had checked and re-checked them. It couldn't have come from something foreign on the negative itself.

The distance to the other wall was short, fourteen feet or so. She began to slide her hands along it like one of the five blind men feeling an elephant. The part of the elephant she'd been given was the unrelenting tusk, she suspected.

Her fingers felt the crack just at waist level before she saw it. She pushed, then tried to pry it open. A section of the frame wall moved. It was a short—very short—door, but one which started a few feet above the floor. She had to hoist herself up onto a concrete floor to go through, then resorted to crawling on her hands and knees to move forward before finally standing upright on the other side.

Once she had stood up, Maggie found herself in a larger space, one where she could not only stand but move around. And while it wasn't bright, there was light, its source a high window to the outside. The light caught dust motes as they slowly wheeled before her. She thought of the dark corners where a rat could crouch and quickly checked the floor around her.

The wall in front of her had another short door, but this one was closer to the ground and opened to the outside, the perfect rabbit hole for Jennifer. Maggie opened it and crawled through. It opened above a bed of thick ivy.

How could Maggie have missed this? Why had she never walked around the cottage on all sides and taken a good look at everything, she chided herself. But the chiding turned to consolation when she realized that even if she had looked straight at it, it would have been difficult to pick out this perfectly concealed door from the weathered tongue-in-groove boards of the cottage. And, from the outside, the window would have looked like it belonged to an upstairs window.

Maggie crawled back through to make her way up the stairs, even though she knew exactly where they'd lead. Another short door took her into Jen's closet.

This time she crawled under the three dresses they'd packed for Jen for the summer, lifting up the skirts as she passed under them.

Could Jen's sneaking around count as a betrayal, she asked herself. But surely a six-year-old can't truly betray you. Only husbands could do that. Six-year-olds infuriated you, confused and bewildered you, but bewilderment was something far short of betrayal. Yet, it was hard to imagine how a child of six could keep a secret like this from her own mother.

Maggie sat down on Jen's bed to think. She'd have to get the outside door secured. She did not want a door to the outside that gave access to a little girl's room. She'd call Jason and ask him to fix it. How convenient. This would give her the perfect excuse to get a nearly boyfriend to come back around.

But talking with Jen was another matter, Maggie reminded herself as she now found herself sitting on the very step Jason had repaired, trying to come up with a plan. The mosquito was still buzzing close to her head. Maggie slapped at her neck. Damn! Too late. She had already felt the mosquito's probe sink into her skin. Her fingers came away with her own blood on them. At least this mosquito had been killed over his meal. She closed her eyes to think. It wouldn't do to challenge Jen. That approach just gave her daughter permission to be even more stubborn.

Maggie was still turning the puzzle over in her mind when Sam came up the walk by herself. Good, she thought. That meant she could put off dealing with the Jennifer dilemma a little longer.

Sam walked carefully, with her arms behind her back. She stopped just short of her mother, eyes wide with expectation.

"So," Maggie asked, "are you going to show me or do I have to guess?"

Sam shifted a little. "You hafta guess."

"Okay." Maggie scrunched up her face as though in deep thought. "You colored a beautiful picture with cotton balls for clouds."

"Uh-uh."

"You . . . collected bark and glued it onto a little board. Then you painted it."

"Uh-uh."

"I give up. You have to tell me."

Sam leaned forward a little to produce the object behind her back.

When she saw it, Maggie had to keep from laughing out loud. "Oh, Sam, this *is* something." Maggie took the contraption and held it in front of her. She wondered whether Annie or Gertie had been the author of this project. "Who helped you with this, hon?"

"Annie's mommy."

Gertie then. Maggie looked at the object again, hoping for some inspiration to identify it. It was a clear Ball jar with two clear plastic funnels fitted neatly inside. The smaller funnel's narrow end was placed inside the end of the other. It was only when Maggie saw the sand sifting quietly, but steadily, inside that she realized what she was holding.

But what had Gertie been thinking? Two rotations of this time machine and the smallest grains of sand would be finding all the imperfections in the Ball jar's rubber seal. And it would just be a matter of time before the sand would be littered on the cottage's worn wooden floorboards. Or the entire thing would get dropped and break, and someone would step on the glass. And that someone would probably be Sam.

Maggie needed to find a way to leave the thing outside. "Okay, I see." Maggie looked up at her daughter's expectant face. "It's an hourglass."

"No!" Sam grabbed for the jar with both hands. "It's *my* glass."

Maggie released it into Sam's hold, only when the child had both hands around the jar. "Of course it is, hon. It's yours. Did Gertie tell you it can help measure time? You turn it over and see how long it takes for the sand to drain from the top funnel into the bottom one. That's why it's called an *hour*glass." Maggie tried to speak distinctly this time. She looked over at Sam and realized her daughter hadn't heard a word.

"Mommy, I made it, and it's mine. It's going to be a present."

"How thoughtful. Did you make it for me or for Jennifer?"

"No. Gertie said it keeps track of the minutes. So, I made this for the Time Being." Sam set the Ball jar carefully on the bottom step and lifted up Maggie's arms from around her knees like a drawbridge so that she could crawl under.

Maggie hugged Sam to her, fitting her chin on top of the child's head, blowing away the stray wisps of hair that tickled her face.

Even though Sam's back was to her, Maggie was careful to hide her smile. "That is very generous, Sam. But, tell me. Who is the Time Being? Do you know what it looks like? Or where it lives?"

Sam pushed her mother's arms away to turn around to look at her.

"No. 'Cept he's old. Very old. He's been aroun' forever. And you might know, cuz you always talk about the Time Being."

"H-m-m-m." Maggie hugged Sam. She tried to conjure up an image of Father Time shuffling off the stage into the wings on December 31, trying hard not to trip over his own long beard. But maybe she was being way too limiting with her imagination—too narrow-minded when it came to the Time Being. For Sam, the Time Being was probably omnipresent, maybe even omnipotent. Maybe this Time Being was something altogether different. Maybe this one was greater than what could be imagined; this one was—was—unfathomable.

Maggie looked down at the Ball jar, where the sand had already drained down. So much for this, Maggie thought. This hourglass would not even be able to time a soft-boiled egg. Dorothy and Toto would have been out of luck if the Wicked Witch had given them only the slim couple of minutes Sam's hourglass allowed.

Maggie held on to Sam while she leaned forward to turn the jar once more. The grains of sand raced each other through the passageway between the two funnels. Tumbling, then gathering, then piling themselves into a hill. Like something that came from beneath the water piling together to form a hill, the heaviest ones sinking first.

Maggie turned the jar once more. Sand may have been one of the original materials of the glass jar she now held in her hand, a very different object from what glistened on the lakeshore. She looked down to the beach to remind herself of the miles of sand in either direction; the water that fell over the horizon; the sky that only very recently in geologic time had been overprinted by airplanes, by human artifacts, large and small. She looked above her to the tallest oak tree above them to see the wind rustle its leaves.

An idea was forming in Maggie's mind. About how someone might ethically justify protecting a beach environment like this one. She hugged Sam to her once more. "Sam, your Time Being may have just helped me solve a very large puzzle."

Sam craned her neck to look back at her mother, game for whatever it was Maggie had in mind: "Okey dokey."

———— ((◍)) ————

Maggie lay in bed that night relieved that things had gone well with Jennifer. Jen seemed to agree with every-thing her mother said. It had occurred to Maggie that more than anything, her older daughter was curious. She also needed to be given credit for her level of maturity. Maggie suspected she needed to involve Jen more in what she was trying to do, and asked if Jennifer was interested in spend-ing some time in the darkroom with her? Jen had jumped at the chance, making Maggie wonder whether, all this time, she had not been giving her daughter enough credit for her interests.

While Jen might be a problem with a solution, Sam had left her with another challenge, to try to picture the unfath-omable: what the Time Being might represent. An excit-ing thought was forming in the back of her mind: Did the concept of time as a power have enough strength to go up against the ambitions of a man like Blailock?

She tried to think of how time, not material stuff, might be front and center in establishing the value of nature. It was difficult. As humans, we learned most of what we knew about our world through eyesight, what we could see. Eyesight took precedence over touch, smell, and sound. Seeing was believing, after all. And who had even seen time; all we could see of the Time Being was what it left in its interminable wake.

Yes, the results, she told herself. But the results could speak volumes. Everything happened within Time. Time's shepherding and heralding and accompanying and marching forward. Maggie searched her mind to remember every biology or geology lesson she had ever heard. Time was situated in every event; time marked change. Change was incessant, yet sometimes so small, no human was aware of it. If humans had been around during the Ice Age, it would have taken us years of the ice retreating before that change would dawn on us, that is, until it was large enough to register, large enough to be perceived. The more time it took for something to change, the more in sync with it were the other things surrounding it. They had had the time to adjust. But what happened when humans rushed things, made changes faster than might happen without us?

Eons of time had passed as the fireball of twisting, turning, and ballooning gasses that would become the earth cooled and altered. The only constants in the picture were the place and events linking each alteration together—increments of time. The Time Being, in other words. Perhaps personifying time *could* make it real.

The mighty processes substances underwent—whether florid gas or boiling liquid—were infused with time, plodding, powerful, unflinching, unswerving Time. Only time could get you from one extreme to the other. Time invested all of itself in that process. Time was necessary to explain how one state could become its opposite, through tiny, imperceptible changes or dramatic, devastating ones. The only way to get to there from here was through time, that patient witness that beckoned and shepherded and bore witness to all discrete events along the long chains of them.

The photoshoots Maggie took of outdoor scenery captured just the briefest of moments in the inevitable linking of them. All that one photo could catch was a single instant in time, yet one never to be repeated, precisely because of the interval at which it occurred. Because of the marker laid down by time.

Maggie knew that the era of ice—what people called the Ice Age—contributed a great deal to the particular small spot that her small cottage stood on. The forces that made their days enjoyable or unbearable were also at work on the face of the earth, like master dermatologists. But the sun, the wind, the waves, the movement of the water, of the atmosphere were not present a million years ago.

Great sheets of ice had flowed across the area and leveled the bedrock which had earlier been wildly flung from fissures in the earth. The mass and weight of the ice helped cause it to flow, covering huge expanses with its chilly blanket.

Where once lava had flowed over the soft rock of sandstone and shale which epochs earlier had in turn quietly, casually been deposited on the bottom of a great sea. They had waited their turn to take part in the next phase, one of giant sheets of ice, slicing through them, carving and carrying them along with the creaking and groaning of thousands of feet of ice on the move.

But the glaciers were still dependent on the Time Being's realm. Given long enough, they, too, would succumb to change. They melted and provided the meltwater to fill the huge basins that they themselves had created. Those hitchhikers, the cobbles, sand, and clay, the glaciers had accumulated in their relentless reach, found themselves without the force of sheets of ice to bind them, and so were now abandoned, thoughtlessly dropped by the wayside.

The glacial hand that had last reached into the area where Maggie's cottage sat had, at an earlier age, pulled back, its fingers curling back under it, digging deeply into the earth's surface, leaving what humans so arrogantly called the Great Lakes. But what had truly been great was what had gone before. It was the chain of events the Time Being had orchestrated by infusing them with whatever time it took—eons—*that* was what had truly been great.

But, of course, it was also false to believe the changes were over and done, just because we could track how huge the differences were by looking back. They might be so slow by human standards as to be imperceptible, but that did not mean they were not happening even now.

The hundred-feet-thick dunes were still being scoured by winds. The hills were nothing but shape shifters at the beck and call of all the forces around them. The changes were slow because they occurred on the back of the patient and ever-deliberate Time Being.

This was the real value of the earth's features, Maggie realized. It was their relationship to time. Because everything partook in the rhythm of time, it was part of a huge, interrelated system, one that moved together, its parts in sync.

It was the poor, ignorant, impatient humans who jumped into the constant, endless march that mixed things up. Humans dallied with new combinations, new creations because it served their purposes, because they were impatient, refusing to include the Time Being in the work, failing to see all the inter-relationships. All in the blink of the Time Being's eye.

Humans were altering things, messing with systems that had formed slowly and surely before their time. Humans could not know the full consequences of what they did. They might never know the full consequences of what they had done. So, they had no idea whether their actions were setting off other hidden chain reactions that would only later show themselves for the lawless forces they were, perhaps altering systems in ways that could cause them to collapse completely.

Of course, some of what humans did was done with the best intentions. Most people sought beneficial outcomes. And then there were some, like Blailock, who basically acted out of greed. All showed disrespect for the Time Being's slow unfolding, its deliberate pace. Humans were good at throwing a monkey wrench into ages of the careful laying down of things, one layer upon the other. Humans made a mockery of age-old processes. And only time itself would finally reveal the longer lasting effects that might in the end turn out to be harmful—to those things humans cherished most.

Disrespect for the Time Being. This was our folly, Maggie decided. Some people were getting rich from it, but everyone would pay for it in the end.

Maggie kept still, her mind fully awake. Conceptualizing time in this way might actually be the solution, she knew. But how in the hell was she going to show this in a photo?

As she lay there, she heard it. The predictable moan of the lighthouse foghorn. Shorter intervals, she told herself, getting out of bed and pulling on shorts. She wouldn't go far; wouldn't leave the girls alone for long. But she had to follow her hunch.

The night was inky black; the moon a small crescent, cradled by drifting clouds. She opened the screen door as quietly as possible, glancing over at the house across the walk almost in anticipation of seeing her neighbor rocking away on her porch. But the house was quiet enough to feel empty.

Maggie made her way to where their walk joined the front one, and crouched to sit on a railroad tie placed there to hold back the sand surrounding a cottage. She focused hard on the lake, trying to pick out anything unusual.

Sure enough, there was a single light some distance from shore. It seemed suspended in midair, though Maggie knew that couldn't be true. Most likely it sat on the bow of a boat heading toward the lighthouse pier. She was too far away to hear waves lapping against the boat's sides, but at least she could tell how fast it was moving.

As she watched, it passed the dune that blocked her view of the lighthouse, but she would have bet her camera—and all the film that was in it—that it had been waiting to hear the foghorn before quietly setting its course for the lighthouse. Standing there under cover of darkness, she knew it didn't take a reporter's instincts to suspect that the quaint red building by the pier might be more than just an historical landmark.

CHAPTER 11

M aggie found herself standing in the creeping myr-
tle and staring down at a bad comb over. Instead
of Jason's baseball cap or his sun-bleached head,
she was watching someone named Ted swing the short door
open, then shut it again, like a toddler entertaining himself.

"So, you trying to lock someone in—or keep someone
out?" The new handyman rocked back on his haunches and
looked up at her.

"Both, I guess." Maggie had expected Jason to be here
and knew she sounded out of sorts. She could have just told
Jason what the problem was, and he'd have known how to
take care of it. "This is a door—sort of a door—that I don't
want to be used."

She'd just stood there holding onto her front door when
the handyman had arrived, she'd been so sure it would be
Jason. "Are you new?" she couldn't help but ask. "I mean. I
haven't seen you before."

"Yup. Just here a couple a weeks."

So, now she had to figure out what needed to be done.
She was focused so completely on thinking about what she
wanted that she didn't notice her neighbor had walked over
and was standing a few feet away from them, her hands on
her hips.

"Hello," she called. Her voice was high, almost a trill. "I'm Helen."

Maggie started. "Oh, yes, of course. Our neighbor." Maggie walked over with her hand outstretched.

Helen patted the back of her bun before extending her hand, and when Maggie went to clasp her hand, she received something closer to a swipe than a shake. Helen immediately went back to looking down at the door.

It was all Maggie could do to make herself turn away from the overpowering birthmark on Helen's face. It was light pink where it approached the center of her face, but purplish as it reached into the roots of her hair. Maggie guessed that in Helen's younger days, Helen would have tried everything she could to hide and disguise it, starting with growing her hair long and parting it on the opposite side so that a large mass of her hair would hang over it. Maggie guessed Helen had been mercilessly teased as a child.

Maggie shuddered and tried to focus on Helen's other features. Maggie realized that from close up, Helen looked older than Maggie had placed her. She also wore a cardigan on an otherwise warm day, a shabby sweater that Maggie imagined was her all-purpose wrap. Helen had missed a button hole, and one side of the sweater hung lower than the other.

"I couldn't help but notice that you've found the hidden door."

Maggie was taken aback. "You knew this was here?"

"Well, yes. The house belongs to my son."

"Oh." Maggie tried to cover her surprise, but then wasn't sure what to say. "We went through a Realtor, Janine Lurie. Why weren't we told about this? I have two young children."

On Little Cat Feet

"Of course. My son hates the bother of renting." Helen patted her bun again, smoothing back some hairs that draped across her temple. "He uses a real estate company."

Was the young man in business? If so, Maggie couldn't imagine how. "So, is a hidden staircase customary around here?" Maggie finally asked.

"Goodness, no." Helen shook her head. "Renters usually don't know it's here. But if they do, it's usually because one of the children—like Jennifer—has found it."

Maggie felt her neck prickle and wondered who the heck this woman was. "You know Jen?"

"Oh, yes. Darling child. She's come over here a couple of times to sit with Ben."

Maggie took a swipe at the back of her neck. "Your son? Why didn't I know that?"

"Oh, *he's* not my son. But I thought you knew. So kind of her, really."

What was going on, Maggie asked herself. "So, Ben is not the son who owns this house? Are we talking *my* Jen?"

"I think so. Jen is your daughter, right?"

Maggie almost felt she needed to hold onto something. She thought she had cleared the air with Jennifer, and yet here was another piece of information Jen had withheld. Jennifer had been sneaking out to spend time with the young man with Down syndrome. The pieces did not add up.

Up to this point, the new handyman had stood idly by, but he was clearly bored with an exchange that didn't make his assignment any clearer. "Sorry to interrupt. But what is it you want me to do?"

"Board it up. That would be the best solution," Maggie answered automatically.

"Oh, I'm not sure my son would like that." This from Helen.

"You're right. I am just a renter. I would need permission before doing that. Or—actually—I should ask my landlord to board it up for me. For security reasons. Helen, maybe you would give me your son's contact information so I can do that." Maggie was beginning to feel combative. Back off, she told herself. She knew that she could get this way when the welfare of her daughters was at stake.

"Oh, I couldn't do that. That's why he uses a real estate company. So he doesn't have to deal with renters. He doesn't even want people to know he owns this house."

"Right. I'm just trying to keep my kids safe—and that includes knowing where they are at all times. I'm sure it's fine if Jennifer visits your son; I would just like to know when she is over there. Maybe we could just use bolts. One on the outside, for sure, at least." Maggie turned to Ed.

"Oh, I'm not sure I should work on this at all. Since this ain't your place."

Ed's reluctance seemed to propel Helen. "No, bolts would be fine. I'll vouch for it. You just need to paint the bolt the same color as the house. It's best if people aren't aware of it. The door, I mean." Now Helen was all business.

Maggie wasn't finished, however. The information about Jen was bothering her. "How long has Jen been coming over?"

"Oh, well, since she discovered the door, actually. When I saw her come out of the ivy, I invited her in to meet Ben. She's good with him. He's slow, you know."

Maggie started to speak again, to tell this woman that she had really baited a child into coming over, then stopped. She wasn't exactly blameless herself when it came to making use of another's child. Ben, after all, was the dune creature who liked to sleep in the shadows of sand whom she had readily photographed without permission. And given that he had Down syndrome, he wasn't exactly in a position to give permission himself. "Helen, you say Ben's not your son. Who is he? Is he related to you?" Maggie knew she sounded too nosy.

"Oh, oh dear. It's hard to say exactly. I'm taking care of him—for now."

A foster parent, Maggie told herself. But she seemed too old for that role. Maybe that was the reason for all the traffic in and out of her house. An effort to come up with a different placement.

"Sorry to interrupt, again." Ed ran his hand through his hair again, making a bad comb-over worse.

"Sliding bolts would be just fine." Helen turned to Ed. "Just paint it so it blends in with the house. We need to keep the door hidden."

Maggie looked at Helen again. How odd she was so interested in the hidden door. She could tell Helen was getting ready to leave. "Helen, if Jen comes over to your house again, would you also make sure that she's told me when she's over there?" How embarrassing, Maggie thought. Needing someone else's help to keep her daughter in line. Somehow Maggie had to get back in the driver's seat with Jen.

"But of course. I hope though that you will let her stop by again." Helen shielded her eyes as she turned into the sun to head back across the walk.

Ed stood motionless, looking from one woman to the other. "Okay. Bolts it is, then. Right? I'll go pick them up and take care of it as soon as I can fit it into my schedule."

"Bolts it is," Maggie agreed. "But tell me, have you ever seen something like this before on the other cottages you've worked on?"

"Mrs. . . . Tell me your name again."

"Dunbarton."

"Mrs. Dunbarton. I try not to ask a lot of questions. But

these cottages are pretty old. Who knows what funny business went on around here in the past."

Right. It was just as she'd expected. This man didn't have
much of a history with Breakwater Bay.

Maggie and Ed were confirming details at the front walk
when Jen came up. "Jen, this is Ed. He's going to put bolts on
the little door so no one can go in or out."

Jen barely acknowledged her mother's explanation.
"Where's Jason," she asked.

"The guy before me?" Ed spoke up.

Jen nodded.

"All's I know he's got another job."

Probably encouraged by his stepmother, Maggie
guessed, surprising herself at how bitter she felt.

———— ((•)) ————

It was fun the way Jen had taken to the darkroom.
Maggie couldn't help but feel a sense of her own pride.
Maggie had decided that part of the reason for Jen's secre-
tive behavior was that she had felt shut out. Maggie saw
the opportunity not only to share with her daughter the
fun of developing a photo, but what could happen when
light-sensitive paper got exposed in a way that wasn't
intended.

Maggie called up the stairs to Jen to come on down to
the darkroom. "Okay, Jen, let's get going. Or, wait. Are you
still Starfish?"

Jennifer came down, taking the stairs slowly, as though
balancing a book on her head. "No, I'm Jennifer now."

"Well, welcome back." Maggie gave her daughter a
quick hug when she reached the last step. "I've missed you."

Maggie decided to start with an easy project: to let Jen choose some objects that she would place on a piece of photo paper and then expose the images. Jen had chosen an old gardening glove from the gardening implement pile in the basement, along with some early fall leaves. She'd arranged the leaves around the glove as though a hand had opened suddenly and tossed the foliage in the air. It was totally charming, Maggie decided, and praised her daughter for the image. Perhaps more than it deserved.

"Now, since you have a wonderful image already, we'll see how easy it is to ruin one. I'll turn off the overhead lights again. You stay here, put another sheet of paper in the easel, and turn the enlarger on again after I've opened the secret door just a crack." Maggie waited until Jen was ready, then walked over and set the door ajar, calculating how many times Jennifer must have stood behind the small door spying on her mother.

"Okay now. Hold on. Take away the glove and the leaves. Wait just a second or so. Now, let's develop it. That's right. Be careful not to dip your hand or the tongs in the stop bath back into the developer, or it will contaminate it."

"Okay." Jennifer's voice was muted, so Maggie couldn't be sure she'd understood.

When the photo was in the fixer, Maggie turned on the light and lifted up the photo a little so they could both look at it.

"There's the spot!" Jennifer seemed almost excited to find the dark mark that slashed through one leaf and part of the glove. She picked up the good version and brought it over to compare it with the damaged print. Then she looked at Maggie.

"The open door does this?" She pointed at the mark.

"Yes, the paper is very sensitive, and even a little extra light can have an effect. It's the reason I put these heavy curtains over the window." Maggie pulled at the window coverings to show Jennifer what she meant.

Jennifer bent down to look at the little cardboard drawers where Maggie stored her prints. "Which photos have marks on them, Mommy?"

Maggie moved in quickly. "Hon, I have thrown most of those away. Let's see." Maggie thought quickly about where she'd put a couple of the damaged photos. She knew she'd kept several, but they were with the Blailock party photo in one of the drawers. How foolish to have not gotten rid of that one. She'd hung on to it, thinking there must be some way to use it against Sheldon. But if Jen got hold of it, she would start asking questions, and Maggie had no idea whether she'd be able to lie her way out of that.

"Let's see. You know I have one of Ben that has a spot on it. Look." Maggie took Jennifer over to the window and opened the curtains some more to look at it.

Jennifer studied the photo and nodded again. "Ben loves the sand. He sneaks out sometimes when Helen is asleep. She doesn't want him to leave without her."

Maggie seized the opportunity that had been handed to her. "Well, you know, it is because Helen is worried about him. She doesn't want him to get hurt and not be able to help him. That's how I feel about you, and it worries me when I don't know where you are. That's why I was upset when I found out you were going over to see Ben without telling me. Why do you think you didn't let me know?"

Jen shrugged. "I dunno. I was walking by, and he waved, and Helen asked if I'd like some lemonade."

Maggie winced despite herself. "Jen, Helen and Ben are very nice people. But promise me you won't ever go into the house of someone you don't know without my permission. You mustn't trust strangers." God, she sounded like her mother. Scaring her children about their neighbors. Maggie knew she should change the subject before she said something she'd regret. "So what do you guys do? Talk?"

"Some. Ben's hard to understand. Mostly we just play checkers. He plays lots of checkers."

Maggie could picture Helen easily tiring of board games. "If it's okay with Helen, it's okay to visit Ben. Just let me know." Maggie decided she needed to let the matter drop. If she sounded too obsessive about it, Jennifer might wonder why.

Almost on cue, they both heard a sound outside and turned to look. Maggie recognized the heavyset legs that she'd seen outside the window before.

"I wonder who that is." Maggie spoke out loud.

"Oh, yeah." Jen was immediately distracted from the photo. She didn't need to see any more than the visitor's legs to know who it was. "That's Ben's Uncle Phil. He sometimes comes to visit. He brings Ben presents. Presents that Helen gets rid of because Ben's father doesn't want Phil to give presents."

Maggie took a step back, to let another disturbing piece of information fall into place in her mind. Had Jen become a fixture in another household? "Jen, maybe it's best if you don't go over to Ben's unless I'm with you. It sounds like Helen has all she can handle." The thought of all the people coming in and out of Helen's only made Maggie more concerned about Jen's visits. Best to try to stop them altogether.

"Okay." Jennifer shrugged.

But Maggie wasn't certain what she'd said had sunk in. Jen's hand was already on the railing to go back upstairs. Maggie waited until Jen opened the door to the kitchen before burying the Fourth of July photo deep in her box of photos. She hesitated a moment, then grabbed the negatives in their plastic sleeves from that roll and two others, folded them a few times, and stuffed them in her sweatshirt pouch. She needed to hide these as well, even though not that much detail could be discerned from a negative. Still, she should put them in a really safe place, like the lining of her suitcase, or between the pages of a book she'd already read and returned to the bookshelf.

―――――《◉》―――――

"That's fine. I'll wait." Maggie tried to sound strong and deliberate as soon as she realized that it was Angie answering the phone. She willed herself not to think about what it meant that Angie felt confident enough to answer the Chicago home phone. The possibility that Angie might move into the house when Maggie decamped to Michigan was unthinkable. Still, the more outrageous Sheldon's conduct, the more likely it was that Maggie would prevail in their skirmishes. She'd finally come to the realization that even though Sheldon's behavior had wounded her, it also gave her the advantage. It was one thing to divorce your wife, and quite another to divorce your own children. Maggie also knew she needed to hold herself together if she were to make the most of this advantage.

She imagined Angie and Sheldon off in another room, a whispered conference taking place about why Maggie would call and what she might want. Maggie knew a call from her could unnerve them. She willed a sense of calm on herself. This was always so much easier to do when she was defending her children rather than herself.

"H'lo." Sheldon sent the first volley her way with his too loud and slightly impatient opening.

"Hello, Sheldon." Maggie tried to speak deliberately and modulate her voice. Gone were the days when he might have gotten some endearment. "I understand from your actions that you are ready to get a divorce and also give up custody of your daughters."

"What the he—who told you that?" This time the tone was accusatory. She could tell that she'd caught him off guard.

"I became aware of this at *Vince* Blailock's Fourth of July party." There was no way he could have known she'd been there.

"Wha—?" Sheldon was silent for a moment. Planning what to say next, she guessed. Taking his time to parley it into power. The pregnant pause in the courtroom, Maggie couldn't help but think—with some irony.

Two can play this game, she thought, staying quiet, careful not to breathe into the speaker end of her phone, in case she was breathing too rapidly.

"You had an invitation?" She detected some incredulity in his voice.

"Yes, I was invited." Matter-of-factly.

"I didn't see you."

"Imagine that." Lighten up on the sarcasm, she thought. No point in irritating him more than was necessary.

His reply—when it came—was the second salvo. "Blailock doesn't really care to have you in the neighborhood, you know."

"And why in the world would he take notice of us? Are you trying to threaten me?"

"No. But I have some information. Call it a warning if you like. He could make life miserable for you."

Maggie covered her mouth to keep from gasping. She knew she had skipped a beat before she could reply, but continued as though she hadn't. "I doubt that. And what does our situation have to do with Blailock, anyway? He's not exactly an expert on marriage from what I gather—or relationships in general, for that matter."

"Just that he might decide to retaliate—if you tick him off."

"Sheldon." Maggie couldn't believe how strong—and justified—she felt. "You're talking nonsense. This sounds more like a threat than a friendly warning to me. But if there's some reason Vincent Blalock needs to be involved in our divorce, then you can mention this to my attorney, who is proceeding to file divorce papers for me. He'll contact you about a settlement—including child support and limited visitation—given that, with a second family and cohabitating with a woman you're not married to, you just may not be the best influence on the girls."

Sheldon's reply was fast. "Then maybe you *should* regard this as a threat."

"I'm totally within my rights." Maybe there was some benefit to being married to an attorney: You picked up on legal verbiage. "I just wanted to let you know what my decision is and how I'm proceeding."

"Okay. And now I know." This was his gritted teeth tone. Maggie knew Sheldon was trying to contain his anger.

"Yes, and it will also be up to you to decide how to tell Jen and Sam. I could do it for you, but I suspect you would not like them to hear my version of this story. Goodbye, now."

Maggie replaced the phone with care. She knew Sheldon would report everything to Angie, and then the two of them would strategize how they'd deal with this latest development. How long did they plan to go along without telling her? How long did they plan to go without Sheldon announcing his own divorce proceedings. Maggie put her hands in her armpits and rounded her shoulders to ease the strain in her back. Well, at least this time she had gotten to be the first to acknowledge the inevitable. It was a small victory at best.

There may have been a degree of satisfaction in it, but not enough to prevent the sharp stab of dread behind Maggie's right eye. She didn't have much time to come up with the name of a good attorney. And that was going to be tough, given that nearly every attorney she knew was either a friend or an associate of Sheldon.

━━━◦◦◦◦━━━

Jen was pulling her pink duffel from the closet as Maggie selected clothes from her bureau to pack. Sam's bag was already packed, and Sam had tucked herself in bed and was asleep.

Strange how life's events never went in any predictable order, Maggie thought. Strange how the best-laid plans got undermined. Sheldon had called the day before to say that Betty had died. It had been a surprise, really. One minute she had been picking the flowers from her garden; the next she had pitched forward, the blossoms scattered around her on the ground. Her service would be on Friday. Sheldon felt it important that the girls attend. He would pick them up Wednesday morning after his meeting with Blailock.

Maggie could not think of how she could refuse to let Jen and Sam go to the funeral. Betty had been their grandmother, after all, though Maggie was wary—more than wary—about letting the girls go with Sheldon. Reggie was not coping all that well, he said. Seeing his granddaughters would help him.

"Jen, this is the dress you should wear to your grandma's service, okay?"

Jen had nodded.

"And will you make sure Sam wears her good dress too?"

Another nod.

Maggie hugged her daughter. "I will miss you. But you won't be gone long. Just a few days." Maggie knew she was consoling herself more than Jen. But there was some comfort in knowing that bringing a pregnant Angie to his mother's funeral service was probably the last thing Sheldon would do. Plus, surely he wouldn't try to mix ideas of a possible stepmother in with his own mother's death. "Now, get some sleep. Tomorrow will be a long day. Okay?"

CHAPTER 12

August had never been Maggie's favorite month of the summer. It usually came and went like detritus floating on some slow-moving river answering to a lazy current. Not a thoughtless flow so much as an absent-minded one.

August had lost sight of any genuine purpose. Unless it was to usher out summer. And the shortened days brought their own brand of sadness, one tinged with regret. Regret at somehow not having fulfilled the early promise of the season. Maggie felt her own regret, but couldn't figure out its source. Whatever she hadn't accomplished—well, it was way too late to go back and fix that now. She had clearly been unrealistic in thinking she could put all of her self-doubt behind her.

Maggie watched the red ember bob slightly across the way, trying to stay in the shadows of her porch. Now that she'd met Helen, it was especially difficult to think of her as a smoker. The woman had seemed to be, well, stoic, proud of her virtues, upstanding in a self-conscious sort of way. Maybe even a bit like Winifred.

Maggie could tell Helen had a guest. There were quiet murmurings coming from the porch. Maggie was fairly certain the other person could not be Ben. By the way Jen had described him, it didn't sound as though Ben was able to hold up his end of a conversation.

Time for bed. The short days made it feel late. The summer sun that usually clung to the Michigan horizon, cushioned and cosseted by puff clouds, had disappeared some time ago.

Maggie pushed the footrest away with her feet and stood up. She missed the girls. They'd only been gone two days, but it seemed like much longer.

When Sheldon had picked them up, he'd been reserved, withdrawn, even polite, standing formally to wait for the girls to gather their things, not barging into the house to fill up the rooms with his presence. Maggie wondered what had gotten into him. Perhaps Betty's death had sobered him in some way that nothing else could. Losing a parent was surely a stunning reminder of your own mortality.

"I'm so sorry about Betty," she'd said, meaning it. "How's Reggie doing?"

Sheldon had shrugged. "Hard to tell. I don't think it's really hit him yet." Sheldon had taken a deep breath and let it out slowly. Nodding and rocking slightly.

That was the thing about being married to someone for so long. You knew all their body language by heart. "And how are you?" Maggie could feel herself capitulating.

Sheldon looked at her for a moment as though debating what to say. "So-so. I didn't see this coming. She'd always been there. Always been a fixture. Then this."

Maggie thought how cold the word "fixture" sounded. But honest. "Do they know what it was?"

"Stroke most likely." Sheldon had looked up to see Jen struggling down the stairs with her pink duffel. He went up a few steps. "I'll get that, princess."

The vision of what this family would be like fractured into pieces filtered unbidden into Maggie's mind. The perfect symmetry of two adults and two children would be shattered. There would be no one else for her to fall back on. She had felt momentarily nauseous, and it took an effort of sheer will to get past her urge to vomit. The specter of how difficult it would be to do everything alone frightened her.

Then Sam had made her own way down the stairs, and Maggie knelt in front of her when she reached the bottom, gathering both girls to her as though she were saying a final goodbye. "Be good, and do what your daddy says now, okay? Hug Reggie for me, and say a prayer for your grandma Betty." When she stood up, she saw Sheldon watching her, his expression sad and unguarded. "Sheldon?" His name came out so familiar sounding.

"Yeah?" This was curt. She knew the moment of his vulnerability had passed. He was now back in control of himself.

"Are my flowers in the backyard okay? Are they getting watered?"

He might have said, "My mother just died, and you're worried about your flowers?" But he didn't. He understood what she was driving at. The flowers were her link to Betty. "Of course." His answer was short as well, so she knew he was deliberately cutting off the route that had, for a moment, seemed to open.

"It's just that I don't want to lose them. Not now."

He had nodded agreement.

She watched as the three made their way down the walk, Sheldon carrying both bags in one hand and herding the girls with the other. They had been backlit by the sun; the light glinted a bright gold halo at the top of her girls' heads. She watched until they turned the corner at the front walk.

At least the girls had called to talk with her while they were gone. Nice of Sheldon, really, to make sure they did.

He had been much better about that than she had. On the other hand, maybe he'd just given in to their begging.

It had been difficult to get Jen to talk on the phone, and Sam couldn't stop. Sam had wanted to describe the physical details of the service, the candles, the casket. Though Maggie was convinced she was really saying "gasket." Sam probably had not actually understood what it meant when she'd been told her grandma had passed away. That was a euphemism that didn't do much to help kids' understanding. Jen, on the other hand . . . Maggie would need to take more time with Jen when they returned.

She rinsed out her wineglass in the kitchen sink, then headed for the stairs.

The knock on the door sounded as soon as she'd crossed the living room, as though the caller had been watching through the window, following her progress through the house. Maggie looked at her watch. Nine thirty. Who would knock on a door at this time of night? This was taking even beach etiquette a little too far.

Maggie opened the door and was stunned to see the woman before her, a stranger, yet someone she knew in an instant. Jersey looked more glamorous close up than Maggie imagined, even though she wore dungarees and a bandanna around her hair. Her face had a perfectly symmetrical look, heightened by the strawberry blonde curls that fell below her scarf.

"I recognize you." Maggie spoke first. "You're Jersey, aren't you? Please come in." Maggie had wished for this. Now she wished she could have predicted it. She needed the time to prepare her questions.

Jersey stepped across the threshold, deftly catching the screen door behind her. She hesitated just a moment to glance around the room. "And I believe you are Maggie." Jersey held out her hand. "Your neighbor told me about you."

That would be Gertie, Maggie decided. More than likely the two of them had met at some point. Maggie stepped back from the door after shaking hands. She knew she need-ed to play her cards right. If she came off as too curious or too aggressive, Jersey might clam up. She breathed in to calm herself, hoping her reporter skills hadn't gotten rusty over the years. "What brings you here?" That should sound like a question one asked merely for the purpose of chatting.

"Oh just family business." Jersey didn't seem like she was in any hurry to give a longer answer. Her voice was low, matter-of-fact.

"Visiting relatives?" Maggie hoped Jersey would correct her, give more of an explanation.

"Um-m-m. Actually that partly explains why I knocked on your door."

Sometime later Maggie would reflect back on this con-versation and realize she had more than met her match in Jersey. For, although Maggie thought she had gotten some valuable information from Jersey, the reality was that she had unwittingly divulged some things that Jersey may have been seeking as well. Still, Maggie would later tell herself, what she had learned during the visit would make all the difference. Though she didn't know it at the time.

Maggie looked at Jersey with raised eyebrows, trying not to appear too eager for more of an explanation.

"We used to live here—in this house—summers, that is. My family owned this exact cottage. Probably hasn't changed much since then."

"You're kidding." Maggie tried to imagine Jersey and Julia as twins living here. "That's a coincidence."

"How so?"

Maggie was thinking fast about how to answer this with-out revealing her motives. "Well, I just recently heard—when

I was learning the history of Breakwater Bay—that you and your sister were water skiers."

"Now that *was* a long time ago." Jersey's face took on a distant look as though focused on the memory.

"Come on in." Maggie swept her arm toward the room. She needed to act fast, she knew, if she were going to get Jersey comfortable enough to stay and talk some more. "I'm surprised you haven't dropped in to visit before now."

"Oh, well, I learned something recently that gave me more of a reason to stop by. But I can't stay too long," Jersey countered as though reading Maggie's mind. "I've never had a real desire to visit. Not all of the memories of this house are good ones. But so much looks the same. Even the furniture down here. As is so often the case with these cottages, when they sell, the furniture goes with them. Sellers don't want to keep cottage furniture— they don't have room in their year-round homes for all the stuff."

"It does serve its purpose. But please sit down." Maggie went over and took a seat herself in one of the chairs.

Jersey looked around again, shrugged slightly, and sat down on the couch, balancing on the edge of a cushion.

"You sure I can't get you some wine. Or just something to drink?"

"No, I'm fine."

"Would you like to look around? On this floor at least?"

"Sure." Jersey was already launching herself from the chair before Maggie finished talking.

Maggie led the way through the dining room into the kitchen. She tried to walk slowly to let Jersey stop and look at shelves and the few knickknacks scattered around.

"It is odd to see some of the same souvenirs we had that are still hanging around here." Jersey stopped momentarily and then, as though it had just occurred to her, "Say, you haven't come across a child's music box, have you?"

Maggie turned in surprise. "H-m-m. We did. When we were cleaning out the basement. We cleaned it out one rainy day to uncover the kids' bicycles that were down there."

Jersey's eyes lit up. "That music box might have been mine. Or my sister's. They were gifts, actually. We got them on our twelfth birthday. June 8, 1935. I didn't really love mine the way Ju—my sister liked hers."

"I'm happy to return it to you." How odd that Jersey had become interested in it after so many years. Well, Maggie had warned Jen that she couldn't keep it, that it wasn't hers. "Let me go look for it. Just one minute. One of my daughters liked it and wanted to keep it in her room. You sure I can't get you something?"

Jersey shook her head, but did sit back down.

Maggie hurried up the stairs to Jen's room. The box wasn't on the dresser as usual. She searched the drawers and the shelf in the closet. Under the bed. There weren't that many places in a cottage bedroom to put things. She wondered what Jen had done with it. Could she have tucked it in her duffel and taken it with her? But that didn't make much sense.

Maggie grabbed the doorknob as it dawned on her. Jersey had said there'd been *two* of them. Two music boxes. That could explain why the one Jen had in her room looked like an immaculate version of the one in the basement. But how could Jen have gotten the second one, unless she had also come across it somewhere in the basement?

Maggie went back downstairs. A plan was hatching in her mind. "Sorry. It wasn't in my daughter's room, but let me look in one more place. She may have returned it to the storeroom in the basement." Maggie tried to sound nonchalant.

Once in the basement, Maggie found the faded box easily enough. It was in her darkroom along with all the other castaways that they had stuffed into a corner. "I've got it," she called as she was climbing back up, catching Jersey studying the objects in the blond sideboard by the kitchen.

Jersey reached out for the box, but then caught sight of it. "No, too bad. This was mine, not hers. I never did take very good care of mine." She sighed. "I just thought I might have Julia's as a memento. Don't you see?"

"Yes. I mean, I'm sorry. I understand your sister Julia died in an accident. We'll keep our eyes open for it. My daughters and I." Maggie would find out when the girls returned if Jen really had somehow come across Julia's box. "My girls are with their dad at their grandmother's funeral right now. Their father and I are separated." That should earn her some brownie points with Jersey. Maybe allow her to open a new line of conversation.

But Jersey wasn't listening. She seemed to be absent-mindedly feeling around the underside of the small box with her index and middle fingers, then smiled when her fingers found what must have been a catch. A small drawer sprang out from beneath the box's inner workings. Without looking up, Jersey quickly pushed it back in with her thumb. "This box holds lots of memories."

Maggie watched, fascinated. "Why don't you take the box with you? I'm sure no one will miss it."

Jersey nodded. "I will. But I do wish we'd found the other one. You know, Julia actually owned this cottage. As an adult, I mean. She had loved this place so much, she bought it back from the family we'd sold it to. She loved it in a way I never could. It was hers until she died. I just thought her box might still be here for some reason."

Maggie began to feel guilty. Should she mention the other box? She might, except that it really wasn't here. Jen might have given it to Ben or to Daphne. She'd ask Jen about it when they got back. "I promise we will keep an eye out for it. But while you're here, maybe you could answer a question I have. You must have been aware of the hidden staircase that opens into a bedroom closet. What in the world was it for?"

For the first time, Jersey gave a genuine smile. "Oh, do I ever remember that. We think it was from the rum-running days on Lake Michigan. Maybe you've heard that history?"

Maggie nodded.

"Actually, that wasn't the only secret passage. There was a second, a tunnel between this house and Helen's house across the way. Not only could they store contraband in one house or the other, but they could secretly move between the two houses—or escape from one or another altogether!"

"That would have been ingenious," Maggie agreed, making a mental note that Jersey knew Helen. "You could live in one house, and conduct illegal activity in the other one. The authorities could be spying on you, and you could still get away with everything—right under their nose! But wait, you say there's a tunnel?" The thought began to make Maggie queasy.

"Oh, don't worry. It doesn't exist anymore. Some of it caved in, so the whole thing was filled up. Too bad. Can you imagine what a heyday kids could have had with that? As a matter of fact, our parents slept in the bedroom with the secret stairs so we couldn't sneak out. We were of that age, you know."

Maggie nodded with empathy. "Believe me, things look so different when you're a parent from when you were a teenager. Or were a six-year-old. I'm trying to get the door boarded up so my daughter doesn't use it."

"Oh, don't do that. Just switch bedrooms. Parents need to be able to sneak out too!" Jersey laughed, and Maggie couldn't help but join in. "Let me know if the other music box shows up. I'd like to give it to my sister's son." Jersey ran a hand on her neck and lifted up her hair, then shook her head. It was done so quickly, Maggie imagined it was a familiar set of gestures, seemingly nonchalant, but in reality, it served to focus attention on her. "Sorry I stopped by so late. Thanks for your help."

"It was good to meet you. I will talk with my girls when they get back. Would you like to leave your phone number in case I learn anything?" Maggie made it sound like an impromptu request, but was delighted when Jersey reached in her purse for paper and found the back of an envelope.

Maggie watched Jersey leave. She headed down the walk and turned toward the parking lot. *Shoot,* she thought. *I should have asked where she stays when she's here. But at least I've got this.* She held the envelope up and waved it as though to confirm its existence.

———◎———

Strange how it worked, really, Maggie decided. Just when she thought whatever power she'd had over her own future choices had been usurped, she had instead begun to feel empowered just by knowing what the future held.

The day began as so many other Michigan summer mornings with low clouds and a heavy haze, the atmosphere seemingly undecided about whether the haze would burn off or dump its payload on the spot.

The air was close and stuffy when Maggie went in to get the girls up. It was hard to know whether to close the windows against the rain or open them up to get some circulation going.

The girls had been more quiet than usual for a few days after their trip to Detroit, though Maggie had tried to get them to talk about Betty's service and their grandpa Reggie. They had instead complained that it had not been very fun. There had not been much for them to do, that there had not been any other kids there. Though Sam seemed enchanted that Grandma Helen "had been returned to the ground," and Jen, for her part, seemed particularly glad to get back into her summer routine.

Nevertheless, Jen had moaned when Maggie went in to wake her up. "I'm too tired."

"Tell you what. You can take a nap this afternoon. After you help me hang the photos in the show."

Jen sat up in bed long enough to give her mother a skeptical look, then fell back into her pillow to emphasize her point.

"Pancakes and syrup." Maggie was not above a bribe today. This was the day she would hang her show in the old armory building's gymnasium, where Noreen and her group staged their summer's end arts and crafts show.

The girls had helped her mount her photos on poster board, then added a colored poster board frame on top. Jennifer had been nearly unerring in her choice of colors, helping to use the colors to set off a mood or theme against the black-and-white photos. The most she could hope for, Maggie knew, was that a reporter from the local paper might cover the event and write about her work. This wouldn't give her a ton of exposure, but at least it would be a start.

Noreen had taken on the role of watching over her, Maggie felt, giving her the name of a good family attorney without asking a lot of questions. Maggie surmised it wouldn't be all that difficult to figure out why a woman spending a summer away from her husband would need the name of a good attorney.

By the time they reached the armory, the parking lot was full of vans and SUVs and people unloading bags or boxes from their vehicles. Maggie had just pulled in and opened the car doors for the girls when Noreen appeared.

"Oh, good. You're here. Since you're new this year, let me show you where to set up. We borrowed some big felt partitions from the high school for your photos. We've also got the reporter from the city paper coming in about half an hour to take photos and do her story. I'll send her over your way."

"Noreen, that is really great of you."

"No worries. I think photography is a good addition. We might make this small town bazaar respectable yet."

The end of Noreen's sentence floated away. She had turned to greet Jason as he approached them. Maggie tried not to seem surprised to see him. "Hi."

Noreen looked between the two. "Oh, you two know each other? Of course. From Breakwater. Good. Jason, then you can pitch in here and help Maggie carry her stuff in."

Noreen's words were shortchanged again when Jen and Sam shot from the car and grabbed Jason by the arms.

"Jason, where have you been?" Jen had his arm in both of her hands to say what had been in Maggie's heart for weeks. "We've missed you."

"Yeah. Our house needs you." This from Sam, who had Jason's other hand patting her head.

"And I've missed you guys." Maggie could tell that Jason was directing this at the girls. She sensed she was somehow standing on the outside of his orbit. "I've got a different job now."

Noreen inserted herself again. "Well, great, if you all know each other, then, Jason and Maggie. I'm assuming this is Jennifer, and this is Samantha? I'll show you where the prints will go. Maggie, did you remember to make out tags with titles and prices?"

Maggie nodded. She didn't trust her voice to speak.

"Okay then. Grab your things and follow me." Noreen

was all business. Maggie suspected her orders were intended to cover up the awkward moment she must have sensed.

Maggie gave Jason a quick smile, somehow managing to keep her own questions at bay. This wasn't the time to talk, anyway. She opened the trunk and reached for the boxes there. "Here, everyone can help carry something."

There was a woman with a camera slung over her shoulder pacing around the empty felt boards at the center of the arena when they arrived with the boxes.

"Oh, Ramona, so they sent you then? A human interest angle, I guess." Noreen seemed to know the woman and took her arm to lead her over to Maggie. "Jason, you and the kids hang the photos while Maggie gets interviewed."

Maggie set down her box and let herself be directed over to the journalist. This might be her only chance for some publicity, even if it meant she couldn't oversee the hanging of her precious photos. Never mind. She could easily rearrange things later if need be.

"What got you interested in photography in the first place?" Ramona began, swinging a hefty camera behind her back so she could take notes on a steno pad she'd pulled from a large bag.

Maggie looked over at Jason and the girls and smiled when she realized Jen was giving the orders of what went where. She turned back to give the reporter her full attention, knowing this would most likely mean Jason would slip through her fragile net once more.

⸺◈⸺

The newspaper was spread out across the footrest in front of Maggie. The profile on the new photographer in town, Maggie DeCour Dunbarton, had made the front page of the paper's Arts and Culture section. The best part was not the interview but the three accompanying photos showing her work.

Maggie wasn't surprised at the photos the journalist had chosen to feature: the menacing one of Blailock's condo building, one of Ben sleeping in the hollows of the dunes, and the shot of the lighthouse's scaffold undergirding.

Maggie put her wineglass down and looked again at the lighthouse shot. It was not the traditional version that found its way onto postcards and amateur paintings, not the full view of the tower light and wind-stiffened flags waving from the roof: historic lighthouse as charming red sentinel. This was more of a behind-the-scenes view, the inner workings version.

Her photo showed the vertical and horizontal lines, a glimpse of the vertical concrete piers that held the lighthouse in place above the shifting waterline of the lake, beneath the horizontal boards of the red siding. For some reason, there had even been a small boat tied up under the pier—more horizontal lines—bobbing in the shallow water, an outboard with its motor pulled up.

Maggie picked her drink back up. The shot had almost had too dear a cost, she remembered. She and Samantha had headed for the lighthouse pier that day by themselves. Jennifer was off with Annie and the older day care children who had gone to town for a showing of *Snow White* at a local theater. Maggie knew Sam would never be able to sit through a feature-length film, even a Disney cartoon.

They had walked to the red light at the end of the pier that jutted out in front of the lighthouse. The pier had a concrete apron on the outside that gave way to huge boulders probably placed there to take the force of the breaking waves.

Their pier was a mirror image of a second one on the other side of the channel. The two piers extended out into the big lake, and then jutted inward toward each other like two arms warding off dangers while beckoning boats back into the safety of Lake Haskell. Beyond the other pier were the wide expanses of beach that were the public state park, with Blailock's condo buildings beyond that.

There were fishing lines spaced all along the pier, some held by hand, some propped in carts that seemed brimming with other fishing gear or in wide blue pipes set in the concrete evenly spaced along the length of the pier. Maggie had her lens cap off and her camera trained on the poetry of the angles of fishing lines when Sam screamed, "Mommy! The little one can't get to his mom," then began to clamber down the concrete apron seemingly with every intention of crawling out onto the boulders.

Maggie immediately saw what had prompted Sam's outcry. A mother duck, with a tight cluster of nearly a dozen ducklings circling her, bobbed on the water several feet from the rocks. She seemed to be herding the young ones away from the smashing waves. A single duckling was stranded outside the fold, seemingly abandoned to his own fate. He was bobbing wildly with the crest and fall of the waves while being slowly washed toward the rocks.

"Sam! No! Stop!" Maggie cradled her camera against her chest and slid sideways after her daughter, yelling over the fomenting water and its spray, "Sam, stop. Sam! You'll get hurt."

Sam had hesitated a fraction of a second when she reached the boulders in order to bend down to hang onto the rocks. This slowed her down enough that Maggie could grab the child and wrap a free arm around Sam's chest.

"Sam, wait. The rocks are too slippery. It's dangerous. That's why it's against the rules to climb on them."

Sam had strained to get away. "Mommy, the little one can't get to his mom."

Maggie held her hard and took a few steps backward until they were well on the concrete, then sat down, keeping Sam between her legs. "Hon, it's too dangerous to help him." Maggie knew it'd be awful if the duckling got washed against the rocks while they were watching, but all she could visualize was her own child's body smashing up against them. Nothing could be worse than that.

Yet, as they watched, the tiny bird began to gain ground on the currents, making his way out of the shoals at a diagonal that would reunite him with the others.

"Lookie! Lookie!" Sam held out her arm and wagged her index finger. "Lookie, Mommy. He's safe. He's okay."

"Yes, and so are you. Hon, those rocks are slippery. Ducks are very good swimmers. Better than we are." Maggie had started to stand up with Sam in her arms when she caught sight of the lighthouse. The meeting of the sets of lines of its foundational piers, the design of it, caught her eye. "Wait, Sam." She set Sam down, but still held on with one arm around her waist, while she used the other to aim the camera at the lighthouse base. "I just need to take a picture of this."

"What about the ducks?"

"What about them? They're all safe now."

"Aren't you going to take a picture of them too?"

"Of course. We will take a picture together. You can press the button."

Sam's concern for the ducks had taken Maggie's mind off the underpinnings of the lighthouse until she was back in the darkroom developing the shot and realized the small boat that fit beneath the lighthouse piers would be hidden both from the level of the pier and from the beach side where a small sand cover and beach grass would hide the lighthouse piers from view. Why was there a boat tied up under the lighthouse, anyway?

As Maggie thought about this question, the phone had rung. She'd hurried to get it before the sound woke up the girls.

"H'lo?" It was Bryan.

"What's up?"

"Mom just heard about Betty. She's been asking me why you didn't call to let her know."

Maggie knew Bryan hated the job he'd been given, and it made him worse at it than he'd otherwise have been. "Bryan. It's been crazy around here. Sheldon took the girls with him to the funeral, and I had to finish everything for my photo show—at the armory in town. The show even got covered in the local newspaper. My photos are good, I think. They show the story of what Blailock is doing to ruin the shoreline. It's not like Mom was actually friends with Betty, after all. It's not as though she would have gone to the funeral."

When Bryan answered her, Maggie could tell he was more irritated with her than she'd realized. "Blailock? Maggie, are you still on that kick? I thought by now you surely would have moved on. I can't believe you are so fixated on that guy. He's probably just a businessman with few or no scruples."

"He seems so shady. He's always trying to bend the rules."

"So, you think he's guilty of some big crime? Don't forget, even when you were a journalist, your instincts weren't always right. I can remember one time when, if your editor hadn't killed the story, you might well have gotten sued for libel."

"Bryan, get off it. I knew that story didn't have enough solid evidence to run."

"And, what's Blailock's crime, anyway? Big buildings close to the beach? Maybe it just means lots more people get to enjoy the water. This isn't exactly a Love Canal after all."

Maggie looked over at the newspaper spread across the footstool. The paper was still open to the story about her truthful photos. She wanted to walk over and crumple it into a horrible ball and throw it into a fire. "Okay, bro of mine. That's enough. Thanks for the advice. I guess Mom has been giving you a hard time because of me."

"How'd you know?"

"I'll try to make time to call her, though you know how much I hate that."

"Only too well." Bryan was quiet for a moment. "Magdalena, I just worry that you're on the trail of this Blailock guy because Sheldon has been such a disappointment. And you think you can get back at him by going after Blailock."

"Yeah, that might be part of it," Maggie acquiesced so she could get off the phone. It would take too much time to push back, to tell Bryan all the circumstances that seemed to add up to some larger intrigue. He'd just tell her she was imagining things and shoot them down anyway. But mostly she wanted to get off the phone because she realized she had been so busy with the show, she had never found out what had happened to Julia's music box. If it hadn't been so late, she would have awakened Jen to ask.

CHAPTER 13

One ray of sun had managed to penetrate the thicket of blueberry bushes and illuminate a single enormous berry just at eye level in the middle of the bush. Maggie wrangled her hand through the tangle of branches to pluck it, and felt it slip from its stem into her hand.

It wasn't Jason's admonishment that they "better pick the bushes clean, and not leave any—or not many—berries on the bushes behind them," and if they did, "they'd get charged more for their take" that made her risk scratched limbs to snag the single berry.

Maggie was after this blue marble because she knew how sweet it would be. She held the orb a moment to look at the deep blue berry whose rounded sides turned silver in the sun. She was not disappointed when she popped it in her mouth and immediately crushed it against the taste buds of her tongue. Sweet and sour at once. The sour made her wince, but the sweet triumphed.

She looked over at Jason on the other side of the row of bushes. He had a baseball cap that shielded his eyes. He had taken his shirt off and had stuck it into the back of his jeans so that it hung down behind him like a tail. How had he done it exactly? Convinced all three of them that the most important thing to do on this particular August day was to pick blueberries under a perfectly cloudless sky.

She wasn't sure how she had gone from washing the kitchen floor and doing the laundry, getting ready to vacate the cottage, to taking a drive out of town to a blueberry farm where you could do your own picking.

Jason had just shown up at their door, calling into the house, "Good morning. Who is up for going on a blueberry adventure?"

The girls, who had been resting on their elbows in the living room in front of the television set, had jumped up and run to the front door. "I do." This was from Jen, showing more excitement than Maggie had seen from her in days. She had told Maggie that her name was now Turtle Dove, and Maggie had to bite her lip not to say, "And does that mean you plan to fly away?"

But Jason had turned their day around.

They had all climbed into his pickup truck, the girls squeezed in the middle of the seat with Jason and Maggie on either side. They'd driven out of town several miles then turned off down a bumpy back road. What was his power over others, Maggie wondered, glancing over at Jason. His mirror glasses just reinforced the image of mystery man.

Once they arrived, Jason had again exercised his powers of persuasion by outfitting them all in the ridiculous get-up they were now wearing, pieces of clothesline tied at their waists with a silver metal bucket hanging down from it in front like they were ready to participate in some pagan ritual. Maggie shook her head when she pictured what she must look like.

"Think of picking blueberries as a little like milking a cow," he'd instructed. "You have to be gentle. Just work your fingers over the berries, and the ripe ones will fall off right into your bucket."

The first few berries landed with a loud ping in the buckets, startling Maggie, who did not want to draw attention to herself. Once the bottom of the bucket was covered in blue, the landings were soft, and they could listen to the far-off voices of other pickers and to the chirps of birds that flew overhead or sat in the line of trees close to the road.

Maggie positioned herself so she could watch Jason. He was finishing his side of the row faster than the three of them could do theirs. Jason had his back to them. His shoulders were narrow and his scapula looked like they were carved out of his back, protruding and retreating as he moved his arms to reach the berries. Maggie wondered what it would have been like to be Jason's father and to watch him go to war. She looked away.

Migrant families worked in a separate field. Whenever their row would open to a pathway, she could see them. The children sat on the ground to pick the low berries. She wondered what they did at night.

Maggie was surprised that Sam and Jennifer lasted most of the morning. But when they had had enough, they let the adults know it.

"My tongue is bluer than yours!" Jen yelled and stuck her tongue out at Sam.

"No, mine!" Sam popped more berries into her mouth, then stuck out her tongue.

Maggie assumed the role of referee. "I think you both win. But that probably means your buckets are not very full." Maggie looked down at her own half-full bucket and realized she didn't have much to brag about. It meant they were dependent on Jason's skill if they were going to have anything to take home. "Remember, Jason said to clean pick. You girls can get the berries that are closer to the ground."

Jason must have heard his name because he was parting the branches of two bushes so he could walk in between to where the three females were.

"How're you comin'?" Both Jen and Sam ran over to show the results of their efforts. "Wow. That's good." He whistled. Then he untied his own rope and poured his bucket into the waiting flat of cardboard containers they'd brought into the field. "We should probably check out now. But, first things first." He took a handful of berries, tossed one in the air, and caught it perfectly in his mouth.

Sam and Jen were delighted. Jen shed her bucket and tossed a berry high above her head, weaving like a seal with a ball on its nose. The berry caught her in the eye. With Sam's toss, her berry flew behind her for regions unknown.

"Hey, you two," Maggie called to her daughters, "you know blueberries stain. Not that it matters too much with what you're wearing," she conceded.

"Okay, then." Jason looked at them in earnest. "I am going to give all of you beautiful women the best berries I have in my bucket." He held one out to Jen for her to pop in her mouth. Then it was Sam's turn. "Okay, and now for you, Maggie."

Maggie started. Was this some show of affection? She was embarrassed in front of her daughters and wondered whether to play this serious or high camp, She chose the latter for her heart's sake. "For me?" She held out her arms in mock ceremony and looked at Jason through raised eyebrows.

"Just for you, m'lady." Jason swept his arm in front of himself in a sweeping bow. "A special blueberry just for you."

Maggie countered with a toss of her head and her own shallow curtsey.

When Jason reached over with her berry, she half-closed her eyes and opened her mouth. With the exquisite care of a mother bird, he placed it carefully on her tongue and again she tasted the sweet and the sour. How fitting, she thought, acknowledging to herself the intimacy of the act. A fitting way to say goodbye to the summer. And probably to this man as well.

Jason emptied their buckets onto the flat, except for Sam's. He said he would use these to "top off" the rest when they got up to the tent. The other berries already in the pints would settle quite a bit, and he didn't want them to pay for a full pint that had shaken down to something less.

The trip home was quiet. The anticipation had gone out of the day, and Maggie was thinking about laundry. Their time at the cottage would be up in two weeks, and she hadn't even made arrangements for what happened next. She had asked Sheldon for at least a month in the house to get things together. Angie and Sheldon would move into Angie's apartment to let Maggie arrange her next move. Maggie and Sheldon had reached a détente that allowed her to do that. Plus, Maggie guessed Sheldon wanted to do that to set things in motion.

Sheldon had planned a trip to visit at the end of the week when he would talk with the girls about what would follow. Maggie knew she would have her hands full after that. They would need time to adjust to the idea of a new home somewhere in Chicago without their father. Maggie was already girding herself against Jen's dramatic reaction.

When they reached Breakwater Bay, Jason parked his truck and walked back with them. At the house, he handed the cartons of berries to the girls to take inside.

"Would you like to come in for a soda? Some lemonade?" Maggie tried to sound casual as she turned to face him. She suspected this would be it. They probably wouldn't see him again. This was most likely about as much closure as Jason gave anyone.

"I don't think so. I have a few things to do, and I'm hoping to sail early this evening. I have to work tomorrow, but before I leave, I want to show you something. Come." He beckoned with his head.

Maggie followed him down the walk to the beach. "We've missed you around here."

"Yeah. Janine says that too. I just needed to make more money. There's a reason I'm telling you this, Maggie. Because I've been working for Blailock."

Maggie felt a contraction in her gut. "You're what?"

"I'm working for Blailock."

"You've sold out." She was incredulous.

"Call it what you like. If not me, then someone else. There's always someone who'll do his dirty work. I'm tired of not having any money. It makes everything harder." He gave her a knowing look. "You know we all sell out in one way or another."

Maggie was shaking her head, trying to imagine what she had just heard and why it hurt so much.

"But that's not why I'm telling you this, Maggie. If I wanted sanctimony, I'd talk to your neighbors. I'm telling you this because I think you're in danger."

"What?"

"Yeah. You don't realize that you may have ruffled a few feathers around here."

"How so?" Maggie brushed at her ear, even though nothing was there.

"I don't know exactly, but I think it had something to do with the photos in your show."

"But they were just art mostly. Photos taken around here."

"Right. Just be careful is all I'm saying."

"Jason, I admired you. Someone who was living out his principles."

"I don't know anyone who does that, Maggie. Especially not me. Life involves other people. As long as that's the case, we're always going to be compromising. When I was in Vietnam, all I did was compromise. It was the cost of staying alive. So I am no stranger to sacrificing everything I hold dear. Here's the reason I did it this time." Jason had walked them close to the water's edge next to the most unusual sailboat Maggie had ever seen.

"What is this?"

"It's a catamaran boat, called a Hobie Cat. What do you think?"

"It's so different."

"Yeah, this boat is all fun. It's really lightweight; the hulls are made of fiberglass. The rest is aluminum tubes. Anyone can launch it, and, in a good wind, she screams through the water. You just head 'er out, pull up the sail, and she catches the wind. And it's also stable. Take a look at the two hulls underneath. You sit on this canvas stretched across the top."

"That looks a little like a trampoline."

"Yeah. Better wear a life jacket when you're on it. There isn't much to hold you in, and you can get a pretty wild ride out of her!"

Maggie tried to focus her attention on the boat, though her mind was still trying to get itself around what Jason had just told her. "I can't imagine why Blailock or anyone else should be upset with the photos. They just show what's there for everyone to see. It just happens to be from my perspective."

"That's probably the reason then." As Maggie's attention shifted, Jason's did as well. "I need to be going."

Maggie forced her attention back to the boat. "But Jason, are you leaving it here?" She patted the canvas top. "Aren't you afraid someone will steal it?"

"Not really. They could sail it away, but they'd still have to trailer it somewhere. Actually, I'm leaving it here so I can sail with a friend."

Despite her best efforts, Maggie couldn't help but think of the woman in the red dress. Why had she ever asked

Jason to take her to Blailock's party? That seemed to have been where everything had started to go sideways.

Maggie was surprised from her reverie when Jason, without speaking, took both her shoulders in his hands and placed a kiss on her lips with the same tenderness he had shown when placing a blueberry on her tongue. "Take care." Before he turned away, he lifted both her hands to his lips and kissed them, letting their hands linger together a little longer before dropping them. Without another word, he waved over his shoulder and headed back across the sand toward the parking lot.

Maggie started to lift her hand to wave back, but then let it drop to her side. Jason already had his back to her.

She needed to get home and see what the girls were up to. Make sure they weren't practicing catching blueberries in the house. Without any bidding, she felt the sadness of August envelop her all over again.

⟞⟝

Strange how sometimes the telephone's ring sounded different, more insistent, when the news was bad. Maggie walked quickly to pick it up. "H'lo?"

"Maggie. Noreen. I have some bad news, I'm afraid."

Maggie felt as though she had already known that. "What's up?"

"It's your photos. Your show. I can't imagine how or why, but they've been damaged. Ruined, actually. Like someone took a knife to them."

Maggie's free hand involuntarily flew to her throat. Her mind conjured up the hours she had spent in the darkroom, the care she had taken to make them perfect. "All of them?"

"Yes, all."

"Who would do such a thing?"

"We have no idea. We've checked. Nothing else in the hall seems to be touched. We don't keep a guard on the premises overnight, because we've never had any trouble. We lock all the doors. One was pried open. We'll have to get it fixed. We've called to report this to the police. They're on their way. Can you come down?"

"Now?"

"Yes, as soon as you can. You need to be here to help make the report. We need to place a value on the damage."

"We'll be there as soon as I can get the girls ready." Maggie's mind began to race. "Who would do this?"

"That's what we're asking." Noreen was quiet for a moment. Then, "Maggie, I'm sorry."

"Oh, thanks. It's not your fault. See you soon." Maggie cradled the receiver before replacing it. She called into the house, "Jen. Sam. We need to change your clothes, and go into town." Maggie headed up the stairs. For some reason, just lifting her feet was difficult. "We need to go back to the armory."

Maggie thought about how when she'd gotten up that morning, she had certainly not planned on this happening to her.

——⫸«(◉)»⫷——

The matte surfaces of the photographs were in tatters. Jen had taken one look and begun to cry. As frequently happened, when Jen cried, Sam joined in. Maggie found herself comforting her daughters while trying to respond to a beefy, bald officer's questions. She was glad for it. It kept her from crying herself. The photos had represented the peak of her work, both the creativity of the conception and the skill of the execution.

She hugged her girls to her. "I think someone was jealous," she told them. "Someone wished they could take beautiful photos like these, and just couldn't stand it."

Jen pulled away and walked over to the photo of Ben. She ran her fingers over a place where the paper had curled back from the cut. Maggie heard a whimper from her. "Who would hurt Ben?"

"Oh, hon. You mustn't cry. You know this isn't Ben. It's just a picture of him. Ben is okay. Ben is fine. And I can always make another picture."

"I know." Jen began to sob harder.

Maggie held her again and stroked her hair. She sensed it was about Ben. But it was also more than that. Jen had to realize this was about her mother as well. Maggie raised her head as Noreen and the policeman walked over.

"I'm Officer Norton, the detective on this case." Maggie shook his outstretched hand. "Noreen, here," he tilted his head toward her, "tells me this is the first year this show has had photos. She wonders if that is somehow connected to the motive."

Maggie turned toward Noreen. "I can't imagine that. Why would someone go to all the trouble over that? I've been going over this in my mind since Noreen called me. Who would do this? And why?"

"Right."

"But I don't think it's about the collection of photos. I think it is about one in particular."

All three adults turned back to the boards.

"Jennifer." Maggie beckoned Jen over. "Sam, you too. Jen, tell me some more about Ben."

"I told you, Mom. He's different. There are lots of things he can't do. And he's hard to understand."

"Right. You did tell me. But I want to know about where he came from. Who's his mom? Is it Helen?"

Jen leaned back to give her mother an incredulous look. "Of course not. She's his grandma."

"Really? Where is his mother?"

"Helen said she died."

A dead mother. Maggie felt something click into place. She knew she had nearly all the pieces of the puzzle before her.

"And Uncle Phil? Who is that, Jen?"

"Someone who brings Ben presents. Except Helen doesn't want Ben to keep the presents in case Ben's daddy sees them. Helen says he doesn't like Ben's Uncle Phil."

Maggie nodded, finishing her thought out loud. "And so Ben gave you his music box to keep so his father wouldn't see it?"

Jen nodded. "So I just kept it for a while. But then his aunt Jersey came over and asked where it was. She said it was important that she find it. So, that was why I needed to give it back."

Maggie knew about tectonic plates. That they existed beneath the upper layers of the earth's crust, how they controlled movements of the earth's crust. They could cause buckling, upheavals, huge fissures. Earthquakes, tsunamis. She imagined there were tectonic plates in her own brain that had just shifted, and all of the unrelated facts began to rotate and rearrange themselves into a new, frightening reality. Why had it taken her so long to make the connections? Falling into the trap of easy assumptions was why.

She had not seen the coincidences though they had been right before her.

Blailock was at the center. Not only was he embarrassed about his Down syndrome son, but he also couldn't be sure that the young man was his. And she had put a photo of him on exhibit for the public to see! The news coverage of her show had probably been her undoing. That was what had tipped Blailock off. Maggie could picture Blailock's goons using a crowbar to gain entry into the armory; their flashlights playing across the floor and walls until they located her photos; then, pulling out their knives, they slashed them beyond recognition. Should she tell her suspicious to the police?

Maggie hugged Jen. "You've been a good friend to Ben." She turned to Noreen. "So, I do think this has something to do with one of my photos. It might have offended someone."

Officer Norton held up a notebook, getting ready to write. "Would you be willing to make a statement so that we can continue our investigation?"

Maggie pictured a policeman approaching Blailock for questioning. The image defied reason. It would make matters worse. Much worse.

"No, I don't think I should do that. This is complete conjecture on my part. I have no proof. I think one of my photos struck a nerve. Probably the story about the show that appeared in the newspaper was what set all this off. If you need to put that in your report, that's fine. But I can't say anything more than that with any confidence." Maggie knew she sounded like some victim in an amalgam of all the bad TV cop shows, but if she shared her suspicions with the police, things could get a lot worse for her.

"Noreen, I wonder if you would let me reprint the photos for the show—all but the one I think is the cause of all this. I think I can do it quickly. I may even have prints of a couple of these ready to go."

"Fine with me. But let's clean off these boards first."

⸻ «◎» ⸻

Everyone was quiet on the trip home. It gave Maggie time to think. She thought back to the time she had caught Blailock inside the cottage, before she'd known who he was. It now cast his intrusion in a sinister light. He'd been looking for something. What was it and why?

Maggie glanced in the back seat and saw that both girls were nodding off. She felt if given the chance, she could fall asleep as well. The emotions of the day had been exhausting.

The thoughts came fast and furious as she tried to scan the reasons Vincent Blailock would pay her a visit. If Julia had owned the cottage at the time of her death, then it now belonged to Blailock. Blailock was her landlord! That was what had been behind Sheldon's implicit threat. He probably felt he had every right to enter whenever he wanted. He couldn't have been after her photos. At that point, he couldn't have known what her subjects had been. Was he checking to see if they'd discovered the secret stairs? But how could he have told if they'd found them or not?

Maggie brought her attention back to the road. She needed to pay attention, she told herself. Think about all of this later. She sensed that somehow she had all the essential pieces of information that, if she could just fit them all together, would implicate Blailock. Would it be enough to take the information to the police so that they could do more than just question him? And he must suspect she already knew this—whatever it was he wanted to keep secret.

This was why he had her photos destroyed. Did this also mean he would come after her? *Calm down*, she told herself. Bryan was right. Her imagination was way out in front of reality. First things first. What she needed to do was find her negatives so she could reprint her photos, if need be. She had intended to hide the one of the party and pregnant Angie from Jen. So, where exactly had she put them? She'd need to look.

———

Maggie stood in the middle of her darkroom with her hands on her hips. All of the lights were blazing. She'd put the girls to bed, but she had no intention of sleeping until she could remember what she had done with her negatives.

She remembered she had wanted to keep them in a safe place, one Jen would never come across by chance. That place did not seem to be her darkroom, she decided. She'd gone through every possible place they might be in this room. She had found replacement photos for the show. But no negatives.

Maggie had done everything she could in this room. She'd save for tomorrow any further searching for the negatives. As she reached for the light switch, she was struck by the thought that maybe someone had beat her to it. What if Blailock had let himself into their cottage, had already located the negatives and made off with them? She might be spending her time searching for something that wasn't even here.

CHAPTER 14

Annie's day care had closed its doors for the week. Gertie and Dave had taken their family on its own summer vacation to Mackinaw Island in Michigan's Upper Peninsula. It was a good time for the trip. School would start in a couple of weeks, and many families were packing up and heading back to their year-round homes. The day care's numbers had already been diminished significantly.

Maggie felt a sadness in the air. The echoing sounds of goodbyes. Everything was about leaving, boarding windows, packing up, moving on. The flowers had shed their blossoms, and their empty, dry stalks clacked in the breeze.

Maggie knew she should be focused on her own exodus. She and Sheldon had worked out the general arrangements; the smaller details would sort themselves out soon enough, she guessed. The toughest part would be sitting down with Jen and Sam and telling them their lives would never again be the same. Sheldon had agreed to come to the Lake next week so that they could talk about the changes, let Jen and Sam know that their parents loved them. Maggie knew she had made some mistakes in her marriage, but she was determined not to make any mistakes with her children when it came to her divorce.

Sheldon seemed to be on board with it, but who knew what would happen when he was a new father with a whole other family.

She leaned in the doorway, watching her daughters watch television. It was *Sesame Street*, but even this made her feel guilty. She'd be hard-pressed to come up with the creative craft projects that Gertie and Annie dreamed up. Then it dawned on her.

"Hey, Sam. Jen. Let's go visit Ben and Helen. I'll come with you. Maybe they'd like a little company just now."

Jen barely turned her head around from her seated position on the floor. "You sure? I thought I wasn't supposed to go over there."

"That was only without permission. C'mon. I'm going over to visit with Helen."

"Okay. This is kind of boring."

Sam looked over at Jen. "Yeah, kind of boring."

⸻ ⊙ ⸻

Even though the front door was open, Maggie still could not bring herself to follow beach etiquette and just open it and announce herself. Instead she rattled the screen with her knock. "Hello. Helen, it's your neighbor Maggie from across the way. Jen and Sam are with me. We thought we'd stop by to say hello."

Jen pressed her face to the screen to peer inside, something Maggie imagined she had done before.

Helen did not appear, but moments later Ben shuffled onto the porch. When he saw Jen through the screen, he lit up. Maggie opened the door for them all, thinking this was probably as much of an invitation to enter as they were going to get.

"Hi, Ben."

By now, Helen had come into view. "Oh, how good to see you all. Come in, come in."

Helen's hospitality seemed so genuine, Maggie felt guilty for her ulterior motives. "Thanks. We just wanted to pay a visit. The end of the month is fast approaching, and we're not going to be around much longer."

"Oh, I know. It's the end of summer. The time of good-byes. Jen, why don't you and Ben go on and play checkers— or another game. And this is Sam, right? You go on with them. Maggie and I can sit out here."

"That's all right. We can be where the children are." Maggie was trying to think of how she should broach the subject. "You know, I was so interested in Ben's music box. The one his mother gave him. There is another one just like it at our cottage. I guess that one belonged to Ben's mom's twin sister. I met her. Jersey."

Helen looked from Ben, then back to Jen, then back to Maggie. "Oh, yes. The music box. The music box has got some mileage on it, all right. I wasn't really aware that Ben had passed it on to Jen for safekeeping. He did it as a favor to me, I think." Helen gave Maggie a puzzled look.

"I learned something about the music boxes from Jersey, something Ben may not realize. I wanted to show him."

"Well, let me go get it. After I learned he had handed it over to Jen, I thought I should keep better tabs on it, you know?"

Maggie nodded.

"Why don't you all come in for some lemonade, and I'll go get it."

What an intrusion this must be, Maggie realized. She began to feel like an imposter, a poseur. She really had wanted to talk with Helen some more, not just use the girls as an excuse to look at Julia's music box for herself.

Ben and Jen settled at the kitchen table with a certain familiarity. Sam and Maggie followed their lead. Helen returned almost immediately with the box. As soon as he saw it, Ben stood halfway up and stretched out his arms. Helen handed it to him, and they all watched as he raised the lid. *Les Patineurs* began at once; the skater began to twirl; white flakes swirled around inside the globe.

This was going to be harder than Maggie had hoped. "Ben," she began, "would you mind if I looked at your box, showed you something?"

Ben smiled and shook his head, but otherwise didn't move.

"Here." Jen reached over and lifted it from his hands. "Here, Mom. Show us."

Once again, Maggie felt odd, like an interloper. Was she taking advantage of someone who didn't know not to trust everyone? It was too late to question herself now. "So, these music boxes have a little secret drawer under them. Let me see if I can find the latch for this one." She began to run her hand underneath, letting her fingers probe the corner, the grooves.

It didn't take long before her fingers felt an extra ridge between the grooves. She pressed this. A drawer sprung out just as it had under Jersey's touch.

All three children gasped. "Wow." Jen was the first to speak. "Let us see." Sam started to stand on her chair to get a better look.

"Sam, stay seated. I'll put it down." Maggie was not sure what she had hoped to find, but whatever it was, she felt disappointed. The drawer was completely empty. She held the box so that each child could see the inside of the drawer like some magician who had made the bunny disappear in the hat. Then she turned the box back over to Ben, with an observation that sounded weak, even to her: "Such a sweet gift to give young girls. They must have loved them."

"Yes, well, let me get the lemonade." Helen left the table again, without remarking on the secret drawer.

Maggie thought she'd try one last gambit, then give it a rest. "Ben, did your mom tell you anything about this box?"

Ben smiled broadly, lifted the lid again to start the music. Only this time he shook the box slightly to stir up the white flakes. "It's snowing! It's snowing."

Maggie nearly snorted in exasperation with herself. Anyone could see that the powder swirling in the globe was meant to be white snowflakes. Of course it was snowing.

⸻ ⸨◊⸩ ⸻

It was probably time to pack up the darkroom. Of everything they had accumulated over the summer, Maggie knew her enlarger and other darkroom supplies might be the most important. The summer had given her the courage to put out her photographer's shingle once she was moved and settled in.

She'd had been collecting boxes from the grocery store. These now sat in the middle of the darkroom. She began by putting her printed photos and extra photo paper in first. She wondered if she would have a home with a room that would lend itself to a darkroom as well as this unfinished basement. What a piece of luck this had been. Maggie smiled to herself.

The moment was short-lived. A child's scream sounded above her. Maggie kicked herself as she took the stairs two at a time. She had left the girls alone too long.

Maggie found Sam standing in the middle of the kitchen, her face in a grimace, her mouth dripping white granules.

"Oh my god, Sam. However did you get into the ant trap?" But Maggie knew full well how. She must have climbed on the counter in search of treats, and found the ant poison behind the flour and sugar canisters.

"Quick." Maggie lifted Sam and set her back on the counter, turned on the faucet, took her index finger, and ran it around the child's mouth, then put her hand under the tap. "Sam, spit out everything you can into the sink, then rinse out your mouth with this water." Maggie handed Sam a glass. "Hon, that stuff is ant poison, and it may not be good for children, either. I'm going to take you to the emergency room to make sure you haven't swallowed a bunch."

Maggie turned around and saw Jen at the kitchen door. "Jen, sweetie. Put on your shoes. We need to take Sam to the hospital to make sure she's okay. Sam, I'll carry you to the car." Maggie grabbed her purse and keys. This was one time she really wished the car were right outside the front door. Her full arms and heavy load reminded her of the day they had moved in. Thank goodness she knew where the hospital was. She'd driven past it enough times on the way to the armory.

<hr>

Palmer had been the name of the doctor on duty. When she had rushed in with Sam in her arms and Jen behind, the staff had immediately taken over.

Dr. Palmer was slow-moving and quiet. Maggie imagined it made him a good pediatrician, calmed kids down. It had worked with Sam. "She should be okay. She really did not get a lot in her system, though even a small amount isn't good. Just continue to watch her. The thing you have to watch out with this are nervous system symptoms like watery eyes, runny nose, loss of appetite, coughing, vomiting.

You don't want Sam to be too active for the next twelve to twenty-four hours." Then he turned back to his patient. "Sam, do you think you can do quiet things for the next couple days? Read or draw or watch TV? Things like that?"

Sam nodded solemnly. The speed with which the emergency staff had run their tests had pressed its seriousness upon her. Maggie was glad. She'd need this memory to keep Sam from being too active. She was already trying to plan what they would do. They had almost made it through the summer with no serious accidents, and then this.

Maggie was angry with herself. She should have hidden ant poison better. Put it in the back of a cabinet. But it had never occurred to her that one of the girls would actually climb upon the counter. Would actually try to eat ant poison.

$$\text{-------}\ll\langle\bullet\rangle\gg\text{-------}$$

Maggie tucked Jimmie in next to Sam before kissing her on the cheek. "Sorry, no story tonight. It's been a long day, and you and Jen need your sleep."

Maggie turned out the light on her way out the door.

She walked across the landing and looked in on Jen. Jen had her pajamas on and was sitting on her bed, carefully brushing sand from her feet. Maggie smiled with the memory of Jen's reaction the first day when she discovered sand in her bed. "Jen, thank you for your help today. You were a big help with Sam at the emergency room. You were very grown up."

Jen looked up, nodded. Maggie could tell she was pleased with the compliment. "We'll need to start packing soon. The summer has gone really fast, hasn't it?"

Jen nodded again. Then swung her legs onto her bed. "Night, Mom."

Maggie walked over to place a kiss on her forehead. "Night, sweetie. Sleep tight."

Maggie knew the girls would fall asleep almost immediately. It had been an emotional day. Maggie also knew she should go to bed as well, but wanted to finish packing up the darkroom. It was cool enough now in the evenings that she grabbed her sweatshirt before heading down. Another reminder that the season was changing and everyone was saying goodbye.

Maggie headed downstairs, flipping off the kitchen lights as she went. No need to waste electricity.

Maggie made sure her chemical pans were clean and dry before putting them into a box. She turned to take a look at the curtain, wondering if she should take that. Probably not. She doubted it would fit any window in another house. She had just decided against packing the curtain when she heard a scraping outside the window. Maggie knew her frayed nerves were on high alert and probably overreacting, but she still switched off the light before lifting a corner of the curtain. It was then that she smelled the gasoline even before she made out two indistinct figures kneeling in front of the house emptying the cans close to the house. The fumes assaulted her sense of smell and sent her fear into overdrive. Surely, this wasn't happening, she told herself. Was someone getting ready to burn down this cottage? *Her* cottage. Then she knew. This was happening because of her.

The realization made Maggie react instantly. She knew what she had to do. She was at the back wall of the basement in three steps, feeling along the wall with her hands as she had when she discovered the door, but now she knew exactly what she was looking for. Even as she lifted herself onto the ledge, scraping her knees on the concrete floor, she felt a wry sense of gratitude for the ruined photos and Jen's curiosity.

Eleven steps. Jen's closet. Maggie shook Jen awake. "Sh-h-h-h. Jen. I think we are in danger. Put on your shoes and sweatshirt. We have to get out of here. We'll go down the secret stairs. Don't make a sound. Wait right here 'til I get Sam. No questions." Maggie held her finger to her lips.

Sam's room was in the front of the house. Maggie glanced down through the windows. The porch was already engulfed in flames. Whoever was out there had started the fire so that it would block the front door. These people were more than arsonists. They didn't care if they became murderers.

Maggie grabbed Sam in her arms for the second time that day.

"Whe-where's Jimmie?"

"Sh-h-h. Put your arms around my neck." Maggie tried to cradle Sam as gently as she could, remembering the doctor's admonitions. No shaking. Damned ant poison.

The fire was large enough to cast a wavering orange glow on the back walls of Sam's room as Maggie carried her younger daughter through the door. They reached Jen's room just as Jen was opening the door to her closet. Maggie followed, sliding on her backside with Sam hanging onto her.

Jen went down the stairs quickly. Maggie felt the wall as she went. Was it her imagination, or were the stones in the wall already heating up? "Jen, go to the back of the house when you get out. Wait there for us." Maggie looked at the three of them. *We're like the refugees whose village is burning, escaping with the clothes on our backs. About to become boat people.* A plan had formed in Maggie's mind. She knew their neighbors' homes were all vacant. And Gertie out of town. "Hang onto my arm, Jen. We need to hurry."

They climbed the steps up the hill to the neighbor's house behind them. Maggie knew they had already left, but if she could get inside, they could hide. Surely, the fire would attract whoever was still in the cottages. *God, I hope Helen's house doesn't catch.* Maybe she'd wake up and call emergency. The fire trucks would arrive in a minute.

Maggie deposited Sam carefully on the stoop before trying the front door. It was locked. She placed her shoulder against it and pushed. Nothing. This wouldn't work. For all she knew, there were other people standing guard to make sure she and the girls didn't escape.

"Okay, Jen. We need to head to the beach. Be as quiet as you can." They rounded the corner of the big house. Setting fire to one of the wood cottages was madness, she knew. They were all old wooden structures, surrounded by trees. Who knew where this would stop.

The night was black except for the flames now licking at the roof. It was too early for the moon to be up, but they'd need to hurry if they were to take advantage of the dark. Once the moon rose above the horizon, the water would light up.

"Mom, what's happening?"

"I think someone has set our house on fire. We need to get out of here, but we can't let them see us because they could be dangerous. Now, stay low to the ground and go straight for the water. When you get there, wait for me."

Maybe there had been some good that had come from her daughters' summer television, because Jennifer took off running, crouched low to the ground. Maggie followed the best she could. Sam was beginning to feel heavy, but the alternative to carrying her was holding her hand and dragging her along the sand. Once again Maggie thought of the doctor's warnings. She fought off waves of nausea.

Maggie could have cheered when she reached Jennifer and the water's edge. "Okay, stay close to the water, but don't splash. We don't want to make any noise." Maggie lifted her eyes to look ahead of her. She could just make out a shape that was darker than the space around it. Sure enough. It was still there. Thank you, Jason. Her lips silently formed the words.

The Hobie Cat was pretty much where Jason had beached it. *Now, we'll find out if this thing is really as light as Jason bragged.* The voice in Maggie's head was taking over, directing her, crowding out everything else,

"Sam. Listen to me." Maggie held her arms over the boat and rolled Sam as gently as she could on the canvas top. She took off her sweatshirt. "Sam, put this on to keep you warm. Jen, help me. We need to get this into the water. I'll pull; you push."

Maggie couldn't believe how lucky they were that the boat was this close to the water. There was a rope attached to the front of the boat. Maggie took hold of this and tugged. She prayed. The boat moved. If they could just get it mostly in the shallow water.

Thin wisps of mist started slowly to lift from the water. Small wraiths circled around her ankles and rose up her legs.

Maggie barely noticed. She walked around to the boat's stern. "Okay, Jen, let me help you get on," Maggie whispered as loudly as she could. She knew the sound could travel. She grabbed Jen under the arms, surprised at how heavy her older daughter felt. She must have grown this summer.

Maggie managed to place Jen next to Sam. "Jen, hold onto Sam." She grabbed the rope once more, pulled the boat in until the water was to her waist, then gave a final pull so that the boat glided past her. When the stern came level with her, she hauled herself on the boat, hinging at the middle, then pulling the rest of her on the taut canvas deck.

"Okay, Jen. Help me get the sail up. Sam, stay where you are." The sweatshirt was a good distraction. Sam was still trying to get her arms into the armholes.

Jen and Maggie fumbled with the rope tied around the sheet, until Maggie realized they could just grab one end and pull. "Jen, grab this rope—sheet—and we'll pull this sail up. Then I need to get back to the tiller to steer."

At the shouts, Maggie's head jerked up. The arsonists— the murderers—had seen them, and were running across the sand. Maggie knew she had to get the boat under sail and away from shore, far enough so that they couldn't be caught.

The sail was not to the top of the mast, but who was worried about small details right now? Maggie grabbed the sheet and pulled the sail in until it filled. Sure enough, the boat began to move! She could hear the wind in her ears, taste her hair as it blew into her open mouth.

She kept the rope in a hand and threw herself at the tiller. She had it. She had it in her hand. She could feel the water beneath the boat move through the tiller and up her arm. All right. This was a start. This was good. But they were going the wrong way. They'd have to come about. Shit. She'd need to do this with her daughters balanced on a canvas surface, a surface without rails.

Maggie knew the murderers on the beach would get the word back to Blailock that they made it out of the house alive. With grim irony, Maggie realized their blazing cottage was the perfect marker to use to steer a course that could save them. She knew she couldn't go back to shore. Or could she? It was a chance she'd have to take. Then she saw the fog roiling toward the beach.

Almost simultaneously, a deep wail sounded. Her head jerked around. The foghorn. Though it wasn't that foggy yet. Was it a signal? Was Blailock sending it? Or was someone else sending it to Blailock? It was a deep, sonorous, roiling sound. Ghostly, like Sam said. No matter. She would use it to her own advantage. It would keep her from ramming the concrete piers. The sound would tell her how far out she needed to sail before heading back. Back to safety.

"Jen, sit next to Sam, would you. No, actually lie down with her. I have to come about. Bring the boat around. The sail is going to sweep across us, and I don't want the boom to hit you."

Maggie realized she was holding her breath. *Breathe*, she told herself. She brought the sail in as she pointed the bow closer to the eye of the wind. She kept her eyes on the lighthouse. If she came about too early, they'd be in a mess. She'd have to tack again, and that would take too long. She pictured in her mind how far away from shore she needed to be to take a position that would take her beyond the channel to the beach that lay beyond.

"Five, four, three . . . ready about! Stay low, girls." She pushed the tiller away from herself as far as she could, felt the boat turn through the eye, then farther. She shifted to the opposite side as fast as she could. Felt the tiller in her hand, let the sail out some more so they were headed straight toward the public beach and . . . dare she hope? Safety.

Maggie kept her eyes focused on shore. She could see lights moving in the distance. Maybe a distant road, she guessed. There were no lights at all on what she guessed was the public beach. She'd have to sail toward it with the wind coming over her shoulder, dangerously close to causing the stern to pass through the wind's eye. That would send the sail whipping across the other way. Maggie held the tiller hard, even as she felt her hands begin to shake. But, if she sailed at a gentler angle, she worried she'd miss the public beach altogether.

Her mind was racing. There could be fog ahead, she told herself. Concentrate. She needed nature on her side. She needed the wind to stay steady. She . . . *But it's snowing.* Ben's words came into her head as though a sharp electric current shot between her ears. Of course. Julia must have known all about Blailock's misdeeds. She may have been too tied to him or too afraid of him to turn on him, but she had left clues for others. Maggie had to keep the three of them alive if only to put a stop to all of Blailock's crimes. Maggie was determined that one of them was not going to include murder.

It may have been a twenty-minute sail, from beginning to end, but to Maggie it was interminable. The tiller seemed both too hard to hold and too wobbly.

Then the shore loomed as though bidden. She barely had time to yell, "Hold on," to Jen before they hit the sand with the bow, moved forward a couple of feet, then got hung up on the sand. There was a flashlight shining in their eyes even before Maggie could get the sail down to stop the boom from wildly swinging back and forth.

"This is a public beach," the voice said. "Not a marina. Boats aren't allowed to dock here—or beach here either." The flashlight moved across their boat's canvas cockpit. "What? You have kids."

Maggie held her hand over her eyes to try to see the person behind the voice. She had crawled over to Jen and Sam and held them close to her. "These are my children. We took this boat to escape someone who is trying to hurt us. Are you security? We need an ambulance. I have a daughter who needs to go to the hospital. And we need to call the fire department in case no one's called them yet. And also the police. We need to report attempted murder. Among other crimes."

"I'll do my best, lady, but the emergency radios are full of it. There's a big fire on the south side, and all kinds of emergency vehicles are racing over there. But I'll do my best."

＝＝＞)((◉))(＜＝＝

Maggie was sitting on the only couch in the waiting room with Jen asleep next to her, curled up with her head in her mother's lap, when Sheldon walked in. He walked over to them and sat down on the edge of a chair next to her.

"What have you heard? I left as soon as I got your message."

"Thanks for coming." Even Maggie could hear the relief in her voice. "Well, it's not all good. This has been a day that may take a terrible toll on all of us." Maggie's voice broke. She took a breath. She knew if she let herself cry, it would come out in huge sobs. And she had to hold it together. If just for her girls. "Sam got into ant poison this morning. Not much, but enough so that she needed to take it easy to prevent any possible damage to her nervous system.

"Taking it easy isn't exactly an option when you're trying to escape from a house someone has set fire to—intending for you to go up in flames along with everything else."

Sheldon pushed back in the chair and dropped eye contact with her. He noticed the policeman leaning against a wall. He looked back at Maggie.

"Security," Maggie told him. "Here to protect us. They're convinced someone was trying to kill us."

Maggie saw the look cross his face that meant she must be exaggerating. "Your client, the guy you think is such a fine businessman, it seems, may have been involved in criminal behavior, and my photos may have been the proof of his trafficking in cocaine."

"Cocaine?"

"Yes. Cocaine. You had no idea?"

"My god. Of course not! How can you even think that?" Sheldon brought his hand to his face.

Maggie watched him come up short. A man who cheated on his wife—no, cheated on his family. It was hard to know where he drew the line on his own morals. But she believed him. She knew if things were going to go well for their breakup, she needed to try to cut him some slack. Not now, but maybe sometime she could even forgive him.

"Are you sure?"

"Well, there will obviously be an investigation."

"I need to call the firm. Drop him as a client. This—" Maggie watched Sheldon struggle with the fear of failure, then realize the true extent of what he had almost lost. "But you. I could have lost all of you!" He reached over to Jen and began to stroke her head. She stirred, but continued to sleep the sleep of a six-year-old, her lips slightly parted, her breath coming out in quiet puffs.

⸻ ((◊)) ⸻

Maggie sat at the end of the pier, holding her knees close to her chest. She imagined herself like Jay Gatsby, looking across the water at the lights, lights that promised wealth and power. Is that where Blailock went wrong? Who knew.

She needed this time to herself. It had been hard to sleep. Hard to sleep since she'd beached Jason's boat onto the State Park Beach within sight of Blailock's mansion, but not within reach. They'd ended up staying at a motel in town, until she could tie up loose ends. Almost nothing could be salvaged from the dark embers and ashen pillars of the house. The single brick wall was mostly all that was left. Even her enlarger was ruined.

The police had asked Maggie to come to the station to tell them what she knew.

There had to be more to the story, Maggie knew, when Ben said that his mother had told him it was snowing when she showed him the music box. The police had questioned Helen, who had been only too glad to talk after being awakened by a burning cottage across the walk from her own. Perhaps it was her son's right to burn down his own building, but not with a woman and two children in it.

Yes, there had been a white powder in the music box. Helen had found it when she'd found the secret drawer. She'd poured it all down the kitchen sink drain, tried not to think too much about what it might be.

The cocaine had led the police to the lighthouse. Blailock had bribed the lighthouse caretaker, who turned a blind eye when the boats from Canada made their way under the lighthouse piers to store their cache of cocaine until another boat from Chicago came to load it up and take it to the Windy City, where it would easily be worth a million on the street. Jason was right: wealth had just made Blailock more greedy, willing to stop at nothing to accumulate as much money as he could.

Maggie imagined that Julia had been conflicted. She loved the wealth but hated that it was ill gotten. She probably knew her husband didn't trust her with his secret, that he would try to kill her. So, she had tried to leave behind the clues that would incriminate him. She didn't count on the possibility that Helen, his mother, would try to protect him.

And it was Sam, bless her, who provided the evidence. When she had tried to put Maggie's sweatshirt back on after being discharged from the hospital, she had reached into the kangaroo pocket and pulled out the negatives in their plastic sleeve.

"Oh, my god." Maggie went over to grab them. "I never took them out of my pocket. That's where they've been all along. Sam, good for you." She carried the negatives over to the police desk. "I think we will find an incriminating photo here," she told Officer Norton. "I have a photo here that shows a boat that was tied up under the lighthouse."

"That could be very helpful. If it's possible to read the identification numbers on the side of that, Mr. Vincent Blailock may have some explaining to do."

Maggie stretched out. She was stiff from sitting on the pier for so long. She knew she should head back. Sheldon had probably had enough time to talk with the girls about their futures. She needed to join them to give her own reassurances.

She gave the lake one last look. The lake stretched as far as the eye could see. It seemed large enough to drop off the face of the earth. Then she turned back to the points of light starting to flicker on shore. Where Gatsby had seen the lights as symbols of power and money, she saw them as lights of hope that might save this small corner of Michigan from the development and degradation that power and money could bring about. At least one dangerous developer was no longer a threat to quiet Breakwater Bay. And maybe others could be turned back as well. Maggie, at least, was betting all her chips, and any photos she could create, on Sam's Time Being.

CPSIA information can be obtained
at www.ICGtesting.com
Printed in the USA
LVHW082045070422
715339LV00018B/982